THE PROBLEM WITH PLANNING LOVE

A SWEET MILITARY ROMANCE

CLAIRE CAIN

Cover photography by Rainbeau Decker

Cover models — real Army couple James Bradley Mason & Michelle A Thompson

Cover design by Emma Robinson

Print: 978-1-954005-01-3

E-Book: 978-1-954005-00-6

To the friends we made in Hohenfels, the real life Kugelfels, for the beautiful gifts of love and friendship from the very beginning. Vielen Dank.

NOTE FROM THE AUTHOR

What is the OCONUS Bonus? First, OCONUS is the military acronym that stands for Outside the Continental United States. So really, it's what military personnel say when they're stationed somewhere other than the 48 continental states.

Any posting in Germany is an OCONUS duty station.

The OCONUS Bonus is an *Unofficial* turn of phrase indicating all the extras that come from living overseas as military personnel. Sometimes this comes with hardships, but many times it's packed with adventure. For the characters in my OCONUS Bonus series? It's finding love. (*Cue rising, inspirational music.)

I hope you'll enjoy a peek at my fictionalized version of being stationed in Germany, which is based on my time living in Bavaria as a military spouse—truly some of my favorite years so far.

CHAPTER ONE

Livie

The-five-year-old boy in front of me took my hand in a firm shake, the wild dark curls on his head shaking with his enthusiasm.

I nodded toward this pint-sized little man. "You must be Robert Wolfe."

The giant smile that greeted me told me I was right.

"Yep. But call me Robby. You must be Mrs. Manderson."

I grinned. "I am *Miss Anderson*, yes. I'm so glad to meet you, Robby."

"I like this room," he said, surveying the large, colorful space he'd spend the next nine months of his kindergarten year in.

The uniformed soldier who'd come in behind him ducked out the doorway before even fully stepping in, cell phone to his ear. I shook my head softly—first strike against that parent, though I tried not to think it. But really, could he not take ten minutes away to meet his child's teacher and make sure his son was comfortable? Some kids would absolutely freak out if their parent stepped outside the classroom when they'd just been introduced to a new adult.

Add to that, this was Kugelfels, Germany. Granted, it was a DODEA—Department of Defense Education Activity—school, so still basically a US public school but run by the DOD rather than a state. Many kids had just moved across the world to come to Germany with their military parents during the summer PCS—Permanent Change of Station—cycle, so this guy abandoning his son with a new teacher at a new school in a new country?

Not great.

I smiled, all practiced warmth and comfort. "I'm glad. There are a lot of fun things to learn and do in here, that's for sure."

He crossed one arm over his chest and brought the opposite hand to his chin, then tapped his cheek thoughtfully as he looked around. "Yes. I can get used to this."

I tucked my lips between my teeth to stifle a laugh. Five was the absolute best age, especially when it came in this kind of little package—one clearly unafraid of his new surroundings. Maybe his father knew he wouldn't have any trouble with me.

"Did you go to preschool, or did you stay home with your mom or dad?" Either was fine, but I'd put my money on this kid being used to leaving home every day.

He turned and shot a thumb over his shoulder at his dad —or where he would've been. "I went to the CDC for everything. My mom is gone and my dad is in the order of the silver leaf so he has to work and can't do school for me. Grams and Ari trade off helping with the driving."

"The order of the silver leaf? That sounds really important." I already loved him.

The glut of information gave me the familiar pang that hit with certain kids. I loved all of them in the end, but some naturally wormed their way into my heart from the get-go. The tendency to over-share was one of many things I loved about teaching kindergarten, though sometimes it led to uncomfortable revelations.

He nodded, eyes wide, a serious wrinkle to his brow.

"It is. He has lots of people to learn from every day, just like I'm gonna learn from you every day." His eye caught on a basket of magnetic tiles in a cubby next to where we sat. "Can I play with those?"

"Sure you can. I have some things to go over with your dad, when he comes back in, and then you can go and I'll see you next week."

He plopped down into a tailor sit, or *criss-cross applesauce* as we call it in class, and dove into the basket with both hands.

I watched him a moment, then movement out the corner of my eye caught my attention and I turned to see...

Wow.

I swallowed down that reaction, pasting a professional smile on my face as I stood, extending a hand. "Olivia Anderson."

His giant hand engulfed mine, dry and warm and a little rough.

"Eric Wolfe. Nice to meet you, ma'am. I apologize for taking that call—I normally wouldn't but it's a bit of a time-sensitive issue."

Ah, manners. The unexpected manners were maybe more lethal than his physical appearance, though that alone was enough to tell me I shouldn't look him in the eye again until the year was over. This kind of reaction to a child's parent was oh so so *so* not appropriate. I'd never had it before—not like this, not even close.

"Well, Mr.—er, uh—" I shot a quick glance at the rank a little below eye level on his chest—ah, the silver leaf, signaling he was a lieutenant colonel, but I reminded myself not to actually say the *lieutenant* because the Army liked to be confusing, or so I'd learned after years working on military bases and learning the conventions, "—Colonel Wolfe, thanks for taking some time to meet with me. If you don't mind taking a seat..."

I gestured to a chair at one side of my teacher's table, a low half-moon shape, and took a seat opposite him.

Then I realized the chair was one of the children's sizes, and this fully grown man in no way fit, but he tried. His knees came up above the table, but his body sat low, only a foot off the ground. Ideal for little kids to sit on and scoot under the table, but for a man who had to be at least six feet tall?

A giggle escaped before I could stop it.

His brutally handsome face didn't crack. "Is something funny, ma'am?"

I blinked rapidly, trying to blur my vision and avoid noticing any of the things that made him so ridiculously attractive. "Uh, um, of course not, I—"

Then he smiled, all friendly humor and co-conspiracy.

And he has a sense of humor.

No. Nope. Not noticing anything. Not the cut jaw. Not the features that easily qualified him to be a model. Not the straight, white teeth behind really nice-looking lips.

"I'm so sorry. I didn't realize I still had the children's size chair there—you're my first parent meeting this year."

And the fact that I hadn't prepped the room would've

made a normal teacher's head explode, but not mine. I didn't mind a fly-by-the-seat-of-your-pants approach as long as I got the job done, and especially if my lack of double-checking chair sizes came on the heels of a summer so full of travel, I'd be living on the highs for weeks. Months. Honestly, probably years to come, especially when I moved back home.

"I spend a great deal of time in like-sized chairs, actually. Robby and his sister Delia have a little table they make me sit at with them. I'm pretty sure it's one of their subtle methods of torture." He shifted in his seat, easing forward so he could rest his elbows on his knees and set his chin in his hands. "Please, do go on."

I laughed freely then. "No, this is insane."

I hustled over and grabbed a larger chair and slid it next to him as he stood, then returned to my seat before I could give into the temptation to smell him.

Not. Okay.

"Thank you. I probably wouldn't have been able to get out of that seat after another couple of minutes." He set a portfolio-type folder on the desk, opened it, and took out a pen. "So, tell me everything I need to know to make this a great year for Robby, and for you."

Resisting the urge to sigh, and ignoring the little leap in my chest when I noted he didn't wear a wedding ring, which confirmed what Robby had declared in saying his mom was gone... divorced? Or widowed? Whatever the case, not my business, so I began my spiel.

Ten minutes later, I'd given him all the information he needed, and he'd nodded, asked two intelligent questions, gathered his items, and then stood.

"Thank you for being here and teaching. I know kindergarten isn't easy. I have to apologize now because I'll be in rotations almost non-stop until Thanksgiving, but my mother and sister will be stepping in to help when needed."

My mouth opened like I'd say words, but none came. How did this man know to say these things? I mean, I knew how—his older daughter Delia would've already been through kindergarten and so must've been familiar with things, but...

"Wow, I'm sorry. People don't normally say that kind of thing, especially not..."

Hot, possibly available, officer dads.

A single dark brow raised. "Especially not...?"

"Uh... hah. Dads, I guess. The moms tend to be a bit more in tune with what teachers need. Around here, half the spouses are teachers as it is. Anyway, I'm sorry, I'm babbling. Thank you."

"Well... you're welcome. I'm sorry I can't be of more help in the near-term." His cell phone buzzed and he pulled it out, silenced it, then returned his attention to me. "I've got to get Robby back before I head to a meeting. Forgive me."

"I understand. My next student will be here any minute anyway. Thank you for making time to come in."

"It was nice to meet you, Ms. Anderson."

He extended his hand, which I took, my stomach dropping to my shoes at the contact, which would've normally made me roll my eyes because talk about off-limits, but then he said, "I look forward to seeing you again."

I sputtered a little, thrown. "Uh, yes. Yeah. Thank you... me too."

Mercifully, Robby appeared next to me and hit me with a large smile as he grabbed his dad's free hand.

"See you soon Miss Anderson."

"See you Monday!"

CHAPTER TWO

Eric

Ariel met me at the door of my house.

"How was your day, big brother?"

I narrowed my eyes. Her greeting was suspiciously cheery, though I knew she was glad to be here with us and not hiding out in her crap apartment back in the States.

"Why are you so chipper? Aren't you still jet-lagged?"

I sank onto the bench just inside the door and bent to untie my boots. I loved nothing more than taking off my boots as soon as possible on a hot August day like today.

"I'm almost over it. It's a lot faster this time than the last time I visited."

She locked the door behind me, then crossed her arms over her chest, waiting for me to finish my boot routine.

"Well... good." I loved my sister, but I was almost out of words for the day, and needed to check on the kids if they were still awake. "How'd everyone do today?"

I followed her into the kitchen, dumping keys, wallet, phone, planner on the counter while she spoke.

"Delia was good—quiet, of course. She started reading a new book series we picked up from the library."

I nodded, washing my hands at the kitchen sink before she spoke again.

"She did great too, Eric." She set a hand on my shoulder and squeezed, then let it drop. "She didn't look like she was clenching her teeth, and I gave her some hand sanitizer when we walked out and she didn't get the look like she did the last time I was here."

I sighed, my heart pinching in my chest at the news. "Yeah, she's been doing better this summer. She's got a new therapist and I think that's doing her some good."

"I can tell." My sister's voice was soft, betraying the love she had for my kids. "And Robby... well, you can guess."

I chuckled and shook my head. "Oh I can, but tell me anyway, in just a sec. Let me run see if I can catch either of them."

She set a plate of food at the table and poured two tall glasses of water, then sat and waited as I took the stairs two at a time to see if either of them were awake. But both were nestled in bed, racked out. I'd be back to properly tuck them in, so I shuffled back down the stairs, took my place, and began eating.

"Well, first he declared he couldn't wait for school to start, and he knew he was going to be the best kindergartener ever."

"Naturally."

She nodded, her long dark hair swishing from its ponytail. The dark shade was not unlike mine right now, without any highlights or other additions, though mine had admittedly veered toward gray more starkly in the last year or so.

"Then he told me about every. Single. Toy. In the classroom."

I smiled as I finished chewing a bite of the grilled chicken she'd made. "Did he mention the *amazing* artwork on the whiteboard?"

She laughed. "Once or twice. And then he told me and Mom that Mrs. Anderson is actually *Miss* Anderson, and he thinks she is the *most beautifullest* lady he's ever seen."

We smiled at each other, at the effusive, delightful enthusiasm Robby had for everything and everyone. My heart thumped dumbly in my chest remembering Ms. Anderson—a task I'd attempted to avoid since I'd left her classroom hours ago.

"So, is she?"

I glanced up from my plate and kept on chewing. I'd ended up hunching over the dish and essentially inhaling the food she'd made—it'd been eight hours since I last ate. I had to get better about taking snacks.

"Is she what?"

"Is she *the most beautifullest lady ever?*" She batted her dark lashes, and her bright blue eyes watched me, full of silly drama.

I dropped my gaze, eyes returning to the last few roasted vegetables. I could try to avoid it, but the part of me that had her sunny blond hair, light brown eyes, and red-painted lips burned across its memory nudged me to speak. "She's quite lovely. He's not wrong."

Her gasp was audible. I chose not to look up, able to guess what I'd find.

"Are you serious?"

I said nothing, finishing the food and pointedly ignoring her. Her ridiculous screeching spoke volumes which I had no intention of addressing after a fifteen-hour workday.

I moved to rinse the dish, then tucked it into the bottom of the dishwasher. Since it was full, I placed a detergent pod into the little holder, then pressed the button to start it.

When I turned, Ariel blocked the way out of the kitchen to the stairs, hands on hips, one dark brow arched like she knew something.

"What?"

"You're ridiculous."

"I am not."

"You are."

"Not."

"*So* are."

Brushing past her, I started up the stairs, Ariel right on my heels.

"You cannot pretend that you saying she's *quite lovely* isn't remarkable. I've been waiting all day to talk to you about this, and you won't even... urgh." She grabbed my arm.

I twisted around and lowered my voice, not wanting to wake either child. "I'm not about to date the woman. But yes. Fine. I concede my noticing her physical appearance is a notable event, and it felt... good."

It had... Good grief, it had. I hadn't looked at anyone and actually seen them, at least not in *that* way, in years. Not since the divorce, and it'd been at least two years before the end of my marriage that I'd felt anything like that for my wife. I'd wondered if that part of my life—being attracted to someone, wanting them, feeling stirred by a person in any way—was long gone. But now I had proof—the divorce hadn't broken me. At least not when it came to this woman.

"That's great. So great."

Her smile was small, but I could see the hope there in her face plain as day.

"Don't get that wistful tone with me. I'm not about to date my kid's teacher, and she's probably married anyway."

Though she didn't wear a ring, and I didn't know any soldiers with the last name Anderson. To be fair, that didn't necessarily mean there weren't any, but the post was small enough, it seemed likely I'd at least know of them. She looked like she was in her later twenties maybe, so odds were she'd be married to an NCO or maybe even a company-grade officer, and in that case I'd definitely have heard of the name.

"I'm not saying anything. I'm just... I'm glad."

"Me too, Ari." I held back from saying *and now it's your turn* because it never went well, and her situation was different from mine. "Thanks for dinner, and taking the kids. I'm going to check in with Delia, and then I'll see you in the morning."

She padded down the hallway to the guest room where she and my mom stayed—a little cramped to have them both here, but Ari was only visiting for a week to get the lay of the land before she left to ditch her apartment and wrap up a few other things, then come out to stay for as long as she could. My mom had spent all of the last year with us, and I'd never be able to thank her for doing that. Our first year in Germany would've been a nightmare without her, but Renee had made it clear when we finalized the divorce that she didn't want the kids.

She'd given me the choice: leave the Army and move with her so she could complete med school, or give her a divorce. She claimed she'd given everything up for me, and after nearly fifteen years, she was done. Since she wanted to pursue her own goals, she didn't want the kids hampering her efforts. The saddest part about it all was that this woman I'd cared for—though I'd come to terms with the fact that we'd had an odd dynamic in our marriage, a kind of coexistence grown out of a flash of lust and the decision to marry quickly— had become a selfish stranger.

I likely wouldn't have cared as much if it hadn't hit the kids so hard. But it had. And it kept hitting.

I shook that off and pushed away the thoughts of Renee as I mounted the stairs to the kids' rooms. The sight that greeted me when I peeked my head into Delia's room made my heart ache—I hadn't looked closely enough earlier, in my haste and the relative darkness, to fully absorb the scene. My little girl was curled into a ball, book open next to her, glasses still on. I flipped off the bedside lamp and carefully extracted the glasses, then took the book and set a bookmark where I thought she'd left off. I'd gotten in trouble one too many times for losing her place when I missed that step.

No clutter anywhere, no extra toys or anything that didn't have a place. I bent and kissed her head, pulled the covers up, and bit back the grumble I felt anytime I saw her poor chapped hands, less bright red lately since she'd been doing better.

Renee had left us when Delia was nearly six. Robby was two at the time, and far too young to be impacted all that much, but Delia had felt it deeply.

In the last two years, she had developed germaphobia that her doctors attributed to anxiety related to the divorce. If anything made me regret and hate the whole thing, it was the toll it took on Delia.

The move overseas had been fairly rough to add on top of things, and without my mom here, I couldn't have done it. She'd moved with us as an official dependent since my father had passed several years ago and she'd said she wanted to see more of the world. Mom would head back stateside in about six weeks, staying with her sister in

Pensacola like she did when she needed a break from the demands her grandkids and I put on her. She wanted a warmer winter, and I couldn't fault her there either since it could get pretty chilly in Germany in the winter months. For now, she was on a little tour of Tuscany with a friend who'd flown in from the States while Ariel visited.

Ariel would take the guest room fully in October and stay at least ninety days—all that was allowed on a tourist visa—and then she'd have to leave again unless we figured out a work-around, which I really hoped we would. My sister had now taken on the task of caring for my family, and she did so willingly and with so much love, it humbled me.

It wasn't a job she should have. She should be making her own family, pursuing her own dreams.

My jaw clenched at the thought of her idiot ex-husband. They'd only been married two years, but had dated for two before that, and she'd given up almost everything for him. I used to fear I'd done the same thing to Renee that Jim had done to Ari. I'd made a comment to that effect not long ago and she'd looked like she'd slap me.

"You gave Renee everything. Yes, military life is hard, but you gave and gave too. Jim only took from me."

Once I found out all the crap that had entailed, I agreed. I hated the way my marriage had ended, but I'd long since given up the resentment and hatred of my wife. I would never understand her refusal to be involved with her children, but I'd had my fair share of counseling to address the anger that came from that, on my own behalf and especially that of my children. It cropped up now and again particularly when she broke a promise or canceled a trip, but overall, I didn't think about her every day, or sometimes even every week. What an odd thing after years together.

Long story short, Ariel's healing would be different

from mine. It'd been a year since she'd gotten out of a situation I wished I'd been more tuned into.

For now, I'd be thankful she could be here and give Mom a break, give me some help, and be another adult in the room when things got crazy. We'd have some fun while she was here, too... it'd be great.

And while I was swamped with work—literally TDY to Ukraine or Lithuania, and that sort of Temporary Duty Travel was tedious, to say the least, then a short trip to Georgia, and several rotations of field training in between—my kids would have my sister here to love them and help them feel secure.

CHAPTER THREE

Livie

A riel Wolfe was a weird, alternate-universe female version of her brother.

Honestly, I would've known she was his sister from a mile away when she initially walked in back in November. Same dark hair, bright blue eyes, dark brows and lashes, though her skin was pale and his a bit darker. Of course she was all woman in the way Eric was, if you don't mind my saying so, *aaaalllll* man.

Don't judge me too harshly. Since our encounter months ago at the start of school, I'd ascertained that he was divorced. Still not great for me to be thinking that way about a parent, but dang and double dang y'all, the man was downright attractive.

I'd not seen him up close since our first and only official meeting. I'd seen him from afar though—he'd walked Robby to the door of the classroom one day after a dental appointment, and another day he'd been in the office talking with the nurse when our class walked to lunch across the lobby area.

He was the quintessential tall, dark, and handsome man. He seemed so serious and stern, but then I'd remember his words from our meeting—his concern over Robby's success in school and making sure I knew his mother and then his sister would be able to support the classroom while he was going through a particularly busy time with his job.

Oh, and of course, he was a battalion commander. I knew enough about the Army after working Department of Defense schools for the last decade to know that meant he'd done something right.

Anyway, point being, I hadn't interacted with him, which was both sad and probably for the best. Sad, because a man like that deserved to be looked at and admired by women everywhere, and I knew most soldiers in his unit tended to be men since it was an infantry unit. But probably for the best because that was just a big fat mess of disappointment waiting to happen for my feelings.

Because a man like that? He wasn't looking for a woman like me.

And frankly, I wasn't looking for a man like him, either. I hadn't dated a single soldier since I'd arrived years ago, nor had I at any other military base. In the end, I knew where I'd end up—when I moved on from the *adventure phase* of life this next year, I'd enter the *family phase*. As my parents' only child, I owed them—they'd given up so much to have stability during my high school years, and then helped fund my college. We were close, and I needed to be there to care for them, and to share life with them. And that did not, I repeat *did not* work with marrying into the military.

But seeing Ariel Wolfe every Thursday since she'd been cleared to volunteer in November? It made me think of *him* and wonder how he was doing, and if, especially now that it was December, he was freezing outside sleeping in his truck, if he even did that on rotations since he was the man in charge.

"It's so cold out there, and there's not even snow on the ground." Ariel rubbed her hands together to warm them.

"It really is. I hope all the kids brought good layers today because we need to get out for recess." Most of them had arrived layered from boots to hats with down-filled coats and cozy sweaters. One or two would be missing gloves, which we could supplement. I made it a point to pick up little extras like gloves and hats when I was out. The German dollar (or, euro) stores were great for that kind of thing.

"I'm staying until lunch today, if that works for you?"

She hung her coat, hat, scarf, and purse on a hook in the little inlet that led to the bathroom for our classroom and where I kept all my things.

"It'd be amazing. I can't tell you how awesome it is that you do this every week. I only have one other parent who comes in regularly."

Ariel had been coming in weekly since she'd first arrived, as soon as her mandatory background checks had cleared. Those were typically an insanely slow process that took months if you needed one for a job, but miraculously, they'd pushed hers through and she'd been cleared to come in just a few weeks after she'd landed.

She settled down at a table where I kept a lot of the easy activities for volunteers—cutting out various craft papers and other menial tasks. The kids were at their host nation language class—German, in this case obviously—first thing this morning, and then Ariel would be able to dive in. I liked this time with her though—we could chat while I took care of paperwork.

Usually, she asked about travel. She hadn't done much, from what I could tell, either in adulthood or since arriving in Germany. Whenever I asked about her life, she'd manage to bring things back around to me, usually asking about the food in a particular place, or most often, just wondering where I'd been the weekend before. I traveled at a breakneck pace in the fall when weather was good. I slowed down in the winter months because usually I was tired, and after whatever trip I'd taken at Christmas, my budget usually needed the rest too.

We sat quietly for a few minutes while we worked, then she sighed. "I wish I didn't have to go back stateside for the new year."

"What? Why?"

She let the paper and scissors fall limp in her hands. "I'm just on a tourist passport—I don't have a visa or anything, so I can only stay for ninety days every one-eighty. We'd planned on me finding a job and then trying to get a visa that way, or even command sponsorship through the military, but so far no luck and it's getting a little late."

"But... *no!* We haven't even gotten to hang out, really. Or see each other outside of school. I was going to force you to hang with me and my girlfriends over Christmas break."

I knew I should've asked her to hang out sooner. But I also knew she'd been busy with her niece and nephew while her brother was working so much, so I didn't want to make her feel bad and ask her to something she couldn't show up for.

She beamed at me.

"Really? I'd love that. I hope to come back, so maybe we

can still hang out, and then I'll be back in April if all else fails." Her smile fell at that thought. "Ugh. If I could just find something even part-time. I think Eric could make a decent case for me staying, especially since I'm essentially his nanny."

I snapped my fingers and pointed at her. "That's it. Why don't you have him set it up so you're officially his nanny or au pair, like, legally. That way you're employed by him, and you're his family care plan too, so it's doubly important you stay."

Her eyes widened. "Oh *duh*. I can't believe I hadn't thought of that. I guess it didn't occur to me that would be real employment, but it might work. I mean, of course it's real employment because obviously he pays me, but, you know..."

"I get it. Seriously, talk to him, and I bet you guys can get this sorted out soon." Then a thought occurred to me. "You know what? My friend used to be a nanny at another post. A little group of us are going out for dinner and the Christmas market in Nuremberg on Friday after work. Would you want to join us? Will your brother be home?"

She set down a pair of scissors she held. "I think so. I think the part of rotation in the box ends tomorrow, and it's usually only a day or so before he can chill out and come home at a normal hour after they're done. The timing might be completely perfect."

I nodded. *Rotation* meant days, or more often weeks, of what felt like every soldier on the base except those in the medical and dental clinics living out in the training area called *the box* and essentially playing war. Usually, they were partnered with visiting US military and other NATO forces units. The soldiers stationed here were the instructors for the visiting soldiers, and then from what I understood, Eric's battalion played the bad guys for any of the training exercises. I was impressed Ariel already knew the lingo, but of course Eric would've taught her what she needed to know.

"Great! We'll take the train so no one has to drive or park. I'll grab tickets on the way home so we have them and can just jump on. Let's swap phone numbers so I can text you the time and everything."

She swallowed, her whole demeanor changed. "Okay, you're going to think this is so insane, but I've lived here for six weeks and I haven't learned the trains yet."

I slapped my hands together and rubbed them as though this sweetened the deal. I loved introducing people to little parts of life here. "Oh yay! I can teach you. In that case, let me pick you up and I'll drive us to the station and I can walk you through getting tickets so you'll know for next time. Then we'll meet up with the other girls and be good to go."

It didn't occur to me to be nervous about picking Ariel up for our girls' night until about halfway up the sidewalk. I would've walked to her house, actually, but since we needed to drive to the train station, I'd parked and let myself inside the gate that lined the yard.

The waist-high green gates almost always signaled military housing—though they weren't on the military base since the post was so small, the government did facilitate leasing homes to servicemembers. I happened to have a place about three blocks away, but happily lived in a small apartment surrounded by other Germans. I liked having other Americans down the street, but still experiencing Germany more immediately nearby.

I knocked on the door, then pulled out my phone in case I'd need to text Ariel. But before I could type a word, gorgeous, tall, dark-haired Lieutenant Colonel Eric Wolfe answered the door.

"Hello, Ms. Anderson."

"Call me Livie, please."

He nodded, widening the door so I could enter. I did *not* sniff him when I passed by, but trust that it took effort. The man was astoundingly good-looking, and the whole worn-in jeans, T-shirt, glasses, beer-in-hand thing *worked* for him.

"Thanks for inviting Ariel out. I feel bad she hasn't gotten to do much travel since arriving."

He spoke as he entered the living room, passing through another door before he did so, which was fairly typical for the military houses around here. He gestured to a man who stood when he saw me. This one rose to a few inches taller than Eric. Slim but muscular, dark gray hair, really nice face.

"This is Nate Reynolds. We work together."

The man extended his hand and I leaned over, kind of awkwardly, if we're being honest, and shook it. Before I could say anything, Eric spoke again, speaking to Nate.

"And this angelic creature is Robby's kindergarten teacher, Livie Anderson."

I did not let the whole *angelic creature* thing upend the Coke bottle in my belly and spill out fizz everywhere. I couldn't dwell on that. So I focused on the other man in front of me, currently shaking my hand.

"Livie Anderson. I like it. Nice to meet you."

Nate smiled and sat back down while I tried not to notice how handsome he was. Not my type, but that was probably because the very embodiment of my type was standing three inches to my right and making me question when I'd become a woman who had a thing for single dads.

I hadn't. That wasn't me. I wanted to start with some-one, do the whole thing—house, dog first, then babies, then eventually remodel the kitchen in our starter home and suddenly fall back in love with it. This was *family phase* in detail and it came next. Of course it came next. It definitely didn't come next with a single soldier dad.

I'd moved a ton as a child, but by late high school, my dad had changed jobs so I didn't have to move during my last few years, and we stuck. My parents still lived in the house now, a decade and a half later. They had married young, and though I'd missed the boat on that whole thing, I could still have it. There was still time.

And okay, *missed the boat* was really more *jumped off the boat* because I'd been serious with my high school sweet-heart after returning home from college and he'd asked me to marry him. I'd said yes, because of course that was what I wanted, what I'd always had in mind. Then I'd gone home, cried my eyes out, and known at a soul-deep level none of it was right. I wanted to *live* more... So I returned the ring and apologized profusely the next day, and made plans to start *Adventure phase* that next week. I bumped around several DODEA schools before getting a job overseas. Decade-long story short, here I was—nearly thirty-five and overdue for the move home to settle down.

"Can I offer you a drink?" Eric asked, pulling my atten-tion from my thoughts and my perusal of the tidy living room.

"Oh... um, sure. I guess we have a few minutes before the train."

He turned to walk toward the kitchen, moving slowly

and canting his body toward me to include me and induce me to follow him—*not that it took much*.

"That's good. Ariel is running a little late tonight. She and Nate got to chatting before she ran up to change—he's about the only person other than you she actually knows here."

"No problem."

"So, beer? Water? Milk? Or I think there's maybe a small secret stash of organic apple juice boxes, if you're that kind of girl."

I smiled, because he was adorable. "Water's fine."

Eric nodded and slipped into the kitchen, leaving me with Nate, who filled the empty space. "So, how long have you been here at Kugelfels?"

"Coming up on three and a half years." Crazy. It seemed like I'd just arrived, and yet my comfort level with everything had grown exponentially each year.

"Were you somewhere else in Europe before that?" he asked, then took a drink of his beer.

"No, I came from North Carolina, and before that, I worked at Stuart in Georgia. I really like working on military bases. Have you been stationed anywhere else in Europe?"

I looked toward the kitchen to see if I could see Eric. I wanted to know his answer to the question too. Annoyingly, I wanted to know everything, and that just didn't make sense.

CHAPTER FOUR

Eric

I mentally rolled my eyes at myself while I poured her water. *Who* was the person who had inhabited my body right now, because this guy was a stranger to me. I didn't say things like *if you're that kind of girl*. The last time I'd flirted with someone was probably over a decade ago, and even then, it'd been with my ex-wife.

Maybe that's why she's your ex.

Soon enough, she sat nestled into the sectional couch right at the corner, which essentially swallowed her small frame, with me a few feet away on one end and Nate on the other.

After a sip, Livie asked, "Am I crashing a guys' night? Where are the kids?"

"They're having a little movie marathon in the basement. Nate decided to keep me company." I lifted my beer in acknowledgement and swallowed, ignoring the little twang of irritation I felt whenever I witnessed Nate and Ariel in the same room. Well, not precisely irritation but... awareness of their interactions.

"Oh good, you're here," Ariel said from the stairs and then trotted into the living room. *Speaking of.*

I should've tried not to see it, but I caught Nate's quick look over her, how he straightened in his seat and sat forward a bit. She did look good, which was a relief. It'd taken her a while to get to a place where she could even stand up straight and meet people's eyes after the divorce.

I stood, ready to usher them out, when Livie spoke.

"Your brother forced a water on me, so no rush. We've still got about ten minutes 'til we need to be at the train."

Her eyes jumped to me, and she smiled. Nothing shy or retiring about her—just frank, happy, open.

What a terribly foreign thing.

Not that Ariel was cagey, but she'd been hurt, and the wind had been knocked out of her, to say the least. Plus, she was my sister.

Renee had been... not like this.

Why are you thinking about your ex-wife right now?

"You two are heading to the Christmas Market in Nuremberg?" Nate asked, congenial and conversational as always.

Livie held up a hand to stop him. "I know what you're thinking. Nuremberg market on a Friday in December... I must be insane. But trust me. We're early enough, and it's much better than attempting it on a Saturday or Sunday... we'll be fine."

Ariel's eyes shifted between them. "Uh, should I be worried?"

I chuckled at her unease, then felt a renewed sense of regret that she'd been here for coming up on two months and hadn't gotten to do hardly anything. "No, no. Nothing to worry about. It's the oldest Christmas market in the world, and well worth the visit. It's also one of, if not the most popular, so it can be a bit intense, but it sounds like you're in good hands."

Livie's face lit up at this small compliment.

"She is." She flashed her brows—a few shades darker than her golden-blond hair—at Ariel. "You are. I promise."

She tipped back her water, and I did not admire the slope of her neck or the stretch of smooth, pale skin that dove down into the vee of her sweater. *No, I did not.*

"Since you're a little nervous, let's just go. I can walk you through ticketing so you'll know for your next adventure."

She hopped up, and I extended a hand for her water glass, which she handed me. The tips of our fingers touched, and a small jolt of... *something*... shot through me.

Was I so starved for female attention that millimeters of contact make me take notice? *Pathetic.*

Though honestly, not a shock. I'd been divorced and single for three years. And frankly, from the moment Robby was born, things had cooled considerably between me and Renee. There hadn't been much marital action, to speak plainly.

The fact that Livie was the first woman I'd found even remotely interesting and attractive since the divorce... that had to be it. I'd let the thought in, the feeling in, and now she'd done something nice for my sister, and she was standing there all short and adorable and at the same time painfully attractive to me.

I coughed, cleared my throat. "Thanks for showing her the ropes."

She patted my arm lightly, her hand warm on my wrist. "My pleasure."

As though that slight touch short-circuited my brain, before I knew it, they were out the door, Ariel raising a brow at me then rolling her eyes as she went, Nate eagerly bidding Ari a farewell, and Livie gamely hollering, "See you soon!"

I shut the door behind them and turned to face a smirking Nate.

"What?"

His brow notched up. "Really? You're going to be coy about this?"

I ignored him on the way to the kitchen, refilled my beer and uncapped another bottle for him, and carried them into the living room. I avoided his amused stare while I filled his empty glass, then sat back and shifted around until the pillows were behind my back enough to make standing without groaning possible whenever I did it next.

"Fine. Get it out."

He didn't even bother hiding his glee. "This is the teacher, right? The one Robby is obsessed with, and Ariel is always talking about volunteering for?"

I nodded.

"And who you clearly want to get to know a little better." He wiggled his brows up and down like a child.

I hit him with an unimpressed glare, downplaying my response to distract from the creep of heat I felt at my cheeks and neck.

He scooted forward, resting his elbows on his knees. "Seriously though, man. She seems great, and she's adorable. You should ask her out."

I snorted. Or harrumphed. Some sound I didn't normally make. "I'm not about to do that."

"Why not?"

"Why would I?"

"Why would you *not*? She's cute, single if I remember Ariel telling me correctly, and you like her. You didn't even really like your wife. You need to date this woman."

My jaw clenched as I glanced at the stairs to make sure they were clear. "I won't dispute my relationship with Renee wasn't rainbows and unicorns. But that doesn't mean I should date this woman. She's Robby's kindergarten teacher."

"Yeah. For what, six more months?"

"It wouldn't work."

Nate looked around dramatically, like someone else in the room would back him up. Then he crossed his arms, and there it was. That know-it-all look. Irritating, but it did effectively banish any embarrassment about his witnessing my interest in Livie.

"Fine. It wouldn't. You're doomed. You'll never get with another woman—Renee will be the last woman you ever love, you ever sleep with, you ever—"

"*Shut it.*"

He shrugged.

I took a pull of my beer, swallowing down the taste. German beer was predictable, but high quality.

"I get the point. Ariel freaked out when she realized I thought Livie was attractive."

Nate chuckled. "You realize you sound like someone describing a couch, right? Like, your level of enthusiasm does not match the events. You haven't even looked at a woman since the divorce. I was beginning to think castration was part of the terms."

I made a face, took another sip of my drink.

"Listen, I'm not saying you have to marry the woman.

Obviously not. But she seemed into you, or at least not repelled by your disheveled, worked eighty hours, old-man glasses-wearing look you've got going on here."

"Remind me... do I outrank you?" I pretended to ponder it. "Yes. Yes I do."

He just smiled and shook his head. "Yeah yeah, you're the boss. But here I am, having a drink with you *in your home* and also one of your oldest friends, so... awkward?"

"I suppose it helps you're decent at your job so I don't have to fire you for crap work *and* insubordination."

He shrugged again, affecting modesty, but he wasn't particularly modest. He wasn't a jerk, but he had enough arrogance for the both of us.

I'd heard someone say that being a leader in the military, especially after a point, takes a fair amount of arrogance. And I could see the point: thinking you can take charge and tell people—sometimes hundreds or even thousands of people—what to do, and even how to live depending on the circumstances, could be considered something requiring arrogance.

My perspective took a slightly different angle. Yes, maybe a little arrogance in one form or another, but also a healthy dose of humility. Being able to ask questions, admit ignorance, admit wrongdoing... these things made great leaders. Of course other things—wisdom, decision-making, clarity of communication... many things go into leadership, and after nearly twenty years in the Army, I'd learned some of it, mostly from great leaders. I had more learning to do, and my current command of the Opposing Force, or "OPFOR" battalion here at the training center, tested everything I knew.

Nate would be an excellent battalion commander when his time came. He'd promote to Lieutenant Colonel in the next year or so. Somehow, we'd managed to follow each other—often because I'd been able to request he join me in a few circumstances. He'd promoted below the zone for major, so that meant he was technically a year ahead of his peers. He had a good chance of promoting early to LTC as well, and it was always well-deserved.

But sometimes, I wanted to knock him down a peg, especially when he was being a Grade A *buttface*, as Robby had recently rather daringly called Delia during a particularly animated fight.

Nate drew my attention back to him as I clicked on the TV.

"Eric. Seriously. I'm not trying to push, but I'm saying... maybe you need a push. So.. here it is. You should go for it."

I did turn toward him when I told him the truth. "Nah. In the end, she wouldn't be interested in someone like me."

CHAPTER FIVE

Livie

I waited patiently as Jen and Nina joined us on the train at the station, then held my tongue to let us all chat and break the ice, but with ten minutes to our stop, I brought it up.

"So... *Nate.*"

Ariel's eyes narrowed.

"Have you guys dated?"

"*No.*"

Wow. Emphatic.

"Okay. Good to know."

Jen, a fellow teacher—though she was stuck dealing with cursive and multiplication tables in third grade, the sucker—asked, "What's this?"

"This is a guy who was hanging out with Ariel's brother, and when she came into the room, he looked like someone had turned on the sun. His energy seriously just... brightened at the sight of her."

Ariel shifted around, pulling her purse over her shoulder and clutching it close. "Nate is an old friend, and he's just happy I'm here. We haven't seen each other much the last few years. I'm more interested in my brother not taking his eyes off of *you*."

"Ooooo," said Jen, the traitor.

I glared at her while she was eye-level, because when she stood, she looked like some kind of Amazonian snow princess at five-foot-eleven, long blond hair flowing over one shoulder with a fuzzy cream-colored knit hat perfectly positioned atop her head. Next to me, she had eight inches and I was always looking up.

Nina, another third grade teacher and dear friend, clapped her hands. "Yes, let's talk about that."

Jen had been my first friend here, and we were very close. Nina had arrived at the beginning of last year, right in time for the coldest, dreariest part of the year. But Jen and I had made fast friends with her and dragged her with us on a few trips, and soon, she'd acclimated. Nina was tiny—even shorter than me. She was petite with dark golden skin and dark features and dark hair—practically opposite to Jen physically in every way, though their personalities clicked perfectly.

"It's been a long time since he's been..." Ariel trailed off, and my stomach took a dive.

"What? Since he's been *what*?"

She gave me a look I could only describe as pointed, then explained. "His divorce cut him pretty deep. I don't want to go into gory details because that's his business and if you end up spending time with him, you'll learn them soon enough. But the key points are these. First, he is fully over his ex-wife. Second, I haven't seen him give a woman a second glance in years... until you."

My belly flipped. "I—we've talked like, twice. Ever. I mean, he's obviously good-looking, successful, seems like a great dad—"

"He's the literal best, Livie. He's just like our dad was, and he's wonderful."

Ariel's devotion to her brother was clear.

Nina rubbed her hands together. "Sounds like a pretty compelling man. I've seen him around and completely agree with the good-looking aspect, that's for sure. Plus Angie Davies' husband is in his battalion and apparently can't stop talking about how shocked he is that the guy is so down to earth—knows every soldier's name, sleeps out in the field during rotations, does it all."

Jen widened her eyes and nodded, confirming the goodness of the news.

"Anyway," I said, exaggerating the word to change the subject. "Jen is the one you want to talk to about nanny stuff, Ariel."

The two of them started chatting, then moments later, we heard the welcome news.

"*Nächste Halte, Nürnberg Bahnhoff.*"

The announcement of our stop saved me from having to respond to their comments about me and Eric, which I was glad for. I had firmly tucked away Lieutenant Colonel Eric Wolfe, put him out of my mind despite his adorable son being a constant source of delight and exasperation in my class each day. I needed to focus on the last few months of *adventure phase* before I moved on.

I swallowed hard against that thought.

"This is us, ladies. Let's move."

~

The Nuremberg Christmas Market covered every inch of the plaza where it was held, plus several side streets. I could tell by Ariel's face she was overwhelmed, but happy. I'd felt the same way the first time I'd come.

"It's just... it's magical." That breathless, amazed quality fit the scene, and her expression, perfectly.

"Isn't it? I love this market. It's not actually my favorite, but I wanted to make sure I got to this one this year because I missed it last year. I've got to get my mug."

I clutched my purse close as we inched our way into the lines of wooden stalls filled with all kinds of wares—the small Nuremberg sausages and semmel rolls with mustard, wooden carved toys and decorations, candies, chocolate-covered fruit on skewers, pretzels, and my favorite, Gluh-wein: red wine mulled with a special mix of herbs, sugar, and lemon.

"What's this about the mugs?" Ariel asked after Jen and Nina had delivered our mugs of wine.

I accepted mine, enjoying the small rounded shape with a painted Nuremberg cityscape and Christmassy details like pine branches and red and white striped awnings remi-niscent of the stalls at the market decorating the lip. "These mugs are different each year. You can keep it as a souvenir, or if you return it you get your *pfand* back, which is like a little deposit on the mug. A lot of people collect mugs each year."

Jen didn't collect them, so her passion for them was lacking. This was Nina's first Christmas here and she'd started her collection in November when the first markets had opened and already had a sizeable showing.

"I get a new one every year, as long as it's either dated or different. Some markets will reuse designs, or will have generic ones. I don't collect anything else, but this just makes me happy." And I'd have them when I settled down to remember my time here by.

I cradled the mug close, relishing its warmth and the scent of the spicy-sweet Gluhwein, the chilly December evening and our walk from the train station to the market area leaving my face cold and stiff.

Ariel inspected her mug, then took a sip of the drink. "Hmm. It's... sweeter than I would've thought."

"It is. It can be an acquired taste for some. I think after my years here, I'll probably always want to drink this at Christmas out of one of my mugs. It just makes me feel cozy and warm." I sipped the drink and closed my eyes, savoring the taste and generally, the experience.

My contract ended this summer with the school here. I'd need to see if I could renew, transfer, or stick to the plan I'd always had and move back home to start the next phase. This might be my last time at this market, which left a film of achy sadness even though I quickly pushed the thought away.

My goal this year was to do the things I loved here, and Christmas markets were high on the list. I loved the little wooden booths, the combination of familiar and unique offerings at each location. I love the warm drinks and the food and the cozy feeling of people gathering together. It was such a lovely, communal feeling. Some markets had this more than others, but overall the entire season just felt kind of, well... like Ariel said, magical.

I linked my free arm with Ariel's. "Alright, you ladies ready to explore some more?"

We milled through the stalls, passing the little figurines made of prunes unique to this market, each buying a gingerbread heart ornately decorated with lace-like frosting and wrapped in cellophane and ribbons. Ariel bought a straw angel from one of the stalls—the things these artists could do with the simplest materials astounded me every year.

After an hour of weaving our way through the rows of vendors, even taking quick tours of the international market and the children's market, we huddled together outside the restaurant where we'd finally eat dinner.

"I didn't realize Germany would be this cold." Ariel tucked her hands under her arms and ducked her chin against a brutal gust.

"Yeah, this year feels like it's colder earlier, but it can be very cold. We don't get a ton of snow usually, but it's very much a real winter." I nodded, remembering my similar thought the first winter I spent here.

She shivered. "Very different from where I was in Tennessee. It'd get cold, but not like this, not even in like January or February."

Jen smiled. "I'm from Kansas, so basically nothing fazes me in terms of winter—until you add a windchill in the negative digits, I'm out in it. I think one difference here is you end up being outside in the cold more than you would in the US—this time of year for Christmas markets, but then you'll also travel and need to walk around and just be out in the world. Unless you live in a big US city or a super small town and don't drive, I find living in Europe makes me much more attuned to the weather because I actually *feel* it."

Ariel and I both looked at each other, then back at Jen. She made so much sense. "How wise, my friend. That's very astute."

She bowed. "I try, I try."

Nina nodded enthusiastically. "I've been thinking that

too! I was in the Carolinas before this and winter was rarely actually *cold* for long. I feel like it got actively wintry before Thanksgiving here."

"That's why so many people try to go to warmer places over Christmas break." I eyed Jen.

"And why we're heading to Portugal." Her smile was almost as big as mine.

We told Ariel about our plans—a fancier-than-we-should-have-booked hotel, food tours and port tastings... I'd been dreaming about it for months since we'd put down the deposit.

Ariel mentioned Eric had arranged for some kind of Santa's workshop adventure in Norway—basically the total opposite of going somewhere warm. Nina didn't seem to have plans for a big trip. She was still deciding if she could afford a quick trip somewhere, but wanted to get to as many Christmas markets as she could. She wasn't sure if she'd be here for more than just this year.

Just when we thought our hands would fall off from the cold, our pager buzzed and we shuffled inside to the blessed heat, hung our jackets on the pegs notched into the posts flanking our booth, and slid in to introduce Ariel to traditional German fare.

Hours later and full of schnitzel and cabbage and three kinds of potatoes, I pulled up to Ariel's house. We'd nearly missed the last train after staying too long at dinner, and I'd thanked God every minute of the ride home we hadn't.

"Thank you so much for this. I feel like I needed this and I didn't realize it." Ariel gathered her purse and set her hand on the door.

"I'm so glad you came. Let's do something again soon."

"Definitely."

She hopped out and scuttled up the sidewalk to the door, then a moment later, Eric appeared, pulling it wide so she could hustle into the warmth. He leaned out the door, raised an open hand, and waved.

I smiled and waved right back, chuckling under my breath at how ridiculously handsome he was. *Yes, hello there beautiful man. Go on back inside so you don't melt me with the relaxed hot dad look.* I really didn't tend to get so caught up on looks, but this guy was striking and nice, which was just deadly.

The door shut, and I made my way back home, all the while thinking over the night. Ariel was such a lovely person, and I'd already been thankful for her help in the classroom. Tonight, I'd gotten a glimpse of her on a more personal level, and it made me both happy and sad.

She had these super bright moments where she just let loose and laughed—especially after Jen and I had gotten her to relax and have a few mugs of Gluhwein—Nina preferred the kinderpunsch, and said she was amazed we could actually stand the wine. But Ariel had made comments that gave me a sinking feeling in the pit of my stomach. Things like "*I haven't had girlfriends in... I can't remember how long,*" and "*I don't think I've laughed like this in years.*"

On the surface, they sounded like things any busy woman in her thirties, or really at any age, might say. But paired with some of the other things I'd noticed—her self-deprecation, her quiet moments when she disappeared inside herself... I couldn't shake the feeling that Ariel had been through something terrible in the not-too distant past.

Maybe I could corner Eric sometime and ask him about it.

CHAPTER SIX

Eric

Robby's energy rolled off him in wiggling waves as he escorted me to his classroom for the class Christmas party. Delia's class would hold theirs tomorrow. Fortunately, the last rotation of the year had gone well, and block leave started in just a few days, so my level of stress would slowly decrease in the next forty-eight hours.

But first, the Christmas party, which for the first time in my life, I wasn't completely dreading, even if I didn't consciously admit it was due to the teacher I looked forward to seeing in her element.

Forgive me for saying it, but going into my child's class and making small talk with other parents I didn't know, then doing little games or activities that never went like the teacher planned, and wondering how long they'd allotted for the event... it terrorized me. Small talk—the worst. Not knowing the schedule—also the worst. Children's activities while dealing with the previous two items and managing the version of my child that materialized whenever I entered his or her classroom?

The *actual* worst.

Delia became even more quiet and withdrawn, like she was embarrassed I was there, but wouldn't let go of my hand. And Robby? Well...

"Dad. *Dad.* This is amazing. It's so great you're here. You're going to love it there's so many decorations Ms. Anderson did such a good job she looks so fancy today there are candy canes and we're going to do a gingerbread house with graham crackers—"

He only stopped to take a breath. He would've kept going if he'd had an endless supply of air. Robby could be high energy, but something happened to him when he got to be around me and other kids and their parents. And this little monster bunny was it.

"Alright bud, let's go check it out."

He pulled me into the room, already packed with parents despite my being exactly on time, and my eyes scanned the room to find the person who kept this from being a chore.

"Colonel Wolfe, so glad you could come." Livie smiled from where she stood hunched slightly to speak to one of Robby's classmates.

We approached, my son nearly jumping out of his skin with excitement.

"This is my dad, Ms. Anderson. You remember him, right? He hasn't gotten to come but we were just talking about it this weekend and he said he would try to come to class more in the spring between rotations."

Her bright brown eyes made their usual assault on my

senses, though something about her seeming genuinely happy I'd come made me feel particularly stupid.

"Right Dad?"

I craned my neck toward Robby, not looking away from Livie until he shook my arm. "Oh, yes. Right. I hope to."

A genuine smile, like all of hers I suspected, spread across her lovely, kind face. Generous lips stretched over white teeth...

"Sounds great."

Her speaking, her sweet voice emerging from that mouth, shook me out of my odd daze and made me return to myself, remembering I was not alone with this woman, not in a place where staring at her mouth like I had permission to made sense.

"What are you going to do first?"

This was directed at Robby, who rattled off his plans while I took in the room—a full-on winter wonderland.

Ariel had brought home supplies for the snowflakes that hung from the ceiling and had spent several evenings cutting them out while we watched TV, so I'd been expecting them, but there had to be hundreds. I caught her eye where she stood doling out punch from a giant bowl and gave her an impressed look. She rolled her eyes at me, but I could see the pleasure on her face.

Something small, but seeing her smiling still hit me and made me thank God for whatever had done it. Today, and so often lately, it'd been Livie and her involvement here in the school.

Before I knew it, I'd been pulled to different stations, as Robby called them—first the gingerbread house construction site, which featured kids mostly eating candy and frosting, then slapping glops of the two melted together onto dubiously stacked graham crackers. Then came every parent's favorite activity—the pseudo-science of slime making, this time with red, green, and white glitter inside.

"I hate to tell you this, but based on your current behavior, you are most likely going to be stolen away by Krampus this year."

My head whipped to the side to see her standing there, festive in jeans and a sweater so hideous and filled with kitschy Christmas flair, only a beautiful person like her could wear it, and I raised a brow.

Robby looked up from his work. "Krampus is creepy and makes Delia cry."

Livie shot me a regretful grimace.

I patted his head. "We learned our lesson at a Krampus parade last year—no Krampus for the Wolfe family."

And it shouldn't have been a shock, but idiot me thought it was some play on Santa, not his foil that would drag kids back to Hell with him if they misbehaved. The old idea of kids getting coal in their stockings had seemed rather benign after that.

Robby returned to his mashing, and Livie raised a brow at me, a small smile tugging at one corner of her mouth.

"You're over here grumbling over slime."

"Correction. I'm over here grumbling over glitter inside the slime."

A laugh bubbled out of her, all appreciative glee. Something in my ribcage crashed together, like cymbals, at the sound.

"So is it the glitter, or the slime, or the combination that is causing you the most pain?" She slid into one of the tiny child seats next to me while Robby worked away, smashing and squishing his slime.

He knew me well enough to know the slime wouldn't make it far in our house—it'd mysteriously get lost or thrown away before it and the glitter inside it could infest every-thing we held dear.

"All three. Any and all of those things would cause this reaction."

She shook her head, a little smirk playing on those lips. "My, my. You might need to lighten up a bit, sir."

Heat flooded my chest at her expression, the tone of voice, and what felt very much like flirting. Could teachers flirt like this in front of students, in the classroom?

No way, but she'd kept her voice low, Robby was tuned in elsewhere, and the assistant teacher, Mrs. Parks, was leading activities with most other kids in the reading circle.

"How would you suggest a man like me do that?"

Her eyes studied my face, and I could've sworn I saw a little flame light behind her gaze. Then she swallowed.

"Get out. See the world. Have new experiences. Play with glittered slime and discover its merits."

I chuckled as I eyed her. "I just might have to do that."

Before she could say anything more, one of the other parents sidled up and began asking questions about their child. Robby and I moved through the other activities, I fought the battle against checking my watch, and finally, Livie rang a little bell and all the students hushed and raised their hands.

"We are so glad you came to join us for our holiday party. Thank you to everyone who contributed to the deco-rations and the food. The kids have been so excited to have you all, and it's great to see such a great turn out. We hope you have a fabulous winter break! We have a regular day tomorrow, a half day Friday, and then you're free! Parents, please don't forget to keep up reading with your student for at least twenty minutes a day, and we'll see you in the new year."

She had great command of the room, and didn't seem nervous speaking to a crowd of adults. Like most things I'd seen from her so far, she was just... natural.

With that, everyone broke, moms gathering children, graham cracker houses, and baggies full of slime before stopping at cubbies to collect jackets and hats. Robby had run to the bathroom, so I moved to one of the stations and started collecting scraps of paper and other trash, replacing crayons into the bucket, and stacking untouched cardstock into a neat pile.

"So how about we get together over break. Are you traveling?"

The man spoke in what should've been a quiet voice, but the words darted straight to my ear. I glanced discreetly at him to find his back to me where he stood, and Livie sitting in her desk chair, which was pushed all the way to the wall, as far away from the man as possible.

More than irritation, a spike of alarm shot through me. Was this guy harassing her?

"I am traveling, actually."

Her flat smile was the first false one I'd seen in our short acquaintance.

"Ah, come on. Not the whole time, right?" He leaned down with one hand on her desk and got right in her face.

She leaned back, her expression tight. "Listen, I don't mean to be rude, but—"

"Then don't."

"I don't date parents. I'm sorry." Her eyes caught mine, then jumped back to the man slowly bending lower.

"I'm sure you can make an exception."

"Um, actually—"

I crossed the room in a blink. "Ms. Anderson, could you tell me where you want these supplies?"

The man visibly jolted when I spoke.

That's right, jackass. You're not alone with her.

"Oh, Colonel Wolfe, of course." She shifted her eyes to the guy in front of her. "If you'll excuse me."

He grabbed her arm. "Just a minute—"

"Excuse me." Livie's voice rose, and she jerked her arm from him and moved around him past the desk.

He turned and shot me a look that said I'd harmed him in some way, like he hadn't just accosted Livie in her own classroom. I stood there, watching him grab his child by the wrist, then jerk him toward the cubbies. "I'll swing by another time, Olivia."

He disappeared out the door, and I watched the tension drain from Livie where she stood at her desk.

"You okay?"

"Yeah."

Shaky.

"Sure?"

She nodded, then let out a breath. "I'll give him one thing. He's persistent."

"That's not persistent. That's harassment."

She gave me a kind smile and reached her hands out. "Thank you for interrupting. I'll take those."

I clutched the baskets of supplies to my chest. "No, thank you. I'd like to help you clean up, if you don't mind. Ariel said she's going to grab Delia so she doesn't ride the bus home."

She eyed me for a moment, then showed me where she wanted things, and so we worked together, moving around each other to clean things up. Mrs. Parks returned from walking the kids whose parents hadn't made it to the party to their busses and to the after-school care lines, and Ariel arrived with Delia.

"If I don't see you, have a great break," Livie said, speaking to all four of us, though her gaze kept finding mine, and I didn't mind that at all.

All the way home, I thought about that—how I kept thinking dumb things like how I *didn't mind* her looking at me. It wasn't that simple though. It wasn't merely that I didn't mind, but rather that for the first time in so very long, I welcomed it. I enjoyed it. I wanted more of it.

And foreign concept though it might have been, I wanted more of her.

But she didn't date parents. Probably a good rule for a teacher in a small community like this one. Good thing I'd heard her say it, or I might have made a fool of myself.

CHAPTER SEVEN

Livie

C art full of fresh organic produce, delicious cheese, high quality meat, and a loaf of heavy multigrain bread, I pushed toward the wine section of my favorite German grocery store to get the last few things on my list.

I surveyed the selection, smiling at the burgeoning cart. I loved traveling, but I did love coming back home. I'd thought of Germany as home for a while now, and returning to these familiar places, finding the products I loved, always made me happy. I seldomly missed American conveniences or products, and I suspected when I left Germany for good, I'd miss it far more than I'd ever really missed America. Maybe because I always knew I'd go back? Plus, I had the advantage of the commissary on post where I could get any American product I wanted. I didn't shop there often, but it kept me supplied with peanut butter and Oreos.

When I left here, I'd leave the language behind,

which was one aspect of a move home that really bummed me out. I'd worked hard my second summer here, taking a class at the Volkshochschule, essentially my nearest German community college, to gain a better grasp. It had made the next two years even better than the first since I could communicate so much better, though I still encountered scenarios when the language proved a barrier. Not too much longer, though.

Shaking off the tug of sadness at the thought of leaving, I determined to savor this big post-travel load up. I still had another few days before school started back, and I planned to use them to relax. Plus I wouldn't be able to shop thanks to the holidays coming up and Bavaria's tendency to shut down completely on the many Catholic and state holidays, not to mention every Sunday.

After grabbing several bottles, knowing I wouldn't venture to this shop again until the new year, I made my way through the checkout line, greeting the checker in decent German and ignoring irritated locals who found my large quantity of items an extreme inconvenience.

I'd never figured out how to only buy a few things at once during the school year. I just didn't have the energy to shop every few days. I supposed it was the American in me or something, but I liked a weekly load-up and knowing I had what I needed. Though admittedly, I loved visiting for fresh *everything* every few days in summer.

Maybe when I moved back, just to celebrate the ability to buy in bulk, I'd get a membership to one of those big box stores and buy my toilet paper by the pallet and my flour by the twenty-pound bag.

I'd also eat Mexican weekly. One thing German restaurants had not mastered was excellent Mexican food. I missed good guacamole more than most things... maybe even more than ice.

I loaded the bags over my shoulders, thankful they were sturdy and reliable, and trundled to the car, walking gingerly so I could keep the wine bottles from clinking too loudly. I popped the trunk and began settling the bags.

"Oh, hi, Ms. Anderson."

My pulse jumped at that voice. I looked up from loading my goods to find Eric standing tall and delectably stubbly next to the car. Military men with beards—who'd have known that would be one of my things too? Though maybe it was just anything he did, which was entirely possible. He must've grown it from the moment he went on leave —what had it been, ten days since the party, and he looked like a full-on mountain man?

"Hey. You really need to call me Livie. How was your Christmas?"

"Good. Great." He stepped around the side of the car so we stood about three feet apart next to my open trunk. "We did the whole Norway experience with reindeer and Santa's village and everything. I figured it'd be better while they're on the younger side."

His cheeks were ruddy in the cold, and he held a stack of neatly folded reusable grocery bags in a gloved hand. Something about that made my chest thump.

"How about you? Did you have a good Christmas?"

"Me? Yeah... yes. It was good."

"Did you travel?"

"I did. I went with my friend Jen—she's a third-grade teacher. We did Portugal. It wasn't exactly warm, but warmer, so I call it a win."

He gazed intently at me, like he had all the time in the world and everything I said proved fascinating. Even though he was busy and had a million things to do, he never made people feel that way—I'd noticed that our first time meeting. I bet that paid off big with his soldiers.

"So you're a warm weather lover?"

"I am. I get cold easily, and I love beaches. I love the mountains too, especially here, but relaxing with the sound of the waves... it's so peaceful."

"True. I'm more of a mountain lover myself, but I'll take what I can get. That's the weirdest part about living here— I've traveled more here in the last ten months since arriving than I had in the last decade combined."

"I'm the same. I moved here specifically to force myself to get out and see the world. I've been to... I think the count is thirty-three countries now."

He stepped closer, just slightly. "That's amazing. You must travel every weekend to make that happen."

"No, not every. A lot in summers, and I've taken two cruises that hit places I wouldn't have seen otherwise like Estonia and Russia on my Baltic cruise." One advantage of being single in Europe? I traveled whenever I wanted, however I wanted. One more reason I hadn't worried about dating while here.

His phone buzzed and he glanced at it. "Sorry, just needed to make sure Ariel wasn't sending me more things for the list. I like this store, and she told me I had to leave the house and not come back for a few hours."

"Why?"

"I'm making them pick up specks of glitter by hand in the wake of a particularly obnoxious glitter-slime incident after your party."

My eyes went wide before he smiled and chuckled.

"No. We're having a new year's party tomorrow night. I can be a little... intense, when I know people are going to be in the house. Nate talked me into it, and while it should be fun, I just have to... gear up for it."

I tilted my head to one side. "Having people in your space?"

"That, and just... all the talking. Home is usually my safe space. I can talk with my family, but I don't *have* to. I don't have to try to be charming or smart or whatever. Anyway, that's way too much information I have no idea why I told you, but you should come."

I blinked. "Uh—"

He held up a hand—not to silence me, but to wave off my concern. "Not like... a date, or anything. *No*. I heard you at the Christmas party say you don't date parents. And that's smart. Very wise. Good for you. I'm just... I know Ariel wanted to invite you. In fact, I thought she said she maybe had? But hadn't heard back?"

The red in his cheeks had deepened, and he was so entirely discomposed, it made me want to hug him.

"I'd love to. I did see her text but I ran out of minutes on my phone plan while I was traveling and just barely picked up some more today. I'll text her when I get home and she can give me the details."

"Great. And, you know, no pressure. Purely as a friendly gesture, because I know Ariel wants you there. So... great." He glanced at his watch. "I better get in there. See you soon, Livie."

I pulled a hand up to wave, but he'd all but jogged into the store and disappeared.

On the drive home, I imagined my car glowed from the smile on my face. I couldn't help it. Eric Wolfe had stumbled all over himself—completely uncharacteristic based on everything I knew about him—and I suspected it was because of me.

Silly, cheery, normal old me.

Don't get me wrong. Teaching kindergarten was nothing to scoff at. I knew I did the work of the angels as a teacher, and occasionally parents were kind enough to express that. But this man was... formidable. Impressive. I didn't know exactly how old he was or what our age differ-ence worked out to be, but he seemed so much more like an adult than I felt.

And it'd been on the trip to Portugal, tasting port wines and stuffing myself with as much bread and butter for breakfast as I could, that I'd decided if Eric was interested, I'd go out with him. Knowing there was no future in it, it wasn't very like me, and yet he was just too... beautiful and nice and compelling. I could push aside the knowledge that I'd be leaving—the time to head home and be with my family, to create my own family, would be here soon. But for now?

He'd mentioned hearing me say I didn't date parents, which I knew he heard because I'd caught his eye when I'd told creeper Bill Cantrell as much. At the time, I'd wondered if it would... affect him in any way.

In fact, I'd spent a fair amount of time in Portugal mildly obsessed with wishing I *hadn't* said anything in his earshot, because if he ever would have asked me out, now he definitely wouldn't.

But Eric had just given me the gift of a blush and a little rambling, and it made me bold. Not that I tended to be the shy and retiring type anyway, but I'd been thinking of him as more of one of those *look, but don't touch* scenarios. Admire from afar, occasionally daydream about closer contact, and know that someday, someone half as handsome might put a ring on it.

At home, while I unloaded my groceries, my wheels

started turning. True, I didn't normally date parents—or anyone, yet that was another point—but it wasn't forbidden. Ethically, it wasn't ideal due to the potential for favoritism, and it was something I'd need to address with Principal Crenshaw if we did go for it. But that was really in the case of it being more than just a date or two. No need to get ahead of myself.

Also true, I had no plans for New Year's Eve, and even without the conversation in the parking lot, I'd wanted to go to the party when I'd seen Ariel's invite.

I quickly dialed in my refill of minutes—though really it was data. For some reason I still called them minutes like the old school system. Anyway, I yet again marveled at how cheap my cell service was thanks to the pay-as-you-go and not the contracted nonsense in the States, and responded to Ariel's invite.

The next job would be figuring out what to wear. What dress would say *No, I don't date parents, but for you, I'll make an exception*?

CHAPTER EIGHT

Eric

Finally back in my car, I rested my head on the steering wheel. Then banged it a few times, amazed at how any sense of calm or composure had *completely* abandoned me at the sight of Livie.

First, I hadn't expected to see her, so it had surprised me. I hadn't been able to mentally prepare, and evidently I needed that. Second, I knew Ariel had been disappointed not to hear back from her friend, and it was also uncharacteristic of Livie. I wanted her to know she was invited, but then had the horrible, screeching thought that she'd think I was asking her out—the very thing I'd fleetingly entertained before I'd discovered how impossible that would be.

Nate would've outright laughed at me if he'd been there. Thank God he'd stayed to help clean. The house had been a disaster after we'd all returned early this morning, and I could admit the exhaustion from traveling, the mess, and the arrival home to no food, plus facing down the party... I'd been less than pleasant.

But now, I had Livie to look forward to, at least. I'd have to get my crap together and not fumble around like an idiot again, but I could talk with her and not become a total dunce. I'd done it before, and I'd do it again.

Tomorrow.

I smiled at that as I drove, my stomach tightening in anticipation, then immediately shook my head. The futility of liking this woman wasn't lost on me, but I couldn't help it. She was just so... friendly, and nice, and beautiful, and easy going, and... just... I liked her. Plus, she was a great teacher, a genuinely kind person based off of every interaction I'd seen and heard about. It all appealed to me. I couldn't turn that off just because I knew I was disqualified from her list of eligible bachelors thanks to my little energetic maniac five-year-old being in her class.

"You certainly look like a changed man. Good trip to the grocery store?" Ariel strung the cord of the vacuum around the pegs on the cannister, then shoved it into the cabinet thing we used as a closet.

German homes didn't provide much in the way of storage, so we had to get creative. Fortunately, the military-leased housing compensated for that in some ways by providing cabinetry and such that acted like closets, and they worked well enough.

The layout of the house was fairly open compared to some homes I'd been in here. The front door opened immediately into a large room that housed both dining and living room. Down the hallway an open spiral staircase went both down and up, and also gave access to the guest room and a door to the bathroom. Just off the living room, through a doorway without a door because I removed it when we moved in, was the kitchen. I wished it connected with the living room so I could chat with the kids when I cooked, but they were old enough now I didn't have to keep a constant eye on them.

"It was," I replied.

"Any particular reason?"

I turned to look at her because something in her voice told me she was up to something.

"It's a good store. I don't go out there often."

"Oh yeah? That's what has you looking like you have all the luck?"

I raised a single brow at her. She knew the look well.

"Fine. I already heard from her. She's coming, by the way."

She flipped around and bustled off to do something else, so I didn't have to hide my smile at the good news.

Around half past nine the next night, my lungs collapsed.

I'd been standing in a small circle with a few people, each sipping drinks and chatting about the year we'd had and what we hoped for the next one. Then, with a flurry of snowflakes and a gust of wind, in came Livie.

She was stunning. Literally, I couldn't breathe when I looked at her. I'd spent the last thirty hours convincing myself I could function courteously and be a friend to her like Ariel was, but as she unbuttoned the five buttons on her long wool coat, each revealing another section of a dress designed to murder fools like me, I knew.

There was absolutely no chance I wanted to be friends with Livie Anderson.

"Look who came!" Ariel declared, like my attention hadn't been focused on her the moment I saw her.

"So happy to be here. Thanks for the invite. Where can I toss my coat?" Livie glanced around, then followed Ariel down a short hallway where we'd hung everyone's outerwear.

I made a concerted effort not to watch her walk behind my sister, not to take in what must be pure magnificence from behind. It would've been too obvious, and while I was attracted to her, I didn't particularly relish ogling her in front of two of my fellow field grades, their wives, and Nate, who would never let me forget it.

"Everything alright there, Eric?"

I gave Nate a look like I had no idea what he was talking about. "Hmm?"

"You look like someone punched you in the gut. I'm wondering if you need to take a seat or something."

The arrogant little sparkle in his eye told me he knew exactly why I looked that way.

Not that I'd confessed just how much I'd been thinking of Livie lately, but he knew me too well. So did Ariel. And they both knew I'd seen something in her I hadn't seen in anyone in years and years, so they were hyper-aware of my interactions with her.

Incredibly annoying.

"Me? Not at all. Just need a new drink. Anyone else?"

Someone's wife handed me her wine glass, which I took and headed to the kitchen.

So far, the party had gone well, though it had started at eight and I'd looked at the clock no fewer than twenty times wondering if and when Livie would show. Like most good military personnel, the fellow soldiers who'd been invited had come right at eight and would likely stay 'til just after midnight, or in the case of a few of the families with younger kids, they'd head home before.

But Livie apparently didn't have that same sense of time, or if she did, she didn't mind stretching it. Some base part of me wondered if she knew it would torture me, but that would require her to know both that I was mildly anal-retentive about time and second, that I liked her and wanted her to be in my house and near me as long as possible.

"What can I get you to drink?" Ariel's voice carried into the kitchen as she and Livie stepped in.

I swallowed, unwilling to turn until I'd finished pouring some wine, but then did, hands full so I had something to occupy them.

"Good evening," I said, like I wasn't struggling to stay an appropriate distance from her.

"Hi, Eric."

"You look... lovely." I almost cringed, but it wasn't a false statement. It just didn't do her justice, not nearly.

Gorgeous. Perfect. Like a dreamy way to start the new year...

Her dress hugged her petite body, draping her curves in dark red velvet. The neckline with its dip at the center of her chest would've seemed daring except it managed to connect up to little sleeves that hung pointlessly, if teasingly, over her upper arms. It did wonderful things for her... *all of her*. The dress was a weapon.

She smiled, her bright red lips highlighted so beautifully by the lipstick she wore, I thought I might not even mind kissing her with it on. I'd never liked lipstick—always looked forward to times when Renee would wear something less substantial. But this... it had the opposite effect. I wanted to be the one to kiss it off her, see it smudged and entirely ruined because I'd taken her mouth with mine and devoured her.

Chill, man.

"Thank you. You look very dapper yourself." Her brown eyes sparkled, and though the line bordered on flirtatious, the smile was genuine and sweet.

"I've always thought New Year's Eve merited a little dressing up. Plus Delia begged to have it be a formal thing. Anytime I can say yes to her, I do."

She asked for things so seldomly, and people always seemed to enjoy getting invited to a party requiring dressing up.

"I love it. I've been looking for an excuse to wear this dress."

"I'm so glad to have provided it."

Ariel cleared her throat. "So, Livie, what'll you have?"

I held up the glass in my hand as an excuse to leave and recover from my very obvious appreciation of her dress and the woman inside it, and delivered the drinks. Then I made my way through—first to the small group of captains who'd come despite undoubtedly having better offers. At any other duty station, I'd be unlikely to invite company-grade officers, but here at Kugelfels, everyone mixed and mingled in ways they didn't at other Army posts.

This was likely due to a few factors. For one, the small community here created a close-knit dynamic that didn't really allow for separation. The idea of fraternizing was in theory still a thing—keeping non-commissioned officers and lower enlisted soldiers from interacting socially with their superiors—but in practice, it just wasn't doable. Perhaps a little more in my battalion because there were a number of lower-enlisted soldiers, but on the critter teams—the teams of soldiers that trained the US and NATO forces that came to the post to "play war" as it was sometimes described—it was nearly impossible.

All of that was to say, I'd invited my NCOs and all officers, because building a bit of camaraderie wasn't a bad thing, and they almost never came and stayed. Tonight, I had three captains in attendance, one of whom had brought his wife, and they were all excellent officers.

"Everything going okay over here?"

"Roger, sir. We're just talking about the rotation in January. Thatcher was suggesting some different maneuvers when we get to x-days," Captain Rob Waverly said, then took a drink of his beer.

"Don't bother the colonel with that stuff right now, Rob." Captain Thatcher Wild nudged Waverly with his elbow, then turned to me. "I'll link up with you after leave, if that works for you, sir."

"Of course. I trust your judgement."

And I did. Wild had to be one of the best officers I'd served with, and he'd only been in for about nine years, give or take. He'd be due for promotion to Major in a year or two depending on the timing, and he was one who should go all the way. His intuition, his management of soldiers—I'd decided within about four months that he'd be someone I'd do everything I could to help. Not that I didn't do that with every soldier I encountered who seemed to *want* help—because as with all of life, many didn't—but he'd stood out early on.

"Thank you, sir."

"And you, Jacobs? Doing alright?" I asked Lieutenant Jacobs, a man of very few words. In fact, so few, I'd had to counsel him about it. He'd have to develop his ability to speak a bit more freely if he planned to lead soldiers. But so far, he seemed like a good kid. As a lieutenant, he was likely the youngest attendee, but I'd asked Wild to take him under his wing so no doubt he was attending both my party and whatever plans these guys would get up to after they left.

"Roger, sir." A nod of his dark blond, close-cut hair, all perfectly regulation, and that was it.

"Good. Good. Well, enjoy." A hand on my back made me turn to find Ariel and Livie.

"These are the captains—Thatcher Wild, Rob Waverly, and Mick Farrell, and this is Captain Farrell's wife Janie. Plus we have Lieutenant Owen Jacobs," Ariel said, fully in hostess mode. I marveled at how she knew their names— she'd asked for a guest list and must've studied it. "And gentlemen, this is Livie Anderson. She's Robby's teacher, and my friend."

"So nice to meet you."

Livie smiled her beautiful red-lipped smile at them, and I may have wanted to smash something when I noticed Waverly's eyes flicker over her.

"She's mine," I said, then the faulty lungs Livie had inspired not long ago kicked in and I sputtered. "My *friend*. She's also *my* friend, I meant."

CHAPTER NINE

Livie

I tucked my lips together, suppressing a smile.

"Of course she's your friend," Ariel said, shooting him a look.

"Are you all enjoying living in Germany?" I asked, hoping to quell the rioting excitement just standing near Eric Wolfe created.

I chatted with them for a moment before Ariel led me to another group. One odd thing about interacting with military personnel was that the turn-over was very high. Without extenuating circumstances, a servicemember couldn't stay in Germany for more than three years, and for most, that timing worked well to provide them a slice of life, a chance to travel, and a return home just before their desperation for Target and Chick-fil-A became unbearable.

Most civilians stayed longer. I'd be wrapping up year

four when my contract with the school ended this summer. I'd been home a handful of times, but Mom and Dad had come to me, too—we'd done a cruise of the British Isles, toured the Normandy World War II sites, and of course they'd come to Germany twice.

Every time I thought of going home, I felt a pang I couldn't identify. It felt a lot like dread, but it had to just be the unknown. I'd scrapped my original plan to return home by thirty when I got the opportunity to come to Germany— I'd left North Carolina promising my parents and myself I'd be back in just a year. That turned into two, then three, and now.... Well, now here I was, surrounded by lovely people I'd miss when I left... or those I'd never really get to know. Like Eric.

I'd wanted to corner him after that little comment burst he'd made in front of his officers, but the man, unfortunately, circulated around the room in the opposite direction. I didn't think he did it purposefully, but I wondered. Was he embarrassed at calling me *his*?

And should I be concerned at the little leap in my chest when he'd said it? "*She's mine.*" I couldn't shake the feeling while meeting the rest of the party-goers, saying hi to a handful of people I knew, and keeping Eric in sight as best I could, that I wouldn't mind if that were true.

I shouldn't have been surprised at the thought. I'd poured myself into this dress, and the Spanx underneath it, in order to get his attention and keep it. It seemed like, just maybe, it had worked. Did it help I was likely the only single woman in attendance, other than the major I'd just met who was ridiculously pretty? Yes. Yes, it sure did.

I'd take the advantage, because I planned to press it and make my case. Yes, he was the parent of a student, but see the explanation of the small community, and things were a little less black and white on that being an issue. We were halfway through the school year. I'd grappled with the implications of who he was, and my role in his and his son's life, and I'd decided it couldn't lead anywhere anyway, so I planned to jump. A few dates wouldn't be a big deal.

And speaking of, I saw Eric excuse himself, presumably to use the bathroom at the end of the hall or to check on the kids, who'd all been corralled by a babysitter in the basement. That was a nice touch, I had to admit. Not that I didn't love kids, and I'd have to go say hi to Robby, but I didn't exactly want to feel the madness that came with a large group of over-tired kids having their run of a house during a party. God bless that babysitter.

I stepped into the kitchen and set down my glass, then scuttled down the hall and took a turn into the bathroom—which meant Eric must be down the spiral staircase in the basement.

I stepped out of the bathroom, and there he was, just four or five stairs from the main floor.

"Why, hello there."

"Hello." Those intense eyes swept over me before returning to meet mine.

My breath became shallow with his attention, but I found my voice. "How many kids are down there?"

He kept coming, stopping just in front of me and making me feel positively tiny all of a sudden. Maybe it was the dark gray slacks and black shirt he wore that made him imposing—all that darkness under an intimidatingly handsome face.

"Eleven." He peered back down the staircase as squeals of glee and laughter radiated up from below. "God bless her."

"I was just thinking the same thing."

We stood there a moment, both a little close for a normal friendly interaction, and yet I had to keep myself from inching closer. He'd smell amazing. He'd *feel* amazing. I'd shaken his hand the first day, and when our fingers brushed the night I picked Ariel up for the Christmas market. That and only that, and yet I felt like my hands belonged on him.

"Can I get you a drink?"

His question broke my dangerous train of thought.

"Yes. Please. Thank you."

The half-smile that played on his lips—lips that were sculpted and so aggravatingly appealing—made me want to lean up and leave a bright red mark on his cheek. If I wanted to be his, I wanted even more for him to be mine.

"What have you been drinking?" he asked, turning a bit in the narrow hallway before we entered the kitchen.

"Champagne, if you don't mind. Here's my glass." I grabbed the flute from where I'd stashed it on the side-board counter and held it out to him.

He pulled a stoppered bottled of bubbly out of the fridge and turned to me, then took the glass from my hand. Instead of reaching for any higher on the stem, he looked me in the eye as he took it right where my fingers held on, thereby forcing our first touch in weeks.

My blood warmed and I no doubt had a flush crawling up the expanse from the sweetheart lines of my dress to my face.

Soon enough, he'd filled the glass and handed it back to me. "To an excellent next year in your life."

I met his gaze and smiled. "To beginnings."

We each sipped the crisp, cool liquid, and I savored the bubbles tickling over my tongue while our eyes locked on each other. If I had any less determination, I'd run out of the cozy kitchen that instant, but I'd come here with a purpose, and now, in the quiet of this moment without anyone else in the room with us, the time had come.

"I wanted to talk to you about what happened at the party."

"Is that parent bothering you again?" He seemed to grow larger at the thought.

"No, nothing like that. I'm sure out of sight, out of mind. I just wanted to address what I said... about not dating parents."

His face unreadable, he nodded.

This must've been his military face. The one that said he was in charge of the situation and wouldn't react one way or another to a briefing or bad news, or whatever the circumstances called for. I wished he'd drop that, just a little, because this impassive front pushed a sliver of doubt to the front of my mind.

"I think you heard me tell Mr. Cantrell that I don't date parents."

He blinked back at me but did offer a nod, still entirely unreadable.

"I just wanted to, uh, make sure you know—"

"I'll stop you right there, Ms. Anderson. Please don't feel you need to spell it out for me. I'm a reasonably smart man. I understood when you said it to him, you meant it applied to everyone."

My stomach sank. *Totally* the opposite of where I wanted this to go. "No, you're misunderstanding me. I'm not rehashing this to reiterate what I said—"

"How we doing in here, you two? Not breaking into the good stuff before the rest of us, are you?" Nate Reynolds burst in, all charisma and smiles and good nature.

I let out a sigh—silently, I hoped. "Eric here stopped me before I had the chance."

I winked, because... well, apparently in the presence of two beautiful men, one of whom I was trying to ask out but who had just shot himself down for me, I became a woman who winked.

"Now that I find hard to believe. In fact, I happen to know if you asked Eric for just about anything, he'd give it to you."

"Okay then, there, Nate. Weren't you going to figure out if AFN is playing the ball-dropping? Why don't you go do that?" Eric shoved him back out the way he'd come and stepped closer to me.

"You know AFN won't have the ball dropping, right?" I couldn't help asking—of course the Armed Forces Network TV channel wouldn't have the ball drop six hours *before* midnight in the US.

"Yeah, I know," Eric said, his voice quieter now.

I smiled, though it was off, I could tell. "I heard some soldiers at the PX discussing it the other day, and one of them was going out of his mind because the other two refused to accept that it *couldn't* be shown here because we're six hours ahead of New York and it wouldn't have happened yet."

My story knocked the tension out of my chest, though his answering smile and low chuckle filled me right back up again.

"Sorry about him. He can be a bit of a ham if he sees a moment that might need interrupting." He gestured with his chin toward the living room.

I glanced over to see Nate gesturing wildly, then leaning in to whisper in Ariel's ear. "You guys act like I imagine brothers would."

"In some ways, we are. We've been through a lot together. He's a good man, even if he's got an ego the size of Texas."

The fizz of the champagne on my less-than-full stomach began to hit, just a little, and I made a note to switch to water before I became too cheery and talkative... Livie on too much champagne, tequila, donuts, or chocolate equaled Livie in a room full of her *very* best friends. Not a good look for tonight.

"Before he came in, what were you saying?" His eyes searched mine.

What intense eyes—the blue so bright, but the lashes and brows so dark.

"Ah, yeah. So, I don't normally date parents. But... I think I'd like to date you."

And... there you have it, folks. Livie Anderson's lessons in tactful delivery.

"You think so?" He inched closer.

"Yes." I fidgeted with my glass. "As long as you would also like to date me."

A half smile, a step forward, and suddenly, my back touched the countertop, and his hands came to rest on either side of me, caging me in. He dropped his head and brought his face close enough so I could see individual lashes and the navy outline offsetting the starburst pattern in his irises.

His arms were long enough that the pose took his body away from mine, and I regretted that—I wished I had an excuse to set a hand on his side and feel the heat through his shirt. I also wished he'd slide his hands over my waist.

It was all coming—I could feel it in the hum around us, the warmth of the kitchen and the racing in my chest. He was just about to say something, just about to *do* something, when—

"Dad?"

CHAPTER TEN

Eric

I moved across the kitchen by four feet, and I didn't even remember choosing to move. I jumped away from Livie like I'd put my finger in a socket.

"Hey sweetheart. Do you need something?"

Delia's face sent my heart to my toes. Under them. She studied Livie, who'd frozen in place, then me as I dropped into a squat to see her at eye level.

"Delia?"

"Um... could you, um, do the popcorn? We're going to start the movie for the kids who are left. Jade asked me to come get it."

"Of course. Give me a minute and I'll bring it down." I patted her head and she shuffled away, past Ariel who entered the kitchen with a small stack of dirtied plates and two wine glasses.

"Is Delia okay?"

"She was asking for popcorn. They're about to start the movie," I said, back to her, and now Livie, who I'd have to speak to soon.

I couldn't not.

I'd been about to whisper in her ear—couldn't even tell you what at this point, but something. Maybe even kiss her. It's not every day someone funny and kind and special like Livie Anderson says she'll make an exception for someone, and today, she'd said it for me.

But Delia's response had done what likely nothing else could have. It had sent my modicum of momentary confidence fleeing.

Did I want to date this woman? *Yes.*

Yes, yes, and yes.

But also... absolutely not.

She'd already proven to be so many things I liked. So many things I admired like sociable and adept at conversing with new people easily, genuine even in small talk and thoughtful in responses to more serious discussions—yes, I'd been straining to hear every word she'd spoken in my house tonight. She was easygoing, funny, a great teacher who loved and cared for her students.

But I had absolutely nothing to offer her. A few dates as long as Ari was around to help with babysitting, and then what? I wouldn't marry again, probably ever, but certainly not while I was active duty.

And that was all assuming it didn't impact Robby and Delia. I didn't think Robby would care, other than he might be a little upset since he'd likely end up telling Livie he was going to marry her and it might register if I was dating her that he couldn't. Granted, that'd mean he'd moved on from planning to marry Ariel, which he still hadn't figured out wasn't happening either.

But Delia's face when she saw me leaning close—close enough that even a nine-year-old would know it wasn't just a friendly conversation—had told me the answer. Or, rather, it had *reminded* me of what I should've been keeping in mind. Even if I was willing to marry again and dating wasn't completely futile, my kids came first.

By the time the popcorn had finished popping and I'd dumped it in a bowl, Ariel had left the kitchen, Livie in tow. I wondered if she'd wanted to stay with me, or if she'd been looking for an excuse to get out of there. Could she read the situation on my face? Or would she think I'd only been surprised, and didn't want my daughter to see me busting a move?

It'd be a lot easier for both of us if she could've read my mind, but I needed to track her down and clarify things before this went any further.

~

"Three!... Two!... One! Happy New Year!"

The small group who'd hung on 'til the end all clapped, hugged, and kissed their partners. I made sure to stand on the opposite side of the group from Livie so I wouldn't be tempted to ring in the new year the way I really wanted to.

People filtered out fairly quickly after that, everyone eager to get home. When I saw Ariel helping Livie with her coat, I dumped the dishes and glasses piled in my hands on the kitchen counter and rushed to the door.

"Can I talk with you for a minute?"

"Of course," she said, her voice rough from hours of use.

The sultry quality of it made me want to hear it another time—early in the morning, or late at night, just the two of us. I shook my head of the thought.

"So... I can't."

She gave me a close-lipped smile that looked more like a frown. "I get it. No problem."

"I really—"

"No, it's fine."

"I didn't mean to—"

"*Really*. It's all good. Thanks for a great party, Eric. See you around."

Her heels clacked down the sidewalk, and she hunched against the cold. She turned up the street, and I realized then she wasn't walking to her car, but along the sidewalk. That meant she lived close... likely very close, because she wouldn't want to walk far in this chill.

Instead of running after her and insisting on escorting her home since she likely didn't want to be around me right now, I shuffled back inside to find Ariel.

Ariel, who was currently getting a very tight, close hug from Nate. They broke apart before I did it for them and she gave him one of her real smiles, so I relaxed.

"Everything okay with Livie?" Nate asked, his hand gently squeezing Ariel's shoulder before falling away.

"Yep. All good. Can you check and make sure she gets home safely, Ariel?"

My sister's bright blue eyes gained focus and narrowed on me. "You don't have her number?"

"I do not."

Her pursed lips told me what she thought about that.

"Will you just check? It's freezing out there, and she walked."

She grabbed her phone from a nearby table, and a moment later pinned me with a sour look. "She's home just fine."

"Thank you."

"I was just telling Ariel I have a good feeling about hearing back on her command sponsorship next week. Colonel Shoales won't be in until the fifth but there's good reason to hope we'll hear soon."

Nate shot her a soft look I didn't want to think about, and she returned it with a subdued one of her own.

"I hope you're right," I told him, then turned to Ari. "I don't know what I'd do without you. Plus you seem... good here."

She set a hand gently on my shoulder to confirm. "I am. I'm really good here, and I hope I can stay."

"Me too."

The three of us circled up the last of the straggling glasses and trash, loaded the dishwasher, and after a hand-shake for Nate who'd leave any minute, I excused myself to go carry the kids up to their rooms. Taking them from the basement to the second floor where their rooms were, or perplexingly the *first* floor here in Europe as I'd learned early in our travels, was no small feat.

Neither child was particularly heavy, but fifty-five pounds of dead weight could add up, especially on the spiral staircase. We'd let Jade leave around ten since the last of the guests with younger kids had left and only my kids and two others who often came over to play had remained. I was shocked Delia and Robby hadn't woken when their friends had departed a half hour ago, but since they hadn't, it must've meant they were exhausted.

Robby didn't stir a bit on the way up or when I tucked him in, but Delia's eyes fluttered open when I set her down on her soft, purple star-covered sheets.

"Did you have fun, Dad?"

Her sleepy voice made my heart clench.

"I did. Did you?"

She pulled the sheet and her comforter up to her chin. "It was great."

With a roll to one side, that was it. She passed out again, and I had a rare moment with her to just sit and thank God for her.

Times like these, I felt hopeful that maybe the divorce and my job and my fumbling through parenting wouldn't actually harm my children. I knew that on one level, particularly about my job and my parenting ability, especially since very often I had help from Ariel and my mom, but the divorce? Renee's... change of heart, or whatever she wanted to call it these days, that kept her from seeing her kids regularly? That, I knew, would have lasting effects. It already seemed to with Delia...

I exhaled roughly, refusing to end the night thinking about all of that. Here she was, tucked safely in her bed after a great night with friends. And I'd had a great night too... hadn't I?

Moving through getting ready for bed on autopilot, I examined the idea. I had. Even if I hadn't kissed Livie like I'd wanted to, I'd enjoyed just being near her. And it always felt good to host a successful party, even if it did leave me exhausted for a day or two after.

But getting into bed on the left side, yanking the covers up over my shoulders and turning out the light, the overarching feeling pressing in on me wasn't that of a great party or fun interacting with friends or seeing Ariel rise to the job of hostess and seeming genuinely happy.

No. It was that before tonight, I'd had a little glimmer of hope I hadn't extinguished, and after? It'd been snuffed out.

CHAPTER ELEVEN

Livie

The phone pinned between my ear and shoulder, I watched Ariel pace back and forth across the reading area where she'd been sorting early level reader books for the kids for the new semester. I'd been eying her on and off for the last three minutes because I'd said goodbye to her and she'd walked out, but she'd snuck back in and clearly needed to talk to me.

But why?

She approached my desk the second I hung up.

"Hi."

"Uh, hi." She fidgeted with her fingers. "So..."

The words she evidently hoped to summon wouldn't come, it appeared.

"Ariel, what's up? Whatever it is, you can tell me. I feel it's too soon for us to be engaged, but if you really insist on it, I'll make a pro-con list and we can see where we land."

She laughed and shook her head.

"I don't know why I've gotten so nervous about this. I had too much time to overthink it while you were on that call." She exhaled and raised her chin, rolled her shoulders back, like she was preparing for some dreaded public speaking task. "I have to head back to the States for a couple of weeks before I can return with command sponsorship for the nanny job officially."

"I remember."

"So... Eric needs help with the kids while I'm gone."

A weird one-two punch of heart-pang and dread got me at that. Similar to what I felt anytime I thought of Eric Wolfe, but with an additional tap on the dread since I suspected what might be coming next.

"I would never ask this of you, but I know for a fact he's out of options. Our mom can't come back right now, and the babysitters can only cover about twenty percent of the time because of school, and one of them is out of town for half the time I'm gone."

I blinked at her. If she was going to make this big ask, I wasn't about to give her the words. Let her make her case.

"I know you and Eric parted ways at the party a few weeks ago, and I don't really know what all is going on there except that I get this would be awkward for you—both of you. But I also know that the kids both know you from school. Obviously Robby loves you, and Delia knows you're a trusted adult and has seen you in a social context at our house at least once."

A sigh escaped. What a moment for her to see me in a social context. That was putting it lightly.

She clasped her hands together. "I'm begging. Not for him—but for me. I messed up, and that's why I have to leave at all. I feel terrible, and he's being so understanding, as always, but I want to help him by getting all the details covered. He doesn't start another rotation until after I get back, so he'll only have a small handful of longer days, he'll be around weekends... it's really just filling in the gaps. I have both kids in after-school so you could just pick them up when you're done, take them to the house, and hang out until he gets home, or in some cases, until the sitters do."

"I can't really say no, can I?"

"Of course you can."

I raised a brow.

"I mean, you *can*, really. Truly. If it makes you that uncomfortable, then please do say no. But if it's just a little awkwardness, I know you guys can get past it. You're both adults, and you were friendly before the party... why shouldn't it be that way again?"

I would've rolled my eyes but since I was a grown up, and that wasn't a particularly grown-up thing to do, I didn't.

Could I swallow my pride and this growing feeling of dismay at the thought of being close to Eric, even for a few minutes a day, in the wake of his complete rejection? If I had an hour to mull it over, I'd say yes. Because I wasn't a sissy, and I cared about Ariel, Robby, Delia, and even Eric for some reason. I didn't want them to be in a bad situation, and I would prove to myself I could be helpful to my new friend. There was no point in dwelling on the embarrassment of New Year's Eve, even though I'd done plenty of that.

I'd always been someone who prided herself on being easy going. I didn't want to say no because I had this mess of silly emotions when my friend needed help. So I wouldn't say no.

My head dropped a little and hung before I gave her the

good news, wishing she hadn't pinned me down at work so I could've really thought it through—too late now. "I'll do it. Text me the dates, make *sure* your brother knows your plan and has no issues with it, and make sure you give him my number and send me his in case we need to work out details beforehand. If I do this, I'm not about to leave Robby and Delia stranded because of a miscommunication or something."

Ariel shook her clasped hands out in front of her and beamed. "You are amazing. I owe you. And obviously, you'll be paid my normal rate."

I waved her off. "No way. You're not paying me to—"

"Stop. It's work, and you'll get paid, and there's no refuting that so don't even bother. Put it towards some fabulous trip you've been wanting to take, and know that you'll be run ragged by the time this is done so you'll be glad for the compensation."

The next Monday, I sat at the Wolfe family dinner table in the quiet of the evening after a long day. A key in the door shook me from the daze that had settled over me as I graded math worksheets. The sound pushed my pulse from barely there to pounding so quickly, it felt like I might gray out.

I stood slowly, one hand on the table to make sure I didn't actually pass out, which would be unthinkable except for the fact that I'd forgotten to eat this afternoon so was probably not working with solid blood sugar levels as it was.

"Hi there," Eric said as he carefully walked in, set a small satchel, water bottle, and mug down just inside the door, and stopped on the rug. "Everything good here?"

"Yes. Absolutely. The kids are downstairs watching their show. They did homework, we had some reading time, and they got a snack before they started their zone-out portion of the evening."

"Perfect."

His voice sounded so... *good*. Wasn't that nonsense? I'd been flatly rejected by the man, and I still liked his voice. His face. His body. His general existence.

I could berate myself for that pathetic reality when I got home. I'd done a little of it already when I'd walked into the house and it faintly smelled like him and my stupid heart had started beating faster. He wasn't home. I was there because he couldn't be home. And yet... there it went, zipping along like it hadn't a care in the world except getting close to Eric Wolfe. But now, seeing him... I needed coping strategies for how not to drown in the irritation I felt for my own mind.

"Let me just get my stuff and I'll get out of your hair." I shoved papers into folders and into my bag, grabbed my water, and shuffled past him to the door, slipped my feet into my shoes and reached for the handle. But before I could exit, he stopped me with a word, the sound of it sending a dizzying jolt of longing through me.

"Thank you."

I summoned that easy, friendly smile I must've used on him the first day we met... before I'd figured out how great he was—what an attentive father and a caring brother and a good leader and a thoughtful person he was—and just how inaccessible. "Of course."

He walked back to me and stood close. "No. This is not a given. I know it's a stretch that Ariel even asked you, and I would've found someone else if I could have. I didn't expect this, and I'm sorry you got roped into it."

"Don't mention it." I turned to go, but his hand on my arm stopped me. My mouth dried out when I faced him again.

"Livie, please." His deep blue eyes searched mine. "I'm sorry. For the party... for all of it."

Somehow, that made my heart sink low, low into my belly, like it might hide from these feelings of disappointment if I only let it. *I wish.* "Eric? I'm fine. I'm glad I can help. I'll see you tomorrow."

I finally managed to exit the house and walk to my car, where Ariel had installed the kids' safety seats she normally used in the vehicle Eric had bought for his mother and sister to use when they were in town. Once I loaded in and took the short drive home, I sat staring at the wintry wreath I'd hung on my front door. I'd gotten it two years ago at a Christmas market. It had dried pine branches, pinecones, old-timey looking miniature skis, and a little sign that said *Wilkommen.*

Why did he have to be so nice?

If he was a jerk—just another arrogant, good-looking soldier? I could stop thinking about him. I could totally dismiss the hurt I'd felt when, an hour after I was sure he would tell me he wanted to go out with me too, and maybe even kiss me, he'd sent me on my way with no more than an "*I can't.*"

I understood, on one hand, how Delia's interruption of the moment might have startled him. But I didn't get how it made it impossible for us to even hang out a few times. I'd made my peace with it as much as I could considering his ridiculously handsome face still showed up in my brain unbidden on the daily, but this new set up would be a major problem.

Because when Eric Wolfe walked in the door looking like every possible good thing in an Army package?

Yep. I still wanted him.

CHAPTER TWELVE

Eric

F our days into her helping me out, I arrived home having prepared myself to be friendly but professional, just like our first meeting. We'd interact on a certain level and keep our personal exchanges to a minimum, so that I didn't have to swallow down the very large pill of how excellent this woman was and how much I wanted her, but couldn't have her.

Thing was, I'd started forgetting why I couldn't again. Of course not forever—I'd never forget about my life and all it would take from someone. But for a little while? Why was it again?

It was only three weeks into January, so three weeks from our interactions at the party, and yet my mind had become an addled mess in the course of the four days I'd come home to find her sitting at the dinner table working, the children perfectly happy sitting next to her or playing in the living room or doing whatever normal activity like she fit right in.

Because she did.

The kids had done so well with her, even Delia. I'd worried about Delia's reaction when she saw me and Livie in the kitchen. But when Ariel and I talked with them about how Livie would be filling in, neither of them had even blinked. Robby thought his life was made, and Delia just said, "Cool, sounds good."

I'd expected... something else. It'd made me call into question my reaction to her interrupting us at the party. Had I blown it out of proportion? Was I reading upset into Delia's startled expression because I felt guilty for the divorce? Was it possible she didn't care?

I couldn't tell, and it didn't feel right to ask her, obviously. I didn't want to put pressure on her about any of her feelings. Generally, she'd been doing really well—her anxiety and germaphobia had been manageable, and her therapist had commented that she'd made important strides in the last seven months. But it was always up and down, and sometimes, unforeseen things really threw her. I'd braced for the change up with Ariel and Livie to set her off, but she'd taken it in stride.

Plus there hadn't been any issue so far, not from what I'd heard. Livie's nightly reports were to the point, but always complimentary and thoughtful. We focused on the kids, and since my useless apology about everything that very first night, it'd been fine.

But today, coming home to her kneeling on the floor with Delia talking about who knew what, patting Geraldo the pig's head where Delia cradled him... the woman must've been trying to challenge my will.

"Everything okay here?"

Delia's red face turned to mine. *Damn.* She'd been crying for a while, if those wet eyes were any clue.

Livie and I shared a look, her face full of sympathy and concern.

"Delia had a rough day. We were just talking through it again."

I dumped my things on the table and knelt down next to her. "Can I hug you?"

Her red-rimmed eyes widened. "Can you—"

I hopped up. "Of course. Give me three minutes."

Back at the table, I shucked my boots as quickly as one can remove combat boots that laced to mid-calf, then sprinted up the stairs... first floor... second floor. Ropes of stress knotted themselves in my gut. If she needed the full clothing change, it'd been a very bad day. It'd been months since one of these.

I hurriedly washed my hands, pulled off my uniform, grabbed sweatpants and a T-shirt, and hustled back down the stairs, holding the railing for dear life just in case today was the day the stairs tried to take me out.

"Come here, sweetheart." I held open my arms from next to her on the couch, and she launched into them. No big wailing and tears, which probably meant she'd already cried them, my sensitive little one. I'd need to calm her and try to talk with Livie about what had happened if Delia wouldn't say.

"Do you want to tell me?"

"No."

"You sure, sweetie? I don't want you to be upset. I want to help."

"It's okay. I'm okay. I just can't stop crying." She ducked

her face into my shoulder and stayed there for a few minutes.

After a bit, I looked up to find Livie sitting back at the table, busy with work and not planning to rush out. She must've known I needed a debrief, and thankfully, she wasn't planning to bolt the moment I stepped foot in the house like she had the last few nights. *Thank God.*

Another minute or so and Delia moved. "Can I go play now?"

I chuckled, my heart immediately lightening. "Of course you can. Go check out Robby's Playmobil creation he's got going... it looked pretty amazing when I ran upstairs."

"'kay."

"Love you, Delia."

"Love you too, Dad."

She trotted up the stairs, and a moment later we heard Robby's battle sounds as Delia's fairy Playmobil people must have invaded his medieval castle. All was well. I moved to the table and took a seat next to Livie, who'd cleaned up her things but hadn't left.

"From what I can tell, it was a handful of small things."

I let out a breath, relieved on one hand that nothing terrible had happened, and yet chest tight from the upset Delia had felt so strongly.

Livie moved like she might set a hand on my wrist, or touch me in some way, but pulled back. "I think she'll be okay. Even at this age, girls tend to have more emotional times each month. I see it as young as my kindergarteners sometimes—really with boys and girls."

I took another deep breath and let it out. "I feel impotent when she's like this. I just... I wish I could fix everything."

She listened, her face all compassion and openness. "You were perfect. You came right in and made it so you could hug her without demanding details. You just let her feel and didn't push her when she said she was okay. I'm guessing changing clothes had something to do with the hugging? I wanted to hug her when she first came down so upset, but she said no, but that I could pet Geraldo if I washed my hands."

"Yeah. When she's upset like this, it's like all her anxiety about germs just skyrockets. It kills me, but it's much harder to connect physically with her when she's upset unless you get rid of the barriers. So the things I know are to change clothes, wash hands, things like that. Normally just washing hands is good enough which is fine because that's just good hygiene, but I've made the mistake of trying to argue around doing some of the things she asks me to do when she's upset and it's a fool's errand. It hasn't been this bad in a while, but it crops up every now and then. Right after Renee left it was a nightmare."

She studied my face, her eyes no doubt taking in the worry lines, crow's feet, dark circles... I didn't spend a lot of time looking in the mirror for anything other than shaving in the morning before work, but I saw it. I was aging, and in the last three years it felt like it'd been exponential. I definitely had more lines and a lot more gray.

She sighed, regretful or... something. "You're a good dad."

I harrumphed, for lack of a better descriptor. "Yeah? I don't know, but thanks."

She shook her head. "I *do* know. I see a lot of kids every year, and interact with a lot of parents. I can't always tell what's going on at home, but I can tell you your kids are wonderful. That tells me that if you're messing up, it's not too bad."

She smiled then, obviously trying to lighten my load.

"Thanks. That's kind of you."

She frowned a bit, then focused in on me, her gaze intent and serious. "I'm being honest. I wouldn't blow smoke about something like this. What Delia's experiencing isn't simple, and you're doing everything you can to support her. It won't go unnoticed by her, and I know how much she and Robby love you."

I dropped my head between my arms where they rested on the table and let my head hang and sway side to side. "Sometimes, I wonder if the divorce has harmed them. If I'd just—"

Quiet rushed in to pack the space where my words stopped. I hadn't meant to go there, not with her, or anyone who wasn't bound by confidentiality or blood.

"Could you have stopped the divorce? Was there something you, and only you, could have done?" Her tone made it sound like she *knew* there wasn't.

And in reality no, not really. But technically, at least according to Renee, there was.

I slowly shook my head side to side. "She gave me an ultimatum. She said it'd been the *Eric Show* for well over a decade of our marriage and she was done. She wanted her turn, and if I wanted to be with her, I had to let it be the *Renee Show* for a while."

Livie focused completely on me, and even though discussing my divorce with this woman ranked about as high as eating eggplant for me—and let it be known, eggplant was a disgusting creation meant only to torture and horrify—I wanted her to understand. I wanted someone other than Ariel, my mother, and my therapist to know.

Crossing my arms at my chest, I remembered aloud. "She said I could leave the Army and we could stay together. She could pursue her MD and support us and I could be the stay at home dad for a change."

Her mouth dropped open.

I scrubbed a hand over my face and had the fleeting thought that I'd never talked with anyone so easily about all of this. "I thought about it... I really did. But I already owed another year at the time—we'd just PCS'd again. So I told her that, and that I was just a few years shy of retirement, never mind that I think if I'd just walked away from my career I would've poisoned myself and our relationship with so much resentment it wouldn't have survived anyway. But *her* resentment, which she'd kept from me for far longer than I realized, kept her from any flexibility. The fact that I couldn't figure out a way to get out right then and there to save our marriage was the deal breaker."

Livie's eyes tracked around the room, then landed back on me. "There's just... so much there. Where to begin?"

I chuckled, surprised at the response considering the subject matter.

"I guess my first thought is, she must be crazy."

"She's not." I sat up, leaned one elbow on the table. "I think she might be a narcissist, after discussing it with my therapist, but she's quite sane. She'll likely make an excellent doctor."

"So she's really doing it? She's in Med School?"

"Yes. Or, I guess not in school anymore. She's at some point in the practical part since she'd already done the undergrad courses—residency or whatever. I haven't tried to keep too close an eye on her."

She nodded, exaggerating the movement to accentuate

her agreement with my choice. Then she inhaled and opened her mouth but stopped.

I wanted it—whatever she had to say. When I first starting talking about the marriage, and my failures in it, I'd feared the therapist's judgement of me at the time, and I'd worried what my mother would say. I didn't get to see Ariel much then, so I wasn't too worried about her opinion. Nate had been firmly on my side, and vocally so, no matter what. But for the first time in a long time, I wanted someone's opinion about the whole mess who wasn't family. "Please. Don't pull any punches."

She smiled at that. "I'm not going to punch... not you anyway. I just... are you still in therapy?"

"Not right now. I was consistently for about fifteen months after the divorce though. And we do family therapy with Delia's counselor once a month." I wished we didn't need it, but I was thankful we had it, and that we'd found someone so good on such a small post.

She sighed. "Then I guess I just want to say out loud that her giving you an ultimatum and you not taking it isn't you choosing divorce and her choosing marriage. She also chose divorce because she could've chosen to stay with you."

"She would say she'd done that for almost fifteen years already." The burn of shame from that thought—that the whole damn marriage had been such work, such a *trial* for her, had lessened over time. But this moment, in the context of a conversation with this woman and on the heels of my daughter sobbing into my chest, it felt vivid again. Not horrible or shameful for Livie to know, though. Somehow, it felt right that she understood how things were. How badly I'd messed up, and how the fallout had affected all of us.

She narrowed her eyes. "No. Nope. Sorry. I don't buy it. I get that you had a hand in it, and of course I'd take your side because I know you, at least a little, and I don't know her. But she prioritized her career and plans by expecting you to give up all of yours immediately. When you wouldn't or likely *couldn't*, she quit trying."

"I try to remember how raw and fed up she was. It wasn't long after Robby and she had a really rough recovery, plus basically the first few years after he was born, I worked a ton. I didn't do as well as I should have, and I've worked hard to be able to see and admit that without hating myself for it. But I haven't quite gotten past my anger with her when it comes to the fact that she has opted out of motherhood almost entirely at this point."

Her eyes went wide. "What do you mean?"

"She doesn't see the kids. She calls every few weeks. It's all under the guise of being very busy with her career, which I of all people do understand to a degree, but she didn't want full or even partial custody. She didn't want weekend visits because she had to take call. She's supposed to have a couple weeks in the summer to counter-balance that at least a little, but she canceled their visit with her this past summer." And that, actually, was the last really rough patch we'd had with Delia. Not a huge shock to trace the anxiety there.

"I don't know what to say. I cannot imagine that." Her tone held grief, regret, sadness.

I shrugged. "Me neither. I'd think it was all a cruel joke except I get to pick up the pieces when she cancels. At this point, I think both kids have learned not to get their hopes up."

She sniffled lightly, then ducked her head. When she

spoke, her voice emerged watery and rough. "They're such sweet kids. I'll never understand that."

The genuine feeling behind her word warmed me, and confirmed that sharing this part of my life hadn't been misguided. Or maybe it had, since now I knew even more clearly how amazing she was.

CHAPTER THIRTEEN

Livie

Each day I spent with the children put me closer to a dangerous edge.

At first, Eric and I exchanged the barest pleasantries and shared only information essential to the kids' care—any issues at school or daycare, any behavioral concerns, homework left incomplete, things like that. But after last Friday's conversation about his kids, his ex... I'd lost the grip I'd had on my ability to emotionally distance myself from the Wolfe family.

By Monday morning, I'd spent roughly sixty percent of my waking moments that weekend thinking about them. I'd vacillated between sincere pity and regret for the children, to anger at some woman I'd never met named Renee who, whether she'd be a good doctor or not, was a crap person for abandoning her kids indefinitely, even if it was to their father. I knew that thinking was too harsh, especially since

Eric didn't seem to feel so intensely—he gave her so much grace, at least in my mind. But still. I hated that she hurt the kids, and Eric.

Some of that harsh response had to come from my own desire for children someday, and seeing other women struggle to conceive, through IVF, through the adoption process. To see someone with two amazing kids essentially cast them aside hurt. And yet what Eric hinted at was true. He'd worked and prioritized his career for years, and now Renee was doing the same. If she was the husband, the criticism of his busyness and focus on success would be far less harsh. Not that I could see a man essentially abandon his kids and still respect him, but who knew what Renee really thought. I didn't know her, but again, I hated that the kids and Eric had been collateral damage of her choices.

And then there was him. I wasn't naïve enough to think he'd had no role to play in the dissolution of his marriage, but he'd clearly worked on himself. Maybe having full custody had forced that on him, though he did have help from his family so in theory that could've kept him doing what he'd always done.

The way he'd been with Delia had threatened to smash my heart with a hammer and leave it pulverized. I'd already been on the verge of tears, so surprised she'd said I couldn't hug her and then trying to bring her comfort by petting her little stuffed animal which in itself broke my heart, but then there he had come. He'd literally sprinted up the stairs—no small thing in a house with a spiral staircase—and seconds later returned in different clothes. He'd scooped Delia up and held her, cradled her, like she was the most precious thing to him.

That was it. *That* was the thing that broke my heart for him. She *was*. And so was Robby. He loved them so much, and I felt no shame admitting that when I thought of Renee whatever-her-name-is-now, I hated her for hurting them.

Something about all of that had set me off-balance, and by the time he came shuffling through the door that evening, my hands were shaking and someone had implanted pop rocks in my stomach.

"How's everyone today?"

Robby sat in the middle of the living room floor building an intricate LEGO house while Delia worked through the last of her homework.

Robby paused his building. "We're good. But Livie said I can't call her Livie at school."

Eric shot me an apologetic look. "She's right, bud. You have to call her Ms. Anderson just like all the other kids."

He made an exaggerated frowny face. "I know. I understand now. I just like *Livie* as a name. It's like live but it's Livieeeeee it's just so fun. *Livie, Livie, Livie.*"

"Okay Robby, we get it." Delia shook her head, rolled her eyes, and then shot a smile at her dad.

His answering smile made my heart thump heavy in my chest.

"And you, Ms. Anderson? How was your day?"

He leaned one hand on the table and set the other on the back of my chair.

It gave me that caged feeling, but the good one reserved for men by whom one might not mind being trapped. Eric was definitely one of those men, and had quickly become the *only* man.

Futile, considering his rejection, but we'd grown closer in the last week despite starting in such an awkward place, and it made *this* moment feel... charged.

Despite the nerves, I smiled as I answered. "A good one.

Mondays can be rough for the kids coming back, but by this time in the year we're cruising."

"Good." He knocked on the table, then stood.

Just before he disappeared into the kitchen, I asked, "How was your day?"

The momentum of his body continued into the kitchen but he grabbed the wall and stopped himself in an oddly comedic movement. "Uh... it was good."

I chuckled at the perplexed tone and wrinkled brow. "Really? Are you trying to convince yourself, or still deciding?"

Shaking his head, he walked back to me. "No. It was definitively good. I just forgot how nice that is."

I tilted my head to one side to look up at him. He dropped into the seat next to me.

"It's kind of pathetic, but I haven't had someone ask me how my day was just... casually like that, in so long."

"Your mom and Ariel don't ask?" I crossed my legs toward him, shifting my weight and body in his direction, all too pleased to have him sitting down, ready to talk again. I couldn't pretend I didn't want more time with him—I did. I craved it, even if it made me pathetic.

He studied Delia's drawing and perused the other items on the table before speaking. "They may. If they do, I don't totally recall. I think we end up running through stuff with the kids and then they're busy with other things and I'm getting settled in... we just don't get there, I guess. Or—"

"Or?"

He let out a little laugh, then an embarrassed half-smile. "Maybe it just felt different because it was you."

He stood again, avoiding my gaze, and slipped into the kitchen.

My heart pumped loudly in my chest, which was a total

overreaction to what had just happened. Only... what *had* just happened? What did he mean? Because if I let myself sit here and dwell on it, I'd think he meant it felt special to him to have me ask him. I'd think he liked me being here to ask him.

I shut my eyes against the temptation toward the feelings and feelings and more feelings just that mere thought created in me. How could something so small send me off into la la land like this? It shouldn't. I had four days left filling in for Ariel, and I needed to keep my crap together or I'd end up doing or saying something stupid and would probably never be able to show my face in this house again.

If I thought Monday was bad, Tuesday brought another challenge. Eric walked in the door soaking wet.

"It is *pouring* out there." He pulled off his patrol cap and wiped a few drops of rain from his face just as Robby skidded to a halt at his feet.

"Really? It must've just started! Can we go, Dad? Please?" He was bouncing where he stood.

Eric nodded, so Delia ran up the stairs, Robby close behind her. I looked to him for an explanation.

"They want to go play in the rain. We moved their rain gear upstairs for the winter since they usually need warmer stuff, but not today." He smiled and scrubbed his hand over his face and then ruffled through his short hair to let the water drop out.

I could've sat there all night watching him wipe the water from himself, but it finally occurred to me I could be helpful. "Let me run and get you a towel."

By the time I brought him a hand towel, Delia and

Robby had come downstairs with their rainboots and jackets.

"If you go out, you're coming right back inside and going straight to showers. It's unusually warm but it is still January so I'm giving you... five minutes. Don't get soaked through like we do in summer." He sounded so stern, but he had a little smile on his face that said he was pleased with their excitement.

They burst out into the yard and the nearly dark evening. He left the door open so we could watch. I moved closer to see, relishing the joy in their giggles as they stomped in a large puddle that had formed on one side of the walkway up to the front door.

"They found a good one."

I nodded, watching them splash. "They did."

"Dad! Come jump!"

He looked at me, with a kind of puppy excitement on his face, and I saw a flash of Robby in the expression. "Excuse me a moment."

He tossed the towel and ran out and jumped, his combat boots splashing both kids up to their thighs and adding a fair amount of water to his own clothes.

I laughed along with them, part of me wanting to run out and join them, but also not wanting to intrude on their family moment. My chest felt full, my stomach fluttery, and leaning against the doorframe watching them, my face hurting from the wide smile that could only grow by the minute as they danced and played together, I had the strangest urge to cry.

Well, not all that strange. This was a perfect example of what I wanted most in *family phase*. It'd been so long since I'd felt the *desire* for that... not since I'd left Virginia nearly a decade ago. Every so often now, though, I did feel a tug.

Which was great, because that would be next for me. Not here. Not with these people. But someday.

By Wednesday, I'd accepted my fate—I would be doomed to like Eric Wolfe, and he wouldn't return the feeling, or if he did he wouldn't act on it for whatever reason, and I would have to live with it.

But that evening he came in, set down his things, washed his hands, hugged Delia, then Robby, and set a hand on my shoulder, looked in my eyes, and said, "You're amazing. Thank you for doing this, and doing it so well."

Gratitude. Of course, it was only gratitude. And the shoulder-touching business wasn't anything to be alarmed about—perfectly friendly area there. But locked into his mesmerizing blue gaze, I struggled to breathe. I definitely couldn't remember the reasons I'd piled up in defense against wanting him. The time with his kids, and even the short interactions we had at the end of his days, only served to add more tick marks in the *pro* column for him.

"Well, you *are* paying me," I said, trying for jaunty and lighthearted.

His serious gaze didn't change, or take the joking bait. "Definitely not enough."

Thursday arrived and I got a call around five, not long after we'd all gotten home, that he'd had a situation arise at work, and wondered if I could stay late. I said sure, both because I could, and because I suspected I wouldn't deny him anything—such was the wretchedness of my crush on him.

But when he came home that night after ten, the kids were in bed, the house quiet, with only the kitchen light on and casting a slanted glow into the room.

He pushed into the door, quiet enough, but I'd been

waiting. He spoke as soon as he was through. "I'm sorry it's so late. Thank you for being willing to stay."

I rose from the couch and met him at the door where he'd set his things and crouched to take off his boots. I could see they were muddy, which explained why he wouldn't take another step inside.

I took his coffee thermos, water bottle, and bag, and moved to take them into the kitchen.

"You don't have to do that," he called out, his voice sounding distant from his bent-over stance.

I waved him off as I walked. "I don't mind. Your cleaning lady will not be happy if you track mud everywhere so I'm really just helping her out here."

The woman was amazing and if I could justify paying someone to clean my house, I absolutely would get her to do it. Alas, I didn't want any of my budget going to something I could manage myself even if it would be amazing not to spend time on weekends I didn't travel cleaning.

I microwaved the dinner I'd thrown together, hoping he'd find it edible since cooking had never exactly been my forte. I could cook, just didn't do it for others all that often, and didn't make much with meat anymore.

When he came into the kitchen, I pulled the plate out of the microwave. "Here's dinner. It's nothing fancy."

He didn't speak, but stepped close and wrapped his arms around me, one hand over my shoulder, and one under my arm, then pulled me into a hug so perfectly warm and lovely I didn't mind I was still holding his dinner plate in one hand.

It didn't last long—not nearly long enough—and when he pulled back, he simply said, "Thank you. Truly, Livie. Thank you."

I left his house that night feeling a muddled concoction

of joy and despair. Joy because I'd done something to make his life easier, and in the last two weeks I'd been given a clear picture, at least in some small way, how challenging being a single parent would be. And despair, because every minute with him made clear just how completely amazing he was, and how much I wanted him.

But Thursday? Thursday was *nothing* compared to Friday...

CHAPTER FOURTEEN

Eric

The pleading looks on Delia and Robby's faces meant I had no chance. I couldn't refuse them when they ganged up on me like this.

Plus, I didn't really want to.

Livie had gone to the bathroom just as I walked in, and the kids rushed me, begging me to invite her to stay and join our movie night. I appreciated their asking me before extending the invitation, and also that they wanted her to stay. This seemed like major progress for Delia, who hadn't disliked her, but hadn't been close to her when these weeks without Ariel had begun.

The door to the bathroom down the hall creaked open and their intensity doubled.

"Dad, please!"

"You can pick the movie, just... *please*."

"Wow, what's going on, guys?" Livie asked, wandering

into the room to then begin stacking her work and filing it into her bag.

"They're begging me to ask you to stay for our movie night."

Her head popped up and her eyes met mine, surprise and... something else there.

"Can you? Please Livie?" Robby dropped to his knees and started a chorus of *please please please*, his hands clasped and raised in supplication.

"You and Dad can even pick the movie. And I'll make popcorn. And we'll probably order Indian food, right Dad?" Delia watched for my confirmation via the nod I gave her, then turned back to Livie, hands clasped together just like her brother.

"That's so nice! I would love to, but..." She faded out then, but her eyes snagged mine.

Ah. Of course. She wasn't sure I wanted her here, and after all, it'd only been about a month since I'd turned her down like I had to. Like an idiot.

I kept her gaze and spoke right to her. "We'd all love to have you join us."

Her lashes fluttered. "Uh, I guess I could, sure. Would you mind if I run home and change into something comfy? I'm assuming a movie night means comfy clothes and lounging on the couch, right? Or is this a formal affair? Do I need a ball gown?"

"What?" Robby collapsed dramatically on the floor, all hard limbs crumpling against the wood flooring, testing the limits of his bones.

"Of course not. Robby and I'll be wearing jammies. Dad usually wears sweatpants and a T-shirt."

Delia's clear excitement made my chest pinch.

"Well, that sounds dreamy. Let me run home and ditch

all my teacher stuff and I'll be back in, say, a half hour?" She extended a hand down to Robby, who grabbed it and rocketed into the air when she pulled him up off the floor.

He and Delia escorted her out to her car and I had to corral them back in so she could actually drive away without worrying about running over toes, though I had to hand it to Delia for remembering to get Livie's dinner order before she left so I could call it in.

The next half hour flew by—we changed, popped popcorn, got the kids' sleeping bags rolled out on the floor in front of the couch, and selected our orders for dinner.

We cued up the movie for the night—*Enchanted* since in the end, Delia did remind me it was technically her turn and unless I had a better idea, that was hers, to which I agreed. The buzzing feeling in the back of my mind, the anxious twist in my stomach... those weren't anything to do with Livie coming tonight. Or if they were, it was more to do with the fact that Ariel had to extend her time in the States another week because she didn't have everything together to come back permanently yet—no one could blame her for that, though she seemed to blame herself. Just the thought made me want to pummel her idiot ex in the face.

When the knock on the door came, my heart jumped in my chest, and I told myself that resulted from being startled. Not because I'd wanted to spend more time with Livie, and the more I did, the more I wanted, and after the last twelve days, I knew I couldn't ignore that feeling any longer.

Maybe it was because Delia had warmed up to her so much, and how Livie had handled Delia's anxiety with so much care. The fact that she had let Livie pet Geraldo even when she was so upset said a lot. Maybe it was the true confessions about the divorce and some of my struggles... I didn't really know, and I'd decided not to care and just to... be here. Now.

"Come iiiiiin!" Robby yelled as he ran, then slid on his socks across the floor and slammed into the door. "Come in, come in!"

Livie hustled into the house, left her shoes by the door, and moved to set her purse on the back of a chair. "What can I do?"

"Choose your seat, though I think Robby may have assigned them already. I'll grab the popcorn."

I found Delia dumping popcorn into three bowls.

"One for me, one for Robby, and one for you and Livie to share." She shoved one bowl into my hand and scampered back into the living room.

I grabbed two beers as well, then went to find my seat, ignoring the little flutter of anticipation. Delia lay stretched on one end of the sectional couch, Robby and Livie sat next to each other on the other side, and the corner seat looked vacant.

I handed Livie the beer as I walked by and dropped into the cozy seat, now wishing Robby would've claimed it. Apparently, he wanted to sit between me and Livie. Fortunately, I knew that eventually, he'd move to the floor and snuggle up in his sleeping bag and then there'd be nothing between us. I didn't know why I felt so glad about that, but I did.

The movie played along steadily until we paused for a break to answer the door for our delivery. A few minutes later, we'd all snuggled up with plates in our laps, the height of glamour, and continued the show. Once Robby finished his food, off he went to the floor, and I knew despite his desire to stay awake he'd be asleep before the movie ended

—if not the first then certainly the second since they'd beg for a double feature.

Livie finished her dinner and she moved to stand and grab my plate, but I hopped up before she could.

"No, I'll get them." I collected the kids' plates and mine and shuffled into the kitchen.

I liked that. She'd become comfortable in my house—at least enough to go into the kitchen. I wasn't about to let her do it in reality, but I liked that she'd offered and it wasn't one of those fake gestures—had I not stopped her, I was certain she'd be in here now, scraping plates and dumping trash. And not that I felt she needed to be the one to clean up after us, but I appreciated her even offering. I prayed she'd stay on the couch, though, because if she'd followed my wishes and joined me in the kitchen, away from the kids' view, I might've... done something.

She'd taken a bathroom break while I scrubbed dishes, and she returned moments after I had sat back down. I hid a smile when she sat down a few inches closer to my spot. Plenty of room between us, and it occurred to me I'd never once wished I had a smaller couch until this moment. But at least she'd cut half a foot of the distance.

I readjusted, stretching my arm across the back of the couch, not yet giving in to the temptation to sweep a finger along the back of her neck and feel the softness of the hair there. She'd pulled her hair into a ponytail but several little wispy shorter pieces fell and grazed her nape and I'd been eyeing the skin there, that smooth slope from the line of her hair down the curve of her shoulder, left bare by the slouchy shirt that hung off that same arm.

Her clothing change had created a problem for me. I couldn't keep my eyes off her... I didn't want to. She looked gorgeous dressed up, she looked great coming home after school, but the woman undid me there on my couch in sweatpants and a shirt that scooped to the side and revealed the smooth skin of her decolletage, shoulder, and upper arm. Smooth. Soft.

I gave in to the temptation and pinched a few strands of her hair between my fingers, then let them trail away when she turned just slightly and caught my eye.

I didn't look away. In fact, some new boldness urged me on and before I knew it, I brushed my index finger over the cap of her shoulder, the smooth, warm skin like a miracle under my touch.

Her lashes fluttered, but she didn't look away. Her eyes seemed to soften and heat at the same time, and she tilted her head, her lips parting just barely, but enough to make my stomach clench and my hand jerk with how much I wanted to kiss her.

"Yes! Got 'er!" Robby's exclamations broke the moment.

I let out a breath, thankful for the interruption on one hand, and on the other, deeply regretting it. Not that I would've kissed her here in front of the kids, but unless I was reading every signal wrong—and that was entirely possible considering how out of practice I was—she wanted me to.

"Can we do a double feature? Please? Livie can you stay for another one? When we do double features we do ice cream." Robby bounced where he sat, begging me, begging Livie, generally releasing enough energy to power a jet engine.

"It's fine with me. What do you think?" I raised a brow at her.

"I'm up for it. Especially if there's ice cream."

And then, if she wasn't already killing my resolve to stay away from her—as if that hadn't been ruined the minute she'd agreed to help me while Ariel was gone—she bit her bottom lip and smiled.

"It's"—I cleared my throat. "It's decided, then. You kids choose the next movie. Livie and I'll get the ice cream."

I stood at the same time she did and followed her into the kitchen, my heart downright racing in my chest at the thought of being alone in the room with her for even a minute. In the last hour, the tension between us had vaulted from subtle to glaring, and I silently thanked God Ariel wasn't here. Though if she were, Livie wouldn't be here anyway, so there was another reason to be thankful Ariel had ended up needing to stay in the States.

Ah. *That.* I did have a favor to ask Livie, and I needed to do it soon so she could plan, and so I could if she said no.

She leaned against the countertop at the far end of the kitchen, conveniently right in front of the cabinet where we kept the bowls. I didn't stop, didn't stutter my steps as I approached and came close, *so close*, to where she stood. She tilted her head up and hit me with brown eyes so inviting and lovely, I physically bit my tongue to keep from grabbing her and claiming the mouth that had just the slightest smile playing at the edges.

"Pardon me," I said, words just above a whisper.

"Don't mind me." Her volume met mine.

I set a hand on the cabinet behind her and looked down at her, suddenly feeling ten feet tall. I wasn't really, but she was short, and crowded together like this, her neck stretching long to look right at me even as close as we were...

"Just getting the bowls."

"Good."

I opened the door and reached in for four bowls, removed them, and set them on the counter next to us. The moment I heard the *clink* of the dishes against the surface, I had a flash—me hoisting her up to sit on the counter, crushing her mouth to mine, winding my hands in her hair, sliding down her spine, the other rising up to touch perfect, soft—

"It's starting Dad! Don't forget the sprinkles!" Robby, inevitably.

And again, I should thank him. Because I couldn't live out that fantasy, not now. So like a man in control of himself, which I definitely was, I stepped away from her, bowls in hand.

"Can you grab spoons?" I asked, rummaging for the ice cream.

I heard an audible exhale, then the drawer pulled out and shut. I glanced at her just as she did me, and just that sent my pulse racing yet again. We smiled at each other like shy teens, then went about piling up scoops of ice cream—vanilla with chocolate sauce for Delia, chocolate with chocolate sauce and sprinkles for Robby, vanilla for me, and chocolate with sauce for Livie.

Some small stupid place in my chest expanded at the thought of knowing she liked chocolatey ice cream. We delivered the bowls and I sat back in the corner, waiting half breathless to see where she'd sit.

Seeing her sit significantly closer, so much so that when I set my arm along the back of the couch it would be around her, made every muscle in me clench. She sat with her knees folded to one side on the couch, bowl resting on her thigh... Honestly, it was a pose I couldn't imagine because I couldn't ball up like that and be comfortable. I pushed away the thought that this evening's intimacies—a family evening together, sharing dinner, dessert, space—all of it was too close to a relationship and not something I should be doing with a woman I had no future with.

At some point, she took the bowls, insisting I'd done the dinner dishes and it was her turn, and returned to sit just as close. I didn't need a second invitation—though essentially, I did and she'd just given it to me, so I rested my arm behind her and indulged in dragging the tips of my fingers along her arm. While the movie played on, she rested her hand closest to me on the couch, which gave me incentive to move and capture it in mine. It was a small enough touch, but as our fingers threaded together, my chest expanded and I let out a great, silent sigh.

The small contact we had felt charged and packed with so much energy and potential, and yet it also made me feel centered, almost peaceful, except for the humming awareness in my blood.

By the end of the movie, the kids were fast asleep, and I'd held Livie's hand for over an hour. If one of us moved, or adjusted our pose, then we released the clasp but returned to one another, always knitting back together like our hands belonged like this.

When I shut off the TV, Delia stirred, mumbled good-night, and dragged herself up the stairs to bed. I'd have to carry Robby myself.

"Don't forget to brush," I reminded Delia as she trudged upstairs, which she waved off with a grunt.

"Do you need any help with him?" Livie asked, smiling down at Robby's slackened face.

"No. I've got him. He'll fall asleep anywhere so I've got good practice toting him around." I squeezed her hand one last time, then let go. "You need a walk to your car?"

She smiled at that. "Thank you, but no—I walked back over. You guys get to bed."

I nodded and followed her to the door. "Thanks for staying."

"Thanks for inviting me."

My heart pounded and my head felt light. The way those big brown eyes looked up at me like she really meant it, like she'd loved being here with us—not just me, but the kids too... It made me want more time with her, made me wish I could ask her to stay longer.

I should kiss her, right now.

"We should probably have a conversation sometime soon," she said, interrupting my scattered thoughts.

"Yes."

"See you soon, Eric."

She waved from the sidewalk and then she was gone, disappearing up the street to her place. I stood in the doorway, the chilly Bavarian air calming my rioting thoughts.

If the last few weeks hadn't clarified it for me, tonight had. Tonight had been the best night I'd had in... years. No more denying it or pretending I could ignore what lay between us. I liked Livie Anderson. I wanted to get to know her better. It didn't have to be more complicated than that.

CHAPTER FIFTEEN

Livie

Eric texted me the very next day.

It didn't quite shock me, but so far, we hadn't communicated except out of necessity. Granted, we had also not held hands and spent hours just shy of snuggling together on his couch before last night, so it made sense things had changed in that regard too.

He'd invited me to join them for the day, but I'd made plans with Jen and Nina and wouldn't break them. He'd then asked if he could call me in the afternoon once they'd returned from their adventures, and I happily said yes.

Nina had had some sort of insane Christmas break, claiming to have fallen for a soldier during the two-week timeframe, and this I had to hear about. We hadn't managed to get together since before the new year, so we were overdue.

The whole time Nina sat, positively glowing across the

table where she ate next to Jen, each delighting in our brunch selection of meats, cheeses, breads, and fruit, I felt a tug toward jealousy, which I quickly banished. Nothing good came from that emotion, and I also felt a stronger sense of genuine happiness for my friend. I'd look forward to meeting the guy at some point... soon, I hoped.

"How has it been with Colonel Wolfe?"

They'd taken to calling him that ever since I'd told them about the rejection on New Year's Eve. We might not have gotten together, but Nina did text often enough and she'd hounded me about it until I'd given her at least the details of my wandering home alone, trying not to cry over something that'd never been a thing to begin with. Jen had heard it in person when she'd cornered me during lunch one day.

"He's... good."

"Oh really?" Nina's interest, along with humor and curiosity, painted her words.

Jen wiggled her brows. "Do tell."

"Yes, really. I don't think he could've managed these weeks while Ariel was gone without me unless he'd taken leave, and I know he's grateful."

"And how are *you* and the good Colonel Wolfe?"

Jen waggled her eyebrows at me again, and I was reminded how much I loved that this woman was such a dork. She was a six-foot-tall blonde with model-level looks and a brain that said *intellectual stimulation* nice and slow for the people in the back—kind of every man's dream, or what we were always told was their dream, except that she was soft and shy and held her hidden places close.

"You seem cagey. This is either very good or very bad." Nina's matter-of-fact approach to life and friendship and all things shone through with that statement.

I spread some chive cream cheese on a slice of fresh

whole grain bread, avoiding their eyes and taking stock of what I wanted them to know. Based on Nina's Christmas break tale of love, she'd kept me in the dark for a while too. I didn't blame her, but it also made me feel justified in keeping some things for myself. I didn't want to tell them everything, certainly, because part of me feared saying it out loud might jinx it.

"We're good. We've had some good conversations, especially after the first few days where things were pretty strained and awkward like I told you last week, but they got better."

Nina's eyes widened and she nodded to encourage me. Jen waved her hand, signaling for me to continue.

"It's good. We're friends, and I'm relieved everything isn't so tense. I always dreaded him coming home and what our interaction would be at the hand off, but now I look forward to it."

"Do you?" Nina's tone made it sound salacious.

I rolled my eyes, sighing for extra effect. "Don't go there on me. Of course I do. It's not like he became a troll, lost all his sweetness, and began hating his children. Everything I like about him is still there. But I'm also relieved that the primary interaction in both of our memories isn't him telling me *I can't*, you know?"

"Makes sense." Jen took a drink of her coffee, then nestled it back into the little saucer. "How about the kids? Did they do okay?"

"Overall yes. Delia had some hard days the first week. I'm not sure if that was linked to Ariel being gone and me stepping in, or just happenstance, but she seems to have had a better week, and she and Robby asked if I could stay for their movie night last night, so I take that as a good sign that she's doing okay with me."

"I'd say so. I'm glad. She's the sweetest child and *so* smart." Nina was Delia's teacher and knew firsthand.

I nodded. "They both are. Robby's great. Delia is too, and I..."

They both stopped, coffee cups halfway to their mouths, and Jen's eyes narrowed on me. "What?"

I crumpled the napkin in my hand, then spread it out again over my lap. "I've really enjoyed the time with them. I thought it'd feel like such a chore, and I definitely needed to sleep in and will go to bed early tonight and make full use of resting tomorrow, but it was kind of nice too. You know?"

Jen set down her cup and reached to pat my hand. Our eyes met and I could see it.

"I do know, my friend. I do."

"How was brunch with your friends?"

I skittered across the floor and dove into my couch, pulling my knees up close and snuggling into the cushions like I was settling in for a good book or a favorite movie. Instead, I was preparing to listen to Eric's voice in my ear through the phone for the first time ever.

"Really good, and long overdue. Have you been to Frühling Haus downtown?"

"I haven't, actually. Seems crazy because I keep hearing people say I need to go, but haven't managed it. I think my mom took Delia one day and they loved it."

I hugged a pillow to my chest and pictured the smile on his face when he talked about his mom and daughter. "You should go. It's really good, though it was insane today and we only got a table because Jen planned ahead and made a reservation."

"I'm glad she did."

I could hear the smile in his voice, which sent my already pitter-pattering heart a-skipping down the lane. I couldn't handle how much I liked this guy, and we'd only gone so far as to hold hands for a while.

"What about you guys, did you have fun?"

"We did, though both Robby and Delia asked why you couldn't join us about ten times."

He chuckled, and the sound, along with his statement, caused warmth to swirl in my chest.

"I'm sorry I couldn't." And part of me was, though the time with Nina and Jen had been necessary. Soul-restoring, even, in the way that only good girlfriends, good food, and long conversations could be.

"Well, listen. I have to fess up and say I have an agenda for this call."

"Oh... okay. Lay it on me." What could this be? My pulse picked up.

"Ariel got delayed another week."

My stomach, and hopes, plummeted. "Oh, I'm sorry."

"*I'm* sorry. Because what I'm about to do is really crappy, but I'm going to ask you if you can help me out again this week. I actually did manage to get a sitter for Tuesday and Wednesday, so I just need help Monday, Thursday, and Friday. Ariel gets in early Saturday and I have a sitter coming until she arrives because I start rotation Friday. I'd need to be pretty late, but then you're off the hook. *If* you can do it. And I don't want—"

"Of course, Eric. I'm happy to do it."

I meant it, completely. I was glad he'd asked. But something about the whole conversation soured in my stomach when the thought occurred that he'd called only to ask that, and not to chat, or catch up, or because he wanted to hear my voice—or, you know, address the whole hand-holding, shoulder caressing while watching a movie thing.

He stayed quiet for a moment. I could hear a rough exhale.

"Thank you. Truly, thank you, Livie. I don't know how I'll repay you for this, although I can double your pay or something, but I hope you'll let me make it up to you somehow."

"You have nothing to make up for and you will absolutely not double my pay—that's insane. Your kids are great. You live three blocks from me, so it's not like you're out of my way. I know the routine, I know the kids, and despite my molten-hot social life, I am free Friday night and can stay late until you get back. You've managed to catch me in a very slow travel season, so you're lucky."

In truth, I'd been relieved for the break. Normally, I took at least a trip a month, even in winter, but I'd been gone so much in the fall, I genuinely needed a rest. Not that taking care of Robby and Delia was exactly a rest, but it didn't wear me out like I would've thought it would. Add to that saving up to make the move back to the States, and the time spent *not* traveling had been necessary.

He thanked me again, then again, until I finally threatened to renege on helping out if he kept at it. We hung up with friendly farewells, and I ended up feeling like someone had stomped on my fifth grade solar system diorama all over again.

Had I hallucinated everything between us last night? Was I that desperate to feel validated and liked by this man that I'd made it all up? I knew I hadn't, and yet the exchange had felt... empty. Friendly, sure, but none of that delicious heat or anticipation had sounded in the words between us. He had been his usual nice, charming self, and even his request for help had come tactfully and clearly only because he had no other options.

But... was that it? Was it all so I would help him out?

Good thing I hadn't said much to Jen and Nina. Maybe in a few weeks, I'd be able to tell them and we could all laugh at what an idiot I'd been.

CHAPTER SIXTEEN

Eric

I t had been one of those days. A Thursday after a week, frankly, that made a person question his choice to stay in the Army, to take command, to say *yes, I'm capable of leading hundreds of people*. I didn't have them a lot at this age and stage of my career anymore, but when they came, they hit hard.

The Army created a unique challenge for leaders. It was the same thing that made Army life so appealing to some, though Renee had certainly never enjoyed it. Perhaps that was one of many reasons she couldn't stand staying together.

Working in the Army created a collapse between the work-life balance. There wasn't a separation. If you got a speeding ticket, your commanding officer would be notified. If you had trouble with finances, you'd pop on one spreadsheet or another tracking liabilities in the battalion. If you had mental health issues, physical health issues, marital issues, even sometimes car trouble... all of these things could and very often would become something the leadership dealt with.

Today, I'd counseled three leaders—one officer, one warrant officer, and one non-commissioned officer—after various incidents that would lead to at least two of them losing their jobs. Truthfully, for two of them, I wasn't as shocked to hear the serious incident reports as I should've been, but for Sergeant Spaulding, it'd genuinely surprised me. His wife had gotten crazy drunk and stirred up enough trouble yelling in the street in front of their house that the military police—the MPs—and the local Polizei had been called. That's what you call a no-win situation.

The other two idiots were clearly in the wrong. The lieutenant was too young to be here, as evidenced by the fact that he'd been pulled over with DWI and ended up testing with a .22 blood-alcohol level. *Super*. He didn't need to be told twice that behavior like that put him on a path to losing his job, though he'd seemed surprised I wasn't giving him another chance.

The Warrant Officer had been under investigation for some missing equipment he'd lost, and the investigating officer had just given his recommendation—unfortunately for him, it meant he'd be drawn up on UCMJ charges for theft of government property, and based on the evidence, it didn't look good for him.

All in all, only Spaulding had been put in a situation he hadn't caused and was something he couldn't control. But this being the Army, and not just a corporation or even an average government job, as his boss, I'd had to have a chat with him.

So when I walked in the door fourteen hours after I'd

left that morning, the weight of the day, the whole week honestly, the relief of returning to my own space, and the little pulse of joy at seeing Livie at the table, all nearly knocked me off my feet.

"Hey," I said, dropping my things, shucking my boots, and padding over to her as she stood.

"Hi, you must be—"

She broke off when I wrapped my arms around her and hugged her to me, arms across her back and head ducking low to rest against hers.

"—exhausted."

The word emerged all breath, a small puff against my neck as she hugged me back.

My eyes closed and I breathed her in, her calm warmth filtering into me and unraveling the knot of stress that'd been winding around my shoulders and chest all week. When I finally did release her, she blinked rapidly, and I wondered if I'd upset her.

"I am. It's been a rough week."

She began to step back, but I grabbed her hand, not ready to be without some form of contact with her. It was selfish, and honestly part of me was pleasantly surprised she allowed it. Our interaction on Monday this week had been short—the kids had been there, and we couldn't justify having the conversation we needed to have. But I'd just *had it* and here she was, and I—

"Bad timing, considering rotation starts tomorrow," she said, watching our fingers weave together.

"So far, it's always been like that. When I know I'm about to go into a phase of working almost nonstop for a few weeks, it's like somehow every single issue, big or small, hits right then." I drew comfort, and more than a little thrill, from feeling her hand in mine.

"I'm sorry."

Her voice had a strange quality to it. She seemed... far away.

"What about you? Rough day?"

She glanced up at me, then let go of my hand and moved to the table, gathering her things like she always did. "It was fine. The usual."

A slow, cold feeling made my hand feel heavy where she'd released me. "Okay. Well... thank you for being here. I'm sorry tomorrow I'll be even later, but I'll do my best to get back as early as I can."

She slung her bag over her shoulder and turned to face me again, finally. The lines at her brow and the tightness around her mouth had me wishing I knew her better—wishing I could guess what she wasn't saying.

"Don't worry. I'll be here whenever you make it back."

She offered a smile, complete with shining eyes and lovely turned-up lips, but it didn't sit right. I followed her to the door, my mind sluggish and stupid at this point.

"Livie, is everything okay?"

I hated to ask it. She didn't owe me anything. In fact, I owed her. But she'd hugged me, and I thought we were... moving in a certain direction.

She took a deep breath before giving me her eyes.

"It's fine. But at some point—probably after the rotation, I'm guessing—we need to have a discussion. I'm toast, and you're clearly too tired, but I have to admit I'm confused. I don't want to feel that way, or act that way, and so I think if we can sit down and talk, it would help."

My pulse raced and I wanted to reach for her, demand she stay and talk to me because I didn't like the look on her face when she spoke of being confused. I didn't know why—I thought we'd been on the same page, but in truth, we hadn't acknowledged being on *any* page. She was right, of course—we needed to talk. And tonight wouldn't be the night for it, especially since we both had work tomorrow.

"Okay, yes. We should do that. Soon."

Twenty-six hours after we'd said goodbye the previous night, I returned home drained and drenched from a downpour that'd hit just as I parked my truck back at the office and was switching to my car. We used HMVs out in the box and somehow, the hop from my truck, into the office, and then back out had left me soaked to the bone.

But none of that mattered once I saw her curled on the couch asleep, face relaxed and so lovely, the sight of it hitting me like a punch to the gut. I'd worked hard not to be distracted by the thoughts of our coming conversation. I'd had to banish her from my mind hourly while I received briefings, observed the initial phase of the exercise, and tried desperately not to wonder what she wanted to say.

But how could I wait any longer? This was my last chance—the last night we'd have alone and without Ariel playing chaperone. In fact, would I ever see her once Ariel returned?

Not unless I made it happen.

I debated running upstairs and slipping into the shower, but didn't want to risk her waking and wondering why I hadn't woken her to let her go home. I ditched my muddy boots and shuffled to the bathroom to run a towel over my hair before I returned to the living room and crouched next to her.

"Livie."

Nothing.

"Livie."

Still nothing. I placed a hand on her shoulder, and she jumped, eyes wide and unseeing for a moment before she focused on me.

"It's me. I'm home. Sorry to startle you."

She huffed out a breath, calming quickly, thankfully. She rolled from the couch and stumbled a bit on the way to collect her bag, already zipped closed and sitting on a chair waiting for her.

"Thank you for staying so late."

"No problem." Her quiet voice seemed small.

One thing I liked so much about her was how unafraid she was—she just enjoyed things, people, food, life. She laughed freely and talked and wasn't shy or held back by a sense of awkwardness. Maybe I admired those things because I didn't see them in myself, but wanted them for my own. Or maybe it was because I suspected she brought those things out in me when I spent time with her.

"Well... still. Thank you." I shook my head at myself, irritated I couldn't seem to confess, to speak the damn words I needed to say before she slipped out into the night and even further away.

She reached the door, but as she pulled the handle, I set my hand on hers and pushed it closed. Her eyes, liquid brown and full of passion even as tired as she was, jumped to mine.

"Sorry, I just... I heard you last night. About being confused and needing to talk. I know this is terrible timing—you're exhausted, and so am I, and you want to get home, but can you give me a few minutes? If we don't talk now, it'll be after the rotation, and I hate to wait that long."

She pulled her hand back and turned to face me, our bodies closer than they'd been since we'd sat side by side, but this felt better. More intimate, to be facing each other and talking. Every cell in my body wanted to be closer, wanted more.

She nodded. "You're right, this isn't ideal. But I'd rather not wait either. I wanted to bring it up last night but you were so frustrated and tired, I knew that wasn't right. But if we wait for perfect circumstances, we'll never do it. So... talk."

For some dumb reason, I hadn't actually thought about what I'd say. I knew I wanted to say something, and make it clear I liked her. But normally, I'd compose myself a bit better, have a plan of attack, so to speak. I didn't have that. I just knew...

"I want to date you."

Okay. One way to do it.

Her lashes fluttered, but her face lit up with a smile. She chuckled like she couldn't believe me. "Well, that's good news."

I grabbed her hand, small and soft. "Is it?"

Her eyes dipped to our hands, then rose to meet mine. "Yes. I want to date you too. That hasn't changed for me."

We sobered then, likely each recalling my one-eighty flip on New Year's.

"Honestly, it hasn't changed for me either." I pulled her with me, leading her to the couch, because having this conversation standing right next to the door didn't make sense. She'd agreed to stay, and I didn't want to rush through anything.

We sat close on the couch, and I continued, still holding her hand, glad she hadn't withdrawn even after remembering my idiocy.

"I'm sorry about how I behaved that night. I didn't mean to... seem like I was leading you on or something. I wanted to pursue something, but Delia coming in... it just reminded me how careful I have to be. She seemed upset, and it spooked me—I couldn't take hurting her any more than I worry I have with the divorce. I'm less concerned about that now after seeing her with you, for what it's worth, though it's not like I've talked to her directly about it. Once I got thinking, the concern for the kids paired with how little I have to offer at the end of the day after work and my kids—I felt I had no business dating someone."

CHAPTER SEVENTEEN

Livie

Eric's ridiculously pretty eyes stared back at me, begging me to understand, but the wrinkled brow and now un-smiling mouth told me he feared I wouldn't.

Silly man.

"I don't need you to *offer* me anything, Eric. I like you. I'd like to spend time with you."

He must've liked my answer, because his response came immediately and decisively, just like I'd imagined it might be with him. His hand rose to cradle my cheek, a look full of promise in his eyes, and he bent to kiss me.

He kissed me once and pulled back, as though waiting for permission to continue. I both liked and didn't like this—it didn't surprise me he'd be respectful and gentlemanly, and yet I wanted him to just... go for it. I wanted him to be out of control, this man who had everything organized and figured out. I wanted to be the reason for it.

So with both hands, I reached up to pull him toward me, and kissed him back. Our lips met and melded together, my stomach flipping at the contact, though it'd been doing that every minute since he'd stopped me from opening the door. Heat centered at my chest spread out, tingling to the tips of my fingers where they smoothed along the close-cut hair at the back of his head.

His opposite hand, the one not threaded into my hair at the side of my head now, urged me closer at my side. The contact there, his warm, large palm on me, his lips demanding in the best possible way, made any remnants of the exhausting week, the confusion between us, scatter.

Just when I was about to climb onto his lap and get serious, which admittedly would've been a bit much for our first kiss in his family's living room, he pulled back, shaking his head and smiling immediately.

Oof. That smile. His smile was truly deadly, and just seeing it, being the cause of it, sent a new wave of giddiness through me.

"I've wanted to do that for a while now."

"Yeah? Me too. Thanks for not being a tease again this time." I winked at him and grabbed him by the collar of his uniform and shook him a little so he'd know I was joking.

He ducked his head before looking back at me. "You have no idea what a jerk I felt like. I didn't mean to be so confusing."

My hand on his arm squeezed in reassurance. "Don't apologize. Just... don't do it again. If something happens you're worried about, let's talk about it. We're both grownups, and we both understand what this is."

His gaze flickered back and forth between my eyes. Man, were his eyes beautiful. The long dark lashes, those almost-severe dark brows... *whew.* This close, it proved an even deadlier combination, particularly after discovering just how soft and skilled his lips were.

"Maybe, for the old guy in the room who hasn't dated in upwards of fifteen years, we should define this."

I laughed at that. "We're dating."

"Good." He continued to study me, like he was waiting for more explanation.

When I didn't say anymore, he spoke in a quiet voice I might've described as vulnerable, except I couldn't imagine how this man would feel that way with me.

"So... that means..."

I couldn't help myself when I leaned in and kissed him again, just one little peck, because something about him wanting to make sure everything was crystal-clear just kind of hammered at my heart.

"That means we're dating, and spending time together, and enjoying each other."

He nodded, but something in his demeanor didn't seem settled. I knew he had baggage, and maybe some of that was coming in to play now. But I couldn't guess, so I waited for him to say what he needed to say.

"That sounds good."

"But?" I prompted. His hesitation, or reservation... whatever it was, made my heart pound in a surprisingly fearsome way.

He exhaled, took my hand in his again.

"This may sound terrible, but I want to make sure I'm clear. I can't offer you anything beyond just that. Just dating and getting to know you. I don't..." He frowned, swallowed. "I just don't have anything to give beyond that. If that makes sense."

Despite the pit that'd opened wide in my stomach, the slight hollowing in my chest, I nodded. "I get it. I promise I do. I get that we need to just enjoy things as they go. Honestly, I may not even be here six months from now. Let's just enjoy the process and having someone to go out with, and not feel bad that we're not planning to run off into the sunset together."

He smiled at that. "Sounds reasonable enough."

I summoned a returning smile, one last thing on my list. "I'm glad. I guess I do just want to say, I completely understand the concern, especially for Delia, and I don't want that to be something that's perpetually bothering you, or that you're worried about."

He exhaled, and his thumb drew an arc over the back of my hand where he held it. "Thank you. Truly. After a lot of thought, I think her reaction was more surprise than upset. She's done so well with you these last few weeks, and you've been amazing with both the kids. Plus, honestly, it's only worth talking to her about if this is going to affect her life, and like we've said..."

"We're just having fun." I'd need to repeat that to myself, because already, it felt like more than that.

He nodded. "Exactly."

"Good. And with that, because it's nearing midnight and I cannot sleep the day away tomorrow, and you *definitely* can't, I need to go." I stood, sad to leave the couch and his company, though I was sure he'd want to get out of his wet clothes and I needed my bed, stat.

He followed me to the door and opened it to reveal an icy walkway and little crystalline flakes fluttering onto a light layer of snow.

"Thanks for staying to talk."

"Thanks for using your words."

We laughed together. "But seriously, I'm glad we did this. That we're doing this. I'm looking forward to it."

His face lit up again, that killer smile making me second-guess my need to leave.

"Me too. The exercise doesn't wrap up 'til end of next week, but then I'll have a more flexible schedule. Can I see if Ariel can watch the kids one night next weekend? We can actually go out?"

After one last peck in answer, I padded gingerly out onto the walk, glad my shoes had decent tread to manage the ice. I savored the short walk to the car and then from my car to my front door—the night felt close around me with only a few streetlights down the block. The village—because it was more a village and less a town or city—lay quiet and still. I didn't remember living anywhere that got this particular crisp, dark stillness in winter. The beauty of the night and the evening's events made me feel like I was gliding up the stairs, breathless in anticipation of what magic might come next.

That week, I met with the principal and we talked through the situation—in the end, she confirmed my understanding that dating Eric wasn't illegal, but that I should ask the assistant teacher to grade Robby's work to avoid bias. I understood completely, and felt relieved to have the discussion behind me.

Having Ariel back was a blessing and a curse. The blessing came in her returning to volunteer in my classroom that week. I hadn't realized how much I valued having her there, both to help, and just for a nice interruption in my day where I got to hang with a friend and talk while the kids were at specials.

The curse? I didn't have to take Delia and Robby home,

or wait in their house until their hot dad arrived home. I no longer had an excuse to see him. Granted, he'd probably not slept at home for much of the week since at the height of most rotations, many soldiers spent the night in their trucks or set up camps, not returning home for hot food and showers for days.

Still. I missed him with an intensity I wouldn't have imagined, and while part of me rebelled against feeling that way, the other part welcomed it. Because I would see him. He'd texted every few days and confirmed Ariel had agreed to watch the kids on Saturday. He didn't tell me what our plans were nor did I ask, instead deciding being surprised would be more fun.

I hadn't dated much while living here. I'd been too busy with school and travel to want to devote my precious days off to trying to get a relationship off the ground, and honestly? I hadn't met or even seen anyone who did much for me. I'd been on exactly two blind dates and a few other set-ups from mutual friends, and all of them had flopped at the coffee or cocktail stage. None had progressed to a full evening meal, let alone anything physical.

Plus, I'd decided soldiers were essentially off-limits, which narrowed the options significantly. I knew I had no future with them, knowing I wanted to return home and live my happily-ever-after there and not moving around constantly, so it made sense not to start. Why tether myself to someone who had a job that guaranteed I couldn't do what I'd always planned to do?

I'd been okay with that, embracing the years abroad as a time to focus on broadening my experiences and expanding my world—fully embracing *adventure phase*. When I moved home, I'd necessarily be done with that part of life— I'd be near my parents, who would make amazing grandparents. I wanted to be close to them, and I owed them that. But after getting close with Eric despite myself, after his kisses and the searing touch of his hands on my face and arm and at my waist—nothing all that intense and yet *so intense*—I felt ravenous for physical attention.

Particularly, from him.

So when seven on Saturday finally rolled around, I'd been pacing the floor for fifteen minutes, doing my best not to check my phone once every few seconds to see if he'd texted and changed his mind or was running late. He hadn't. He wasn't. In fact, he was probably about thirty seconds early, which was good, but not nearly enough according to my over-eager mind.

I swung the door open before he knocked, because I'd been spying on him from the window in my living room that overlooked the walkway to my door. He paused, hand in the air ready to knock, and smiled a sheepish, delighted little grin.

"Well hi there, Livie."

"Why hello, Eric. Would you care to come in?" I admired the dark jeans and button-up black shirt, relieved my own jeans, sweater, and heeled boots matched his outfit choice.

"I'd love to." Then a moment later, "Wow, this is great."

It was great. I loved my apartment. I'd had decent places to live in Georgia and North Carolina, but this place was amazing—natural wood, solid walls, a huge German tile-work stove that heated so well in winter. Though it was hard to imagine settling down in a home and just... staying there. I'd gotten used to adjusting quickly and embracing the faults and annoyances of a given place, knowing I'd leave it again soon enough. "Isn't it? It's so reasonably priced too. I'm going to be so sad to leave it."

We chatted a while longer and I did my best not to let nerves overwhelm my ability to speak—he looked so good. He smelled so good. I was in danger of sighing, all kinds of mushy for him, but thankfully, he pulled out his buzzing phone and held it up. "Alarm. Time to go."

I stifled the giggle at this man who'd set an alarm to make sure we left on time. Not a shock considering his tendency toward being regimented which I'd become more familiar with since watching the kids. Everything was meticulously organized in his house, and the family worked off a schedule written on whiteboard calendars lined up three at a time for a ninety-day view of everyone's plans. I admired it, and guessed it ultimately simplified life.

But alarm for a date? Adorable and a little odd—just like him.

Soon enough, we were nestled at a tiny table in the *wintergarten* of a local brewery and restaurant. The food was amazing, and I never got tired of eating here.

I smoothed the white tablecloth next to the plate. "Perfect choice."

His eyebrows rose in expectation, and there came another flash of his son. "Is it? Good. I was afraid maybe you came here all the time, or it wasn't very original. You'll have to tell me what you like and, you know, how I can improve."

I blinked back at him.

He nodded encouragingly. "Think of it as an AAR— after action review. What you'd keep, what you'd want to do differently next time. It'll help me do a better job for future dates. I don't want you to feel like you're wasting your time with a slouch."

"You know I'm not grading your performance, right? You don't have to worry about that."

He unwrapped his silverware and placed the napkin in his lap. "I don't want to take you for granted."

A little star burst in my chest. "I know you won't."

The waitress in traditional modest dirndl of cranberry and hunter green with a white blouse arrived and offered us menus. She took our drink order a few moments later, and in what felt like a blink of an eye, I took my last bite of a delectable meal of *jaegerschnitzel*—thin-pounded, breaded, and fried pork cutlet with the most gloriously rich mushroom and herb sauce—and salad.

During the meal, he'd offered to share bites of his food—a steak with some kind of fancy vegetable strudel on the side, the generosity of which had pleased me to no end. He didn't do the weird thing where he held out the fork and I'd have to bird-beak over to taste—he took a plate and dished up a decent helping and really shared it. I did the same, and he raved about everything.

"Do you have room for dessert?"

"Regrettably no, but if you ever bring the kids, make sure you get dessert." Their desserts were usually homemade ice creams with unique flavors or different kinds of dessert rouladen or fritters. Always delicious and a little surprising, usually with a twist on a more traditional German dish.

The look he gave me then sent another flash of feeling through me—something I couldn't quite pin down but that felt warm and lovely and a little sad, almost. That, and a bit nervous too, because next came the part where he'd take me home.

CHAPTER EIGHTEEN

Eric

Our conversation in the car on the drive home centered on our favorite things about Bavarian life—the forced quiet on Sundays when mostly everything shut down except restaurants, the generally slow pace of life, the occasional happening upon a herd of sheep blocking the road to one's destination.

She'd lived here three times longer than I had and had great stories. Our back and forth flowed easily all evening, and too soon, I'd pulled up to her apartment and opened her car door.

Anticipation thrummed in my limbs, swirled in my gut, and I inhaled slowly to calm the galloping in my chest.

It was late. I would leave her at the door. It was our first date. I would leave her at the door.

I did *not* want to leave her at the door. But I could not go in, however much I wanted to, and I suspected she wouldn't ask even though I sensed she might want to as well.

"Thank you for a great night." She turned to me in front of her door, both hands holding the handles of her purse.

"Thank you too. I'm glad we did this."

"Me too."

A pause, our eyes searching, and my heart pounding, then propelling me forward. She moved for me at the same moment, our hands reaching for each other, feet stepping close. With my hands in her hair and at her shoulder, I guided her two paces back so she rested against the door. With nowhere to go, she pressed into me, and I into her.

Our lips moved together, slow but searing, eager and yet willing to savor these touches, this moment. The winter moon glittered down and cast us in shadow. The air around us was cold, but with no space between us, I only felt heat and the building desire that came from an evening shared with someone compelling and beautiful. Someone I'd wondered about since the moment I'd met her, and wanted since the moment I'd let myself.

"Well..." she said, voice breathy and almost a sigh as we pulled back from the intimate sharing of breath.

"Yeah." I agreed, though she hadn't said much. But I knew.

I wondered if she'd been stunned by our kiss the other night too. I wondered if she'd obsessed about it like I had. But now I knew... it hadn't been a fluke. Our physical connection was alive and well and the more I had, the more I wanted.

I leaned one hand against her door, keeping our bodies close and my head dipped to hers. "I should go, but I don't want to."

She rose on tip toes to kiss me again, too quick, then

lowered and set a hand on my chest. One I wished I could feel on my skin, and not through a shirt and jacket.

"I don't want you to either, but you should."

I squeezed her side where my other hand rested, then released her. "I'll see you soon. I'll call you tomorrow."

I drove home and parked, unwilling to leave my car and face the inquisition that no doubt awaited me inside. Ariel would want details, and I wouldn't be lucky enough for her to be asleep, despite the late hour. I closed my eyes and savored the memory of the kiss... though had to cut that short or I wouldn't be able to think about anything else.

No sense putting it off... Time to face Ariel, and apparently Nate too, since his car sat nestled right behind hers in the driveway.

I stomped my boots just inside the door and hung my coat.

"So..."

Nate sounded like he'd been waiting a lifetime to say that word that way, and when I looked, he sat, elbows on knees, hands cupping his cheeks, a dippy little look on his face.

Ariel busted up laughing and saved me from responding. I dropped my keys, wallet, and phone on the table and didn't say a word as I moved to the kitchen, got a beer, and plunked down on the couch in the corner seat.

"But really, what happened?" Ariel asked, her voice softened in a way that made me think she must be really trying to contain herself.

"What happened? We went out. It was great. I took her home. Now I'm here with you two goons."

She and Nate both flopped back against the couch, and the movement struck me as something an old married couple might do. They had known each other for years at this point, and been good friends all along—or all excepting the four years her ex had dominated every part of her life. I'd never noticed them picking up each other's mannerisms quite like that, though.

"Are you really not going to tell us anything?" she asked.

I enjoyed a sip of my beer, looking at the screen of the TV where they'd paused whatever they had been watching. After another drink and a long inhale just to torture them since they were both staring at me, I finally spoke. "It was great. I really like her. I'm looking forward to doing it again."

Ariel's smile could've lit up a city block, and Nate clapped his hands together like *he'd* been the one to go on a good date. I should've been annoyed, maybe, but in the end their reactions only confirmed why they were both fixtures in my life. They were excellent people who loved their friends and family well. I counted myself lucky indeed to call them mine.

"You two are ridiculous. It was one date, and it's not like it can actually go anywhere."

Out of the corner of my eye, I saw them shoot questioning glances at each other. Then Ariel piped up. "Why's that?"

She couldn't actually be surprised I wouldn't sentence another woman to the apparent misery of being married to me while I served in the Army, could she? After everything I'd been through with Renee, and everything I'd shared with my sister about that mess, she had to understand. But tonight wasn't the night to get into that. So instead, I used the more obvious reason.

"She's not going to be here much longer. We didn't get into specifics, but she mentioned she'd be gone by this summer. Obviously, I'm not about to bring someone into our lives in a serious way only to have her leave again... I don't want to deal with that, and I refuse for the kids to have to."

That shut it down, and if they had any more concerns, they didn't voice them. Nate clicked the remote and the TV came back to life, distracting us all from the surprisingly grim reality of my statement.

I stayed with them for a half hour or so, then retreated to my room, my thoughts inescapable.

I didn't want to feel so strongly for Livie already, but I did. Our first date hadn't felt like a first. It had felt like a twentieth—smooth conversation, no awkwardness, just fun and warm and good. Maybe a few more nerves than a twentieth date, sure, and probably more anticipation for the doorstep scene, but I already felt close to her. Everything I knew about her, I liked, and I felt sure that whatever else I'd find out, I'd like that too.

My mind filtered through snapshots from the evening. Her listing her favorite dishes from the restaurant, seeming genuinely joyful to recount how delicious each one was. Her ordering in what seemed to me to be perfect German though she told me how rough hers was compared to her friend Jen's. Her devouring her food and claiming she'd lick the plate if it were socially acceptable because she loved the *jaeger* sauce so much. Her confusion at my statement that she could give me feedback on the date, like it wouldn't occur to her to be grading my performance in that regard.

I wondered about that. Could that possibly be true? I had baggage in this area, of course. Renee had been critical of nearly anything I planned, usually because it was something I'd thought of without consulting her. I'd always imagined it'd be nice to be surprised, and somehow her hatred of being surprised took years to penetrate. Granted, often, especially after the kids, we were attending work functions for my job—hail and farewells, military balls, changes of command... not dates with just the two of us. That had certainly been a failure I had to own.

It was also one I didn't intend to repeat. I'd learned the brutal lesson that being consumed with my job would cost me. I'd changed my ways, not without some difficult growing pains for sure, but I had. And this time with Livie was a great opportunity to practice what I'd always imagined I should do if I were dating someone—if I ever took another chance. Make time for them. Do things for *them*, not just drag them along with my life.

I finally drifted off to sleep well past midnight, mind full of possibilities, worries, and more than a few plans.

"It's weird. I'm not accusing him of anything, I'm just saying, it's weird."

Command Sergeant Major Allen leaned back in the chair across from my desk, perfectly at home.

"Agreed," I concurred. "But we don't know their story. Have you asked him?"

For the second time in a month, Allen had mentioned his concern over a few soldiers in the battalion and his suspicions about their marriages. Here again was something that other industries and vocations wouldn't have anything to do with. But when you get housing allowances based on whether you're married, let alone often determining where a soldier could live depending on rank, the Army did have an interest.

Last summer at Fort Bragg, there'd been a big sting operation of what the news had called a *military marriage fraud ring*—soldiers marrying people and, in one way or another, cheating the government out of money. Because of this, all command teams had been tasked to keep their eyes out, and Allen had identified a few questionable situations. The current topic of discussion, Sergeant Miller, had pinged on his radar one too many times lately.

Allen crossed his arms over his chest. "She hasn't visited once, from what I've heard. That's odd, no?"

I leaned back in my chair, and pushed away from the desk a bit. "It seems like it, but maybe she's ill? Maybe she can't travel? Maybe she has a sick relative she's responsible for. We don't know. If you're getting serious about this, you've got to ask him. You can't really nose your way in there without a good reason, and though it blows my mind, not living together, especially at an OCONUS duty station, isn't actually a red flag."

Allen grumped a little but acquiesced, and we moved on to other discussions until the alarm on my phone buzzed.

"I've got to run over to the school. I'll be back for the briefings this afternoon."

Gathering up my keys and patrol cap, I hustled out the building to my car, anticipation jumping through me.

It was Wednesday, four days after my first official date with Livie. We'd texted every day, and I'd already asked if she could go out again this coming weekend. But I hadn't seen her, and after seeing her nearly every day for the past few weeks before our date thanks to Ariel's being gone, I felt like I'd been deprived of something essential.

At the school, I parked, checked in at the office, and caught Ms. Anderson's kindergarten class as they plodded along single-file to the cafeteria led by someone I didn't recognize. I knew by this point in the year I wouldn't be likely to see Livie on a lunch visit unless I went out of my way to do so since she had a prep period while the kids ate.

"Hey Robby, is that your dad?"

"What? *Dad!* You're here! Why are you here?!" Robby was jumping and lunging toward me, then pulling back to retain his spot in the train, nearly shouting but clearly doing his utmost to keep himself under control in accordance with the lunch line rules.

My heart ached at the sight, as it so often did when I got to see him bubble over with happiness at the mere sight of me. The boy was all energy and delight, just pure joy sometimes. He could drive me insane, sure, but there was nothing better than to surprise this guy. I never told the kids when I was coming to visit for lunch just in case it fell through—I'd learned that lesson the hard way once and the fallout of *not* making it to lunch, even though it'd been a true emergency, had taught me well. Now I tried my best to come once a month for each kid, but it was always a surprise.

I held up a finger to my lips to remind him to be quiet. "Hey, bud. You keep going in your line, you're doing great. I'll be there in just a minute to eat lunch with you."

"Really? Oh, really!?" He jumped in place, hands flailing around until he stopped and literally ran in place like he had to burn the energy somehow or it'd swallow him whole.

I waved to a few of the other kids who recognized me and dared to smile or greet me, then nodded to the stern-looking woman who ended the line and followed her. Minutes later, I sat sandwiched between Robby and his friend Rhiannon, across from Jaya and Darrol, and being frequently hugged by my little sidekick while we ate.

The first ten minutes of their lunch period were done in

silence. They'd instituted this after a wild lunchtime the day before, apparently, so we couldn't actually talk, but it gave the kids a chance to focus on their food. By the end of the tenth minute, when Mrs. Parks released them from *silent lunch* so they could speak, Robby was practically writhing with unspent words and energy.

"Dad I'm so glad you came today this is so perfect. After can you come see my artwork Liv—uh, Ms. Anderson hung up in the hallway? I've been waiting for it to be displayed because it's *amazing* and you're gonna love it. Then you can see Liv—uh, Ms. Anderson and say hi and maybe take her on another date."

I wasn't prone to blushing, but my face heated and I chuckled, ducking my head and speaking softly to my son. "I'll come see your artwork, for sure. But go easy on talking about Ms. Anderson and me in school, alright bud?"

In a stage whisper, he said, "Oh, is it a secret?"

I chuckled again, chin at my chest and wondering if anyone in the entire cafeteria hadn't heard him. Realistically, probably very few people had considering the low-level hum of voices chattering now that *silent lunch* was over.

"No, buddy, not a secret. But let's keep home stuff at home, okay? Just like we only call her Livie at home?"

With wide eyes, he nodded, chin swooping from ceiling to chest and back again for emphasis. One of his classmates started asking me questions, and in what seemed like a remarkably fast twenty-five minutes, the kids were marching back to their classroom.

The closer we got to the classroom, which was located in its own wing of the school in a kind of little kindergarten haven, the faster my heart beat, just at the thought of getting a glimpse of Livie. She wouldn't be expecting me, which somehow made the anticipation greater.

We rounded the corner and with a nod from one of the line escorts, Robby jumped out of line and pointed to his artwork stapled to the bulletin board on the wall outside the classroom door. I oohed and ahhed over it, pointing out my favorite parts, asking him which were his. Then he named every person in his class and pointed to theirs—he loved knowing his friends' names and I'd been working on not rushing him. I so frequently pressed him and Delia to be somewhere at a certain time, to get ready to run out the door for school, to hurry up and get ready for bed... I didn't want to be that parent, and this moment had been crafted for him to take his time.

"I heard we had a special guest."

Livie's voice at the doorway sent a warm rush through me. I stepped closer to her, then stopped myself a few feet away.

"Can I go back in now? It's free play time, right Liv —*nowaitMs.Anderson?*"

His big blue eyes blinked up at her, and I could see her fighting a smile.

"You're right, Robby. You better give your dad a big hug before you go though."

He immediately plastered himself to my legs, arms wrapping around my waist. "I love when you come for lunch. You should come again tomorrow."

I ruffled his hair. "I can't tomorrow, but I will definitely come again in a few weeks, okay? And you'll see Ari tomorrow when she's here helping Ms. Anderson."

"Okay Dad. See you after school!" He skipped off into the classroom, leaving me with his teacher.

Would it be wrong of me to say I was glad for a moment

alone, and currently fought the impulse to satisfy my days-long craving for her right there in the hallway?

I leaned forward, just a little, toward her. "I know I can't touch you, but let me just say... I wish I could."

A bright smile covered her face and she clasped her hands together in front of her. "I wish you could too. But I couldn't really waltz into your office and grab you by the collar and take what I want either, now could I?"

Hot, burning desire shot through me even as I laughed at her boldness. "Oh, but you could. And how I wish you would."

"Really?"

I inched closer, still not touching her, but close enough I could speak and only we would hear. Close enough I could smell her minty shampoo and see the sheen on her lips like she'd slicked them with gloss before coming out to see me. Something about that pleased me and set my mind more wholly on the subject of what would happen if she came to visit me.

"I do have a door that closes, and I don't have a class-room full of twenty kindergarteners when I do."

The collar of her shirt, a crisp white button up, rose and fell with the rest of her when she took a great breath and let it out.

"You're dangerous, Colonel. I cannot be seen making out with a parent on school property and plan to keep my job, so you need to back away." She bit her bottom lip, and her hand slid along the wall as she backed up. "But I hope you'll deliver on all of that—" she raised her chin as though to gesture to all of *me*, "—come Saturday."

"I shall aim to please, Ms. Anderson."

With one more incredulous smile, she slipped back into her classroom, and I resisted the pull to peek inside and watch her walk to her desk, or even to spot Robby one more time and wave. If I did that, he'd need another hug, and I didn't want to distract him if he'd found something to focus on.

The stupid smile on my own face lasted the rest of the day—even through Nate's incessant ribbing and a rousing round of "Livie and Eric, Sittin' in a Tree."

CHAPTER NINETEEN

Livie

A full four weeks after our first date, Eric and I made it out on our second. The second date that should've happened the weekend following had ended up being a movie night in with the kids since Ariel had come down with a nasty cold and couldn't babysit the kids by herself.

Then, he and the kids and Ariel took off on a trip to the Black Forest while Jen and I made our way to Madrid. I hated the sense of longing and even mild regret I had when we'd said goodbye, each having planned our trips weeks ago before we would've considered factoring in the other person. Plus, it was far too soon to travel together.

Then he had another rotation, which essentially took up another few weeks of his life, weekends included. Such was life here—it was both the blessing and curse of things at this post. The schedule was planned and shared months in advance so everyone knew when soldiers would be occupied and in many ways essentially non-existent for anything but their time in the exercises. But that also came with longer weekends and that did seem to make it all bearable for the Army families.

But to say I'd been eagerly anticipating getting him alone was an understatement. We'd texted, even talked on the phone a few times a week, and I'd stopped by to drop him lunch twice during his rotation. I hadn't actually seen him, but had left the food on his desk, which he'd texted and thanked me profusely for.

He always seemed so surprised by stuff like that, like he didn't deserve someone going out of their way for him. It certainly made me suspect that his ex never did things like that, but maybe he hadn't for her either.

Whatever the case, when he knocked on my apartment door on a snowy Bavarian Saturday night weeks after our first date despite our best efforts, I happily opened the door, wrapped my arms around his neck, and kissed him as I walked him through the doorway.

"It feels like it's been months since we were alone together," I whispered against his neck, the snow outside making the moment feel hushed and intimate.

He pulled back enough to look in my eyes. "It has been. A month, anyway. A few stolen kisses is not enough."

"Agreed."

That earned me one of the smiles that sent my nerves bubbling, happy and excited to be near him and be the one causing that expression.

I took his head in my hands and pressed another kiss to his lips, then stepped away. "We are actually going to be late—we need to run up to the restaurant and pick up our food. I decided we're ordering in so we don't have to worry about the snow."

And so I could be as affectionate as I wanted and not feel the censure of the local crowd.

Twenty minutes after leaving, we returned to my apartment, bags of delicious German and Vietnamese food in tow. I'd already set out plates and utensils at the small table tucked into a corner of my living room.

After surveying the spread, he chuckled. "Do you think you ordered enough?"

"Never. This place is the absolute best."

"I've only eaten there one other time. I remember someone mentioning it when we first moved, raving about their crispy duck and their schnitzel and praising their Bolognese sauce. I thought it was an insane combination—German, Italian, and Vietnamese. But silly me, because it's amazing."

"It is. Just like the Indian and Italian place. I feel like if these were in the US, it'd all be gross, but here it's just kind of... magical." I sighed, relishing the tableful of food and his enjoyment of it as well.

After a few moments of happily gobbling food, a look crossed his face, but he didn't speak. I couldn't quite tell what it meant, but I couldn't let it slide.

"What?"

He finished chewing a bite, seeming to do so slowly, like maybe he needed to buy himself time. "I want to ask you questions, but I don't want to come off like I'm interviewing you."

A chuckle escaped. "What would I be interviewing for?"

"Well, it's not an interview, so *macht nichts*, right?"

I smiled at his use of the German phrase—*matters not*. "Then you should ask."

"Can you tell me about you? Where you grew up, your

parents, your siblings, your... life. I'll show you mine if you show me yours."

"That phrase has always kind of creeped me out. It has a... crotchy connotation."

He coughed, continued chewing, coughed again, his face red. Once he'd swallowed, he took a drink of water, then a low inhale. "Wow. Okay. Wasn't expecting that."

"The *crotchy* part?"

He laughed, shaking his head at me. "Yeah. Didn't see that one coming."

"Well, sorry to make you nearly choke. But it's a weird turn of phrase." I pointed my fork in his direction to emphasize the point.

"I promise I'm not trying to... you know what? That can go nowhere good. I'll just say *tell me about your life and I'll tell you about mine*. How's that?"

"Acceptable."

We smiled at each other, and my chest tightened at how cute he was. Hot, handsome, gorgeous, yes, but also... maybe a little prudish? Or, not quite that, but just kind of... shy about some things. I liked that about him. This dashing, accomplished, seasoned soldier of a man who'd still blush at my made-up word. *Adorable.*

I shoveled a few more bites, then finally felt the food hit bottom and sat back. "I was raised moving around the country. I was born in Georgia, but we lived in eleven states before I was in high school."

"Were your parents military?"

"No, but it wasn't unlike a military kid's upbringing, minus the whole community, pride, sense of purpose. My dad worked in oil and gas for a company that I don't think exists anymore. I never really understood what he did. He left that industry and started teaching high school sciences in a little town outside Richmond, Virginia, and that's where I think of as home. That's where my folks still live, and that's where I'll end up one day too."

Eric shifted, settling his fork on his plate and resting back in his seat. "So you ended up liking where you guys landed?"

"I did. I liked things about some of the other places—I remember really loving one place we lived in North Carolina, and a few others, but I hated never knowing how long we'd be there. I could never guess. I got to the point where I could hardly stand to make friends because I hated to leave them." And it crushed me. Every time I had to say goodbye. I got better at that, and as an adult, especially in a world full of digital connection, it got easier to manage. But I tended to only make a few really close friends—friendly with everyone, sure, but only a few who I let all the way in.

His brow furrowed and he straightened his knife on the table. "I worry about Delia and Robby in that regard. This last move was rough on Delia, but I think the largest part of it was that it was our first huge move without Renee. When we leave here, they'll both really feel it, and I don't want to... damage them any more than I already have."

My heart clenched at his tone, his words, and the expression of worry on his face. I took his hand in mine.

"No, Eric. It won't be like that for them. I know it's hard on kids, but there are so many great examples of resilient, strong, amazing military kids. Talk to the high schoolers and so many of them will say how much they love their lives, even when it's hard. I never knew when I was leaving. I didn't have anyone else who had the same life. Your kids will be surrounded by fellow military kids, and I do think that helps. Plus, you're a great, engaged, thoughtful father,

and you have a support system with your mom and Ariel...
you won't damage them."

He let out a little sigh and started to stand. "Should we
clean up?"

I held tight to his hand. "Seriously. Your kids are great,
and while I'm sure they'll be sad to leave, they get to go with
you, and they have the security of knowing they're off to
whatever great Army adventure is next."

He offered a reluctant smile. "Okay, Pollyanna."

"Okay, Eeyore."

His eyes widened. "I am *not* Eeyore."

I laughed and began gathering plates and containers
from the table. "Not usually. But just now? Had a very
morose feel to it. I can't blame you for the train of thought,
but I hope you'll go easy on yourself."

"I can get a little down-in-the-dumps about stuff like
that, I guess. I've talked to other military parents who
struggle with the same thoughts, so I know it's not unique to
me. I think I just have the added guilt of putting them
through a divorce too."

I stopped and turned to him, frustrated by his statement
even as I ached for him and his kids regarding the aftermath
of their experience. "You didn't plan on that. That wasn't
your Plan A, or I'm guessing B or C."

"Definitely not."

"So don't let the meanies in your head trick you into
believing it's all your fault. You know it's not. You've told
me that."

One brow rose and his eyes lit up. "Meanies?"

I shrugged a shoulder. "You know 'em. The mean voices
in your head you have to ignore. They tell you all your
mistakes, all your failures, all your problems, and they don't
stop. They don't allow for logic or understanding, for

forgiveness or growth. They only want to rehash the bad stuff and keep us struggling. They're mean, and they need to be shut down."

With another look I couldn't quite decipher, he reached out and tucked a few strands of hair behind my ear, then let his hand glide down from there to my shoulder, down my arm, and squeezed my hand at the bottom. "I like you."

Butterflies burst in my belly. "Good. I like you too."

CHAPTER TWENTY

Eric

After dinner, we curled up together on her small couch and watched a movie. She apologized for the lack of originality and joked I could give *her* an AAR for the date, which I promptly did.

"I wouldn't change a thing. It's just what I needed, and what I wanted—uninterrupted time with you."

I watched her smile, a look so lovely it made me want to wrap her up and not let go.

"Well, we have had that, haven't we?"

Her eyes didn't leave mine as she leaned her elbow on the back of the couch and angled toward me.

Immediately, the change in her tone, the serious look in her eye, the press of her arm against mine had my pulse racing. "We have."

And now, my voice had dropped, low and slow and so full of wanting, she had to hear it. We hadn't had time alone, and I'd been waiting for it. Not just for this. Not only for the physical, but so we could talk openly and like we had at dinner and on and off through the movie. I'd arrived determined to find out more about her tonight since the times we'd had together in the past had largely been spent on me and the kids.

But now... now we were alone in her quiet apartment, the snow covering the sidewalks and Ariel manning the house so there was no rush for me to get home. Heat curled in my gut as I brought her face close to mine with one hand threaded into her hair.

"Have I mentioned how beautiful you are?"

She let out a breath, then smiled before she bit her lip to cover it. "I'm not sure."

I grazed her lips and along her cheek, then kissed a trail around her ear before returning to her mouth to kiss her properly. As usual, she responded with enthusiasm and joy.

We kissed for minutes or hours or both—my mind solely wrapped around her and making her feel the same joy she did me.

It was a strange thought to burst through, but it did as our lips moved together and our hands mapped each other's bodies. I thought how I'd never been *happy*, I'd never felt like I was having *fun* while kissing someone.

Frankly, it'd been a really long time since I'd really kissed someone to begin with, especially since once Renee and I were married we sort of just... got down to business. I'd never really thought about how it could or perhaps should have been different. It just was from the very beginning with us. We married young and it'd always been like that.

But just kissing Livie made me think I'd missed an

entire dimension of the physical expression of love and care for someone.

Not that I loved Livie. I didn't. But I did care for her, and the more time I spent with her, the more care I had for her. Which should probably have been a warning to me, but I'd wasted time and hurt her in the process, heeding my paranoid warnings. We'd date. Enjoy each other. And she'd leave, or do whatever she had to do, and I'd continue on with my life and always remember her fondly.

She pulled back, a hand at my chest, and we breathed together. I ran a finger lightly over her bright lips and down to her chin before kissing her once more. "I should go, but I promised Robby and Delia I'd ask if you want to join us for a hike at Kallmünz tomorrow."

"Sure. I'd love to."

"Then we'll come grab you at ten."

I forced myself up off the couch and away from her, knowing if I stayed much longer I wouldn't leave at all, and though my body wouldn't mind that eventuality, my heart and mind had promised myself I wouldn't rush. Not any part of this. Especially if I planned to make it out intact.

As I drove home, I reviewed the night, much like I had the last time, nearly turning back as the memories of our time together drew heat into my lungs again. But I parked, turned off the car, and let my head fall back against the seat. She was funny and fun and beautiful and easy to talk to. She was smart and had an odd mix of sweet and brash that kept me guessing and on my toes. And her lips, her hands, those deep brown eyes...

Yeah. When all was said and done, I'd remember her fondly. *Right.*

〜

Livie bounded down her walkway with the energy of at least two normal people. Another thing that amazed me, and yet seemed just right for someone who taught five- and six-year-olds day in and day out.

Robby began talking immediately, one long string of words tumbling out of his mouth like an endless run-on sentence. "Hi Livie I'm so glad you're coming Ari and Nate are in the car behind us because we couldn't fit everyone and didn't want to be illegal so we'd get pulled over and go to German jail so you get to sit in the front and then we'll be in the back and then Ariel and Nate are in the car back there and we'll all go to the hike and get out together."

"I'm so glad I get to come with you today. Thank you for inviting me." She turned to smile at him and Delia in the back seat, but also reached over and squeezed my leg in acknowledgement.

She chatted with the kids on the way—asking Delia about her reading and how she was getting along with times tables. She knew all the lingo and what the kids were learning—maybe because all teachers knew what kids learned in each grade, or maybe because she'd made a point to know for Delia's sake. I didn't know, but either way, a swell of tenderness for her, for my kids, and gratefulness for this time together washed through me.

The half-hour car ride flew by. I hardly spoke since Livie kept the kids talking, occasionally entertaining them with a story of crazy things that'd happened in her teaching career. She got along so well with them. I couldn't help but wonder if she liked them, particularly, or if she was just naturally great with all kids.

Probably both, but some not-small part of me wanted it to be the former—that she cared especially for *my* kids.

"There it is!"

Robby's announcement heralded our arrival. We pulled into a small road-side parking area situated across from the trail head. Nate pulled up behind us, and Ariel's door popped open immediately after. Before I could wonder about that, Robby began jabbering away again about how fast he would make the hike to the castle ruins at the top.

By the time I'd loaded up the small pack I carried whenever we went out and about with water bottles, double-checked for snacks, wipes, and tissues, Livie and Ariel had hugged and talked, and Nate had ended up restraining Robby by letting him jump up for a piggy-back to avoid Robby running across the road to get to the beginning of the hike.

Finally ready, we all crossed and Robby jumped down, then ran ahead. Fortunately, the majority of the hike's initial incline was visible as it climbed the side of a large hill, so he could run free and I could keep an eye on him without having to leave everyone else. This hike, in particular, suited our group dynamic that way.

The March day proved to be a perfect choice for the hike. Though it was a little cold, and the trail a bit muddy in places where the gravel had washed out, the snow hadn't stuck and everyone had come prepared. I shouldn't have been surprised that Livie had sturdy-looking hiking boots, and I'd made Ariel get some in the fall. Though I hadn't managed to get her out much, we had done this and a few other hikes and walks.

Before long, we reached the castle ruins where little patches of snow lingered in shady spots. Long grasses flanked the sides of the pathway we walked. An arrangement of carved stones created a mini maze near a lookout that showcased the view of the winding river and the quiet town below. Robby and Delia trotted through the stones a few times before running back to peek through ancient windows.

I stood on the path between the stones and bench and the castle, enjoying the view, but closer to the kids just in case Robby got too bold for his own good.

"What's the deal with those two?"

Livie spoke from right near me and I startled a bit, thinking she'd been taking her own walk around the stones. Now she gazed down at the bench where Ariel sat and Nate stood behind her, not touching her or even angled to look at her and yet somehow even from here we could see his attention focused on her.

I reached for her hand and twined our fingers together, glad for the sun that'd made gloves unnecessary for the moment. No doubt we'd be back to freezing temps and ice in a day or so.

"Great question."

She turned a wry smile to me, and I wished I could tuck us away from prying eyes and kiss those upturned lips.

"You really don't know?"

I let out a sigh that sounded every bit the forty-year-old man I was. "I don't. Not really. I think maybe there's some unrequited feelings there, but I can't get in the middle of it, and I don't think she's ready for that anyway. They've been friends almost as long as Nate and I have."

Livie stood quietly by for a moment, her thumb brushing over the back of my hand.

"What happened to her?"

A familiar fierceness rose in me, but when I looked at her face, ready to snap at her, I saw only concern and care on her features as she looked down at the scene of Ariel staring off at the view, and Nate doing his best to do the same, but if I knew him at all, mostly staring at her.

"She was in a toxic relationship for a long time. She's only been divorced about a year. Still lots of recovery ahead of her. You can ask her about it at some point. It might be good for her to talk about it with someone who isn't her brother or her therapist." I summoned a smile, my lungs tightening at the thought of the pain she'd been through.

"I'm so sorry. She's such a beautiful person, inside and out. I hate the thought of her being hurt."

I pulled her hand up and hugged it to my chest, then kissed the back of her hand.

"Thank you. I'm glad you guys have become friends. She needs that."

And though it wasn't my job to protect Ariel, not really, it still felt like it. I tried to, anyway, and the fact that I'd failed for so many years made it all the more my role now. Knowing Livie cared for her with her big, lovely heart only made me cherish the woman next to me all the more.

CHAPTER TWENTY-ONE

Livie

After picking our way back down the mountain, after gorging ourselves on pizza at a small café open in town, after driving the country roads home and unloading the kids and seeing Nate off, after being invited to stay for dinner and excusing myself regretfully since I had prep work for a meeting with my principal that week to do before Monday... I sat alone with my thoughts in my living room.

The day had done its damage almost more effectively than had the night before. The combination had most certainly been deadly.

I was a strong woman. I didn't need a man—had genuinely never felt that. I'd wanted one often enough. But once I'd moved here, especially, knowing my plan to return home and stay, I'd never really considered dating seriously. And even with Eric, I'd wanted to date him while knowing being together wasn't truly an option.

But yesterday and today had felt like we were together. And I'd liked it. I might've been able to walk away just liking it until the conversation about Ariel, hearing the worry in his tone and the pain even thinking about his sister's history caused him.

I was strong, but not against seeing him like that—the doting father, brother, friend. The one thing I was fast discovering I couldn't resist was him being so darn sweet and loving. The part of me that had always believed in great love, in huge, life-long love stories, wanted him to be part of mine. The main part. The other half. Even the kids—not that I'd know how to jump into parenting elementary-aged kids, not even close, but I already loved them.

And *that* was why I had to get some space and come home and remind myself what could and could not happen with this man. He was in the Army. He was not someone who was going to settle down in Podunk, Virginia and live happily ever after. From the sounds of it, he had no plans to end his Army career until they made him. And even then, what would he do when he retired?

That didn't fit in my life. Plus I was leaving... wasn't I? Maybe I'd missed my *settle down back home by thirty* initial goal. Then I'd blazed by thirty-one, thirty-two, and flat-out ignored thirty-three. I'd loved the travel and adventure and no part of me had felt it was the right time to lay that all aside and start that next phase—the *find a husband, settle down* phase. Family phase. So I'd stayed.

But I'd promised myself that before I turned thirty-five, I'd be nestled down the street from Mom and Dad, a life of worldly adventures behind me. Their only child was too far from home—I felt it every time we talked and they ended with *"we miss you like crazy, kiddo"* and *"when are you coming to visit again?"* Which meant this year, *this* summer,

I'd move home. If I felt a little swarm of unease bleed through the sunny thoughts of home when thinking about that—about settling down back home—it was only because I did love life here so much.

Too many thoughts flooded in at that. I loved the ease of travel—that was obvious enough. I loved being able to *hop over to Prague* or *take the train to France* or *drive three hours to the most glorious mountain range in the world*. I loved the sense of adventure even small things could cause, like reading what oddball "American" treats the local stores put out during football season (hotdog stuffed crust tex-mex pizza, anyone?), and the emphasis on rest in the afternoons, and especially on Sundays.

I loved the German insistence on walking—just *walking*. Not with spandex and sweatbands, but to be out in the air, to see. Often, the pace seemed maddeningly slow as healthy Germans from my age to their nineties plodded stubbornly down paths cutting through the farmlands of Bavaria. And though I wouldn't miss feeling like I didn't belong, which happened even after years of living here and developing my understanding of the culture and language, I'd miss the beauty of life here.

All of that meant I needed to pump the emotional brakes. It would only make leaving harder if I had to say goodbye to Eric after giving him part of my heart. I had to guard against that. I didn't want to stop seeing him—just the thought made my chest ache. But I couldn't keep doing it so often or so... intimately. Whatever that meant, since it felt like every glimpse of him turned into a close, heart-punching look at the man.

Fortunately, the schedule for his battalion, and there-fore him, would be insane right up until spring break. Then

I'd be off to Paris with Jen, and after that, the downhill slope to summer and my moving back... It'd fly by.

Hours later, Eric called. I'd planned to text him good-night like we often did when we didn't get to see each other, but I'd gotten my head on straight about him, so I answered.

"Did you have a good afternoon?"

My stomach dropped at the sound of his voice. He had a really great voice.

"I did. Just pecked away at the planning for the meeting." *And sat around thinking about you, but NBD.*

"That's good." He paused, and my heart thumped out of control. "Listen, I wanted to thank you for coming today. It was great to have you with us."

"Yeah, thanks for the invite." I slid a container of left-overs into the fridge.

"So... I have another rotation but it shouldn't be too crazy until it ramps up next week."

My jaw clenched, but I said the words. "Yeah, it'll be a busy week for me too. Maybe we can talk this weekend."

"Uh... yeah. Sure. That sounds good."

"Great. Have a good week, Eric."

"Yep. You too."

I wouldn't worry about the fact that his voice, usually so warm and appealing, sounded hollow, maybe confused, maybe even hurt. If I wanted to make space between us, the weekdays and busy times for his schedule were the easiest, least conspicuous way to do that. Maybe I hadn't been that smooth, but I couldn't just say, *"Hey Eric, I think I might be getting dangerously close to having real feelings for you that go way beyond fun and dating, so I need to not be around you as often or I'm doomed."*

Somehow, I suspected that wouldn't go over well either.

~

I made it all the way until Thursday before I broke down and texted him. He didn't contact me, which I'd basically told him not to do, but even so, it made my heart sink.

I hated this. I wanted to just... enjoy things with him. But I could feel it happening, bit by bit, every time I had even the smallest interaction with him... and if I let it keep going, I'd be leaving Germany with a broken heart on more than one level. I'd already be horribly sad to leave this little town, my apartment, and this country that'd shown me so much in the last few years. I couldn't make the trek home feeling like my heart also belonged to someone else.

But I hated not talking—not even texting. So Thursday evening before bed, I sent a small message. Just a *Hope your week is going well*. I couldn't say what I'd expected in return, but his curt *you too* was not it.

I scrubbed my hands over my face and sighed at my idiocy. Did I really think he'd be all warm and friendly when I'd shut us down?

By Friday, the prospect of not seeing him felt like a punishment that I knew full well I'd imposed on myself. Having Robby's boundless energy in my class made me both happy and desolate. I loved the little boy, as I did all my students, but he had a special place. He'd had it right from the start, and the fact that he looked so much like his dad made it all the more bittersweet to interact with him. The assistant teacher still did all his grading, and though I wouldn't have purposefully had a bias one way or another, I was glad none of his hard work could be called into question because of me. Especially since I was potentially ruining everything with his father.

With a half hour left in the day, the kids were working

on clean up at their stations. Robby stopped me when I wandered past his area.

"Ms. Anderson, are you coming over this weekend?"

My eyes darted to the students nearby, but they were all busy chatting with classmates. "Uh, I don't know, Robby. Why?"

His little face turned into a large frown. "Dad seems sad this week. He's always really happy when you come over, so I thought that might help."

I didn't know how to react to that, and so many thoughts flew through my mind at once. I loved that he'd recognized his dad was happy when I was around. I loved that he wanted me to know it, and wanted me there.

"Oh, I'm sorry to hear that. I hope he's okay. I'll call him tonight and see if I can cheer him up, okay?" I patted his shoulder gently.

Accepting the offer with a nod, he returned his focus to cleaning up his space, and I began mentally rehearsing what I'd say when I called.

The afternoon slipped by, and even though I knew he wouldn't be late getting home since he'd mentioned the weekend wouldn't be too busy, I waited to call until after eight that night. The phone rang, and my pulse pounded with nerves. Our last conversation hadn't ended well. I could tell I'd confused him, maybe even hurt him with my refusal to... well, my backing off. I didn't want that. I didn't want him hurt or confused or anything other than happy.

"Hey Livie." He sounded tired.

"Hey. How'd your week go?"

A pause. Maybe he was excusing himself from family movie night.

"It went just fine."

His speech wasn't clipped, his tone normal, if still that

tired-sounding version of his voice that made me wish I could hug him.

But he didn't say anything else.

"Robby mentioned you'd had a hard week." Maybe a cheap shot, but in the end, I wanted him talking to me. Even if that made me a ridiculous hypocrite.

"Uh, yeah. Hasn't been one of my best, but everything's fine."

"Ah. Well... good. I guess..."

A hollering in the background, probably Robby, and he spoke again. "Listen, I've got to go. Have a good night."

"Okay. Yeah. You too..."

He hung up, and my little heart slumped in my chest, even though I recognized I'd gotten what I wanted. We had space between us now, and he wasn't asking me to come over, and I wasn't snuggling down into bed talking with him 'til I fell asleep.

Just like I wanted.

Right.

CHAPTER TWENTY-TWO

Eric

Maybe I needed to get back to therapy. Based on the rage that descended every time I spoke with Renee lately, I probably did. I didn't actually normally feel much of anything except mild frustration with her anymore, but now?

"You can't do this again, Renee. You can't." *Calm. Stay calm.*

"I don't know what you expect from me, Eric."

I closed my eyes and prayed for patience. For grace. For understanding. "I expect you to do what you say you'll do. I expect you to make time to see your kids this summer since you refused to see them last summer or over Christmas."

"What do you want me to say? They can come late April for two weeks. Otherwise, it just won't work for me. I can't change my entire life for this—I already gave you nearly fifteen of them. You literally cannot ask me for anything else."

My throat closed, unable to swallow down the anger, sadness, and frustration cinching it shut. "How long will that be your excuse? The kids can't miss two weeks of school—that's why their visits come in the summer."

"Excuse? You've got to be kidding me. You know damn well I gave up everything for you. *Everything.* I may have gotten my undergrad and masters while you were flitting off on deployments, but what about *my* dreams? I'm taking my turn, and I'm not apologizing for it. I love the kids but I can't be flexible on this."

I balled a fist and pressed it into the cinderblock wall, letting the pinch in my knuckles distract from the over-whelming anger that ballooned at every single one of her words.

"If you can't understand how that's inapplicable to the current situation in which you refuse to make time for *your own children*, I can't explain it for you. Even if I deserve your resentment, they don't, and you know it. I'll call you back tomorrow, and we're going to figure this out. If we don't, I'm not going to be the one to tell them you won't make time for them. You'll do that this time."

I tapped the end call button aggressively like it'd punctuate my statement any more effectively than a light touch. I almost wished I was the type of person to scream into a pillow or punch a wall or break a plate to let off steam. I wasn't, and that's maybe what'd made therapy so necessary in the first place.

Ariel stood right outside my bedroom door, leaning on the frame. "Did she do what I think she did?"

"Yep. Along with a heaping helping of *it's my turn now* and referring to me *flitting off* on deployment during the pre-kid years like I was on multiple Caribbean vacations." I pulled in a huge breath, then let it out, willing some of the stress and tension to go with it.

She shook her head and crossed her arms tight over her chest like she was holding herself. "I never really loved her, but I didn't see this coming."

I sighed again. "Honestly, maybe I should have. We lived such separate lives before the kids, and then really only came together for bigger things—vacations, parties, work events. It all seemed kind of like a highlight reel, but I think that's all there was. The more I've thought about it over the years, the more I realize how seldomly we actually did stuff together just quietly at home. If we did, she was working on her masters' or I was, or... whatever."

"I never saw it." Her face darkened. "I guess I have a proven track record in that regard."

I set a hand on her shoulder and dipped my head to catch her eyes. "If you do, I do too. Except I don't think she ever deceived me, and what Renee and I did to explode our marriage is nothing like you and Jim. She was fine with life when she got to do what she wanted, and for a long time, that worked for us. We both wanted kids, but I know it took a much larger toll on her—of course it did. And it happened to hit right when I promoted to major and the semblance of a home life I had disappeared into the ether of the Army's needs and my ambition. I don't think we would've stayed together if I hadn't been so clueless and focused on work, but I might not've been blindsided by her resentment in the same way."

The doorbell rang and shook me from me musings. Probably time to switch gears rather than spend the next precious few hours at home stewing over the end of my marriage and my maddening ex's refusal to parent.

"Is Nate coming for dinner?" I asked as we trotted down the stairs.

"Uh, no. I think he has a date."

I eyed her, looking for any sign of... anything when she said that, but nothing.

"Huh. Well... good for him."

"Yeah. He seems to have a lot of them lately. Good for him."

It wasn't exactly a heartfelt protest, but the agreement seemed weak. I couldn't decide whether Nate and Ariel would be good together or not. I mean, I loved them both, and Nate was a good guy—one of the best. But I would've been shocked if Ariel was ready to date or even think about another man yet. But then... she seemed like herself with Nate, and I hadn't seen that in so long.

Robby had opened the door before Ariel or I reached it. I'd have to talk with him about that again.

"Hi Livie! I'm so glad you came. Delia and I are making a picture for Grandma. She says she misses us and can't wait to come back to see us. She wants to meet you and said she is very curious about you."

A laugh bubbled out of Livie, and my heart clenched.

She smiled wide and bent down to talk with Robby, right on his level. "What have you been telling her to make her curious?"

I wondered the same. They often did video chats with my mom and I didn't supervise them—she knew them well enough and they did pretty well not to make her dizzy, especially if Delia controlled the device they used.

Robby waggled his head side to side before speaking. "I told her you make Dad smile and you're my teacher and Ariel's friend and you live in our neighborhood and you're really pretty and Dad holds your hand and kisses you. Come in!"

Livie's face turned red, just like mine must have. Not that we'd hidden physical affection for each other, but I hadn't realized he'd seen us kiss. I didn't think he was tuned in to that kind of thing.

Delia giggled, but said, "Hi, Livie."

Livie defeated her embarrassment enough to offer a hello back to Delia with a small wave.

"Hey, Robby. Can you come show me the picture you're working on?" Ariel flashed her brows at me as she said hey to Livie and pulled Robby along with her to sit at the table.

I moved to the doorway where she still stood. "Do you want to come in?"

"Sure. Yes. Thank you."

For some dumb reason, I stepped forward to do... I didn't know what, just when she moved to walk through the doorway. She put a hand up to stop herself and touched my chest, which made my pulse quicken and my throat dry out.

"Sorry. I—I don't know what I'm doing." I slid back out of her way, and she entered the house, taking an exaggerated step to the side of the door so I could close it.

"Are you okay?" She tilted her head, inspecting me.

I scrubbed a hand over my face. "Yeah. Sorry. I don't know why I'm so frazzled."

She tucked her lips between her teeth. "I never would've used a word like *frazzled* to describe anything about you."

I chuckled, a little jolt of the warmth I always felt around her squirming its way into my chest. "I guess that's good news."

"I don't know. You're kind of cute when you're frazzled, if that's what you are."

Her brown-eyed gaze tracked over my face, and my heart thumped.

I'd done my best to avoid thinking about whatever was happening between us this past week. We'd had an amazing weekend and then something changed. I had no idea what, and by the midpoint of the week, I didn't have it in me to figure it out. She seemed to want space, so I'd let her be.

Her call last night had made me ache and wish I understood what she wanted. I hadn't even been angry about the shift from what felt like very close to stiff-armed in less than twenty-four hours. I just felt sad.

But here she was. Not pretending like nothing had happened—in her tentative smile, how she hadn't touched me yet... She wasn't sure what to do here either.

"Can we talk for a minute?" She kept her voice low, obviously not wanting Ariel, Delia, and Robby sitting across the room, coloring, to hear.

I wished it wasn't such a dreary day and we could step out on the porch and chat. Instead, I nodded and walked her into the kitchen just as I heard Ariel suggest the kids run upstairs and get their pajamas on. God bless her, she was trying to give us space without my having to drag Livie up or downstairs.

I ignored the memories of stolen kisses, of her in that dress on New Year's Eve, and leaned against a counter to face her. She hit me with those gorgeous brown eyes before she spoke.

"So... I owe you an apology."

CHAPTER TWENTY-THREE

Livie

His expression gave nothing away—back to the totally neutral command mode, evidently. Not a great sign for me, but I could understand him guarding himself against whatever was coming next. I certainly hadn't been acting predictably.

"I'm sorry. I wigged out a bit last weekend, and just... needed a minute. I should have just told you that instead of shutting down." My breath followed the words, shaky and fraught with nerves.

His chest rose and fell under his crossed arms. "Should we talk about what happened to make you *wig out?*"

Yes. No.

No. I didn't want to scare him, and talking through my out-of-control feelings wouldn't help keep them under control. We didn't need that kind of intimacy bringing us even closer.

"No. I'm good." His gaze exemplified *piercing*. But I held my ground. "No, really. I am. I just... needed a minute. But I didn't want to miss seeing you this weekend and then end up going another week or ten days while the rotation is crazy."

"I'm glad. I would've been disappointed not to see you—"

"Hey, Eric? Can you... come here a sec?" Ariel rushed into the room. "I'm so sorry to interrupt but Delia must've heard... something. I don't know. But she wants to talk to you before she goes to bed."

He nodded at Ariel, then turned to me. "I'm sorry. Give me a few minutes?"

"Of course." Just then, my phone rang. "I'll just grab this."

I walked into the living room and into the far corner, trying to get as far away from the stairs in an effort to give them privacy even though they were already up with Delia on the second floor.

"Hey Jen, what's up?"

"You're going to hate me."

"Oh no, why? What's wrong?" I'd seen her just yesterday at school, though we hadn't had a chance to talk.

"So... Jason wants to take me to Malta for spring break."

My stomach sank. "Oh. Wow. That's... exciting."

"I wouldn't normally do this. You know I wouldn't. But I think... he's... *it*."

I swallowed down the lump forming in my throat, disappointment thickening in my chest. She'd been on again, off again with a contractor. I'd honestly been terrible about keeping track of their relationship, but apparently they were *on again*.

I forced a smile so I wouldn't sound glum. "It's great. It'll be great. I'll cancel the Airbnb and change my plans, no problem! Just promise you'll show me photos!"

"Of course. I love you, friend. Thank you for not hating me."

I reassured her yet again and ended the call, then wandered to the couch and slumped onto the first seat I could. Ariel walked in just then.

"What's wrong?"

"Jen just called. She had to cancel our spring break trip." I smoothed the denim over my thigh, funneling my frustration and sadness there, my brain scrambling for some way to turn this into something good and fun.

Ariel sat next to me on the couch and grabbed my hand. Her lovely, kind eyes caught mine and she gave me a small smile. "Come with us."

"Uh... what? Where are you guys going?"

"We're doing Paris too. A few days at Disney Paris after the city for the first three, I think. Come with us! We'll have enough space—you can share a room with me. It'll be great." As she spoke, her smile widened, and the idea seemed to grow on her with each word.

My heart sank. In truth, I kind of loved the idea, but an invitation like this should come from Eric. And on the other hand, it was a terrible plan based on my very recent freak out about how much I liked him. "That's... so nice. But I couldn't intrude on your family vacation."

She patted my hand. "Nonsense. You fit right in. Eric will completely agree with me and insist on it."

"What will I insist on?"

My eyes jumped to him as he strode into the room, his face serious.

"Livie's spring break plans fell through. She was supposed to go to Paris, actually. So I told her she should just come with us!" She elbowed me excitedly as I watched Eric's face.

Unmoving, as always, except a few rapid blinks when she said *she should come with us*. And now, an awkward silence in the wake of her statement. No hearty agreement. No joyous accord. Just quiet.

I cleared my throat.

"Again, Ariel, that's so nice of you. It sounds amazing. But I definitely can't do that." I checked my watch, which I was thankfully actually wearing because that wouldn't have been obvious at all if I'd checked my bare wrist. "I actually have to run. I'll catch you guys soon, okay?"

"Wait, weren't you going to—"

"We're good! I'm glad I caught you. I'll get out of your hair and we'll talk soon." I literally shut the door while speaking the last words, thankful I hadn't brought a purse or taken off a jacket. I'd arrived in jeans and a hoodie and I'd left in the same.

I jogged up the street, thankful for the chill to distract me from the train wreck of the last few minutes. Spring break plans done. No real reconciliation, or repair... whatever the right word was, between me and Eric. And now the invitation from Ariel which was clearly *not* one Eric would've issued.

Just thinking of the silence that had followed made my eyes burn and my throat ache. I didn't like feeling this out of control and sad and torn. I should've been glad he didn't clap his hands and yell *hooray!* at the thought of me coming. Me joining them would be a lot for my little heart, and though the disappointment of not having him react that way hurt—hurt a surprising amount—I needed to embrace that it had turned out for the best.

I closed the door to my apartment and rested against it, wishing I could keep it together, that my emotions weren't so out of control. And now I couldn't even escape to Paris and stuff myself with cheese and *tartes aux fruits* to make up for it.

~

Three hours later, after giving myself a good twenty minutes to cry and then ordering in a larger-than-I-needed pizza from my favorite place and watching my favorite dumb comedy while sipping champagne because *I do what I want*, Eric called.

My heart started pounding so loudly in my ears, I got dizzy at the sight of his name on my phone. I could barely breathe as I picked up. "Hello?"

"Hey. Do you have a few minutes?"

"Well, I'm normally super busy on a Saturday at nine o'clock at night, but for you? I'll clear my schedule."

His low chuckle made me hug my knees to my chest, an odd mix of longing and nervousness and satisfaction flooding my mind.

"Thanks for making some time for me."

I could hear the smile in his voice. I smiled too, little butterflies flitting. If he was smiling and chuckling, he wasn't calling to say he never wanted to see me again, so that was something. "So, um, what can I do for you?"

"I wanted to talk about spring break."

I exhaled. "Oh."

"Can you tell me why you ran out of my house today?"

I shut my eyes against the tide of embarrassment. I guess I couldn't say I was surprised he just... *said it*... but ugh.

"I felt weird. I didn't want to stand there and make you feel like you needed to find an excuse for me not to come. I don't want you to think I expect that, and I don't—"

"But I do want you to come."

"What?" That didn't make sense. "You looked... unhappy at the prospect of me joining you guys. And you don't need to explain that."

"Livie, seriously. I want you to come. I love the idea of you being with us in Paris. I was coming out of a tough conversation with Delia, and before you came I had a pretty bad one with Renee which was the cause of the stuff with Delia. She's fine and actually took Renee's flakiness better than she ever has, but I couldn't shake my frustration with Renee. Add to that the odd dynamic between us the last week, and I just couldn't quite process it."

"Oh."

"Honestly, I thought you'd need an escape hatch. You said you wigged out, and I assumed traveling with us would be the wrong direction if a date and a hike put you over the edge."

I laughed at that, then sighed, releasing a good bit of the tension. "I'm sorry. I really confused things."

"You have nothing to be sorry for."

"So if you thought I wouldn't want to go, why are you calling me now? I mean, not that I'm not glad, please don't misunderstand that." I pulled at a loose thread at the seam of my sweatpants, working to tamp down the hope, the excitement bubbling up at where this might be heading, even if part of me knew this would mean no going back.

"Because Ariel told me in no uncertain terms that I

needed to call you and make sure you were okay, and make sure you knew you were welcome. Apparently, she thought my facial expression was less than delighted. Please tell me you'll consider coming with us. I want to be with you in Paris."

CHAPTER TWENTY-FOUR

Eric

In retrospect, I wondered if she took me literally. Like I wanted to *be with her* in Paris, and that was how I chose to say it.

I didn't mean it like that. Fortunately, she hadn't seemed too fazed by the expression of my wanting her there with me—of course I did. How could I not want to be around her? I'd found it impossible to think of anything else, even when exhausted, frustrated with my ex's flakiness and irritated with myself for being so affected by not getting to talk with Livie as often as I wanted. The last week had been long.

After Saturday's conversation, she'd asked to think it through and get back to me. I figured that was a way for her to get some more space before she rejected the offer, but by Tuesday night, she messaged and asked if I really meant it. I confirmed I did, not being a man who said things he didn't mean.

And she said yes.

I may have let out a *whoop!* in the office. Both Nate and Sergeant Major Allen peeked in the doorway.

"Everything okay in here?" Allen raised a brow, displaying his usual dry humor.

"Yeah. Whatever that sound was that just came out of your mouth makes me think maybe we've got an alien invasion on our hands." Nate flashed his obnoxious little *I'm so funny* smile at me as he sauntered into the office and slunk into a chair.

"Everything's good. Livie just said she's coming to Paris with us."

Allen nodded and held up a hand, departing for his desk, while Nate's eyes narrowed on me.

"What are you doing with this woman?"

I bristled. "What's that supposed to mean?"

Nate straightened in his seat and speared me with the earnest, concerned eyes of a friend. "I seem to recall you said you were keeping it casual. I know you have no plans to marry anyone after what happened with Renee. So I'm just wondering. Because traveling together sounds pretty serious to me."

"Does it? I thought it sounded like a step up from going for coffee."

He blinked slowly, evidently unimpressed with my sarcasm. "Seriously. I'm not trying to be a jerk, I'm just asking."

I pulled in a slow breath and let it out, my thoughts tumbling around untethered in my mind. After a moment, I leaned an elbow on the desk.

"I don't know. We did say we'd keep it casual. It has started to feel pretty... *un*casual. She took a step back last week and I tried to tell myself it was for the best, I should let it happen, but when she showed up this weekend apologizing, all I could feel was relief. And when Ariel suggested she come with us, I jumped at the chance to share that experience with her."

Nate studied me, but didn't interrupt. After well over a decade of friendship, he knew when I had more to say.

"I definitely have feelings for her. I'm trying not to worry about it. It really can't go anywhere, but I don't want to ruin something between us just because I like her so much. So I'm just... enjoying it while it lasts."

I closed a notebook that had been sitting open on the desk, lined up the mechanical pencil I'd been using so it sat parallel to the notebook and desk calendar. Anything, really, to avoid looking at Nate and reading whatever he thought in his expression, which he would definitely let me see.

He sighed, more resigned than frustrated or disappointed. I looked up to see compassion in his face.

"I know things with Renee sucked. I'm sorry for it. I wish you'd consider that you don't have to just be done at a certain point, especially because you seem to like Livie so much and she gets along with every part of your life."

"She's leaving anyway." And I wouldn't ever ask her not to. I wouldn't risk holding someone back again. Not again.

Nate stood and moved to the door, stopping just shy of exiting before leaning on the doorframe. The grave expression on his face surprised me—I'd been so happy moments ago, but he'd sent my thoughts scattering over things I'd tried not to think about. Namely, the end of my time with Livie, which would be here before I knew it.

After a few moments of silence, maybe while he gathered his thoughts, he finally spoke. "Then I guess you enjoy it while it lasts. Take what you can get when you can get it. I can certainly understand that."

"Uh, sir? Do you have a sec?" Sergeant Noah Miller and Captain Rob Waverly stood at the door.

"Come on in. I'm just leaving." Nate slipped out of the office, and the other two men stepped inside.

"We wanted to talk with you about the tasking for upcoming TDYs. Wild's taking the next one, but I wanted to make sure you knew we're both available anytime and happy to take any assignments that'll let the family guys get more time with their kids."

Waverly spoke for himself and his sergeant. My battalion didn't typically do many TDY assignments, but the new post commander had placed an emphasis on the OPFOR—my battalion—doing their fair share. *Sure.*

Doable, except we were often run ragged by the rotations, even with a recently added company of soldiers. Still, I appreciated the gesture. These men were stepping up, trying to alleviate the stress on the soldiers with families who'd seen their loved ones even less when they were TDY.

"You're a *family guy* right, Miller? The wife won't miss you?" I entered the password on my computer and clicked through to the long-range training calendar.

He straightened a bit. "Uh, no sir. She's stateside."

"Really? For how long?" I skimmed through the calendar, eyeing the TDY obligations each company commander had made assignments for. I knew his wife was stateside, but since Allen had concerns, here was an easy way to have him verbalize his situation to me directly without seeming like I was staging an inquisition.

Miller cleared his throat, his weight shifting side to side. "Permanently, sir. She had to stay stateside. So she won't miss me any more from here than she will in Ukraine or Poland or wherever's up next."

"Ah, I apologize. I'm sure you've told me that already. I'll make a note of your names and have Nate take a look at the lists for me. We'll get you guys slotted for some adventures this year for sure. I know we've got quickies to Afghanistan three times in the next six months—I'd like you to consider being on each of those for consistency's sake with the training, if you're up to it."

"Sounds good."

"Absolutely."

With that, they left, and I sat back, thoughts of Miller's stateside wife and my own kids muddying my thoughts.

Weeks later, Friday and the night before we planned to leave for France, I jogged up the stairs to Livie's house. She'd brought me lunch, but as fate and the Army scheduling powers that be would have it, I hadn't seen her since our awkward conversation about her coming to France with us. *Not* ideal. We couldn't exactly talk intimately in my office even if I had seen her, even with the door closed. It wasn't the best place to reconnect.

So I needed to see her before we found ourselves surrounded by the moods and mayhem of traveling with kids... and my sister. Livie wouldn't be with us the entire time. She'd decided to take a tour of Reims she'd pre-paid for when she'd planned the trip with Jen, which I wished I could join her for, and then join us in Paris for two nights. *Just two.* But I think for her, that was her way of saying yes without committing to too much time with me and my brood.

We'd make the most of it. And part of how we'd do that is by not drowning in weirdness left over from the last few weeks of non-contact.

"Hey. I didn't expect to see you until Tuesday." Her beaming smile assured me it hadn't been the wrong choice to come.

I brushed a hand down my uniform top. "Yeah. I guess I should've texted or something, but I wanted to see you before we're in the midst of the madness."

She stepped back, the door swinging wide. "Come in."

"I only have a minute."

I followed behind her as she shut the door and took a seat on her couch.

"So?" She bounced a little where she sat, that cheerful energy drawing me in as usual.

I ate up the sight of her. "I just... wanted to see you. I feel like the time is going to fly, and I suspect the first few days without you might age me prematurely, so I wanted to see you one last time before I go fully gray."

She laughed freely at that. "You'll be a hot silver fox. Fear not."

"Really? *Silver fox?*"

Her brown eyes sparkled with amusement.

"Oh yes. I've always liked a good head full of gray. Though I do take issue with the fact that culturally it seems to only work for men." She reached up and brushed her fingers along one side of my head where my hair, I had to admit, was more salt than pepper lately. "This part here, I particularly like."

The touch had brought us closer. In fact, other than bumping into each other weeks ago in my living room, we hadn't been this close since we'd held hands on the hike— even before. My body raced with anticipation and a heightened awareness that pushed intense thoughts into my mind.

Thoughts like *please touch me again*. Thoughts like *you're mine*. Thoughts like *I don't think I'll be able to stop kissing you if we start*.

Before I could say something stupid and ruin the moment, she leaned in and touched her warm, soft lips to mine. Heat flooded me, overwhelming all thoughts except how much I wanted her.

I held her to me with one palm at the back of her head, but she pulled back, huffed a little, and smiled.

"I know you can't stay long because I'm guessing you're leaving super early, right?"

I nodded, struggling to keep my attention on her words when her lips were so near.

"Hey." She snapped twice. "Eyes up here, sir."

Her delighted smile gave her away, and I laughed. Obviously, she'd caught me staring longingly at her lips, which I couldn't even be embarrassed about. The force of being alone with her after so long paired with the warmth of her greeting, the relief that the absence of awkwardness brought... it'd shaken all sense from me.

I cleared me throat. "Sorry. I just... like you."

We both chuckled at my dumb statement.

"But yes. I do have to go. Thanks for answering the door."

"Thanks for coming to the door in the first place."

CHAPTER TWENTY-FIVE

Livie

T he metro zipped along underground toward my stop. I'd get out and take a ten-minute walk and arrive at the Airbnb where I'd spend the next two nights with Eric, Ariel, Robby, and Delia. It was only about fifteen minutes from where Jen and I had planned to stay, but at this point, I didn't care. I just wanted to get there and see them. Him.

Eric. Goodness, I could not get the man out of my head. I'd enjoyed a lazy Saturday with a bit of prep work so I didn't have any obligations when I returned, then chatted with my parents and caught them up on everything—even this whole Eric Wolfe is dreamy but a dead-end situation.

Then Sunday, I'd cleaned my apartment top to bottom before an oddly timed flight out of the Nuremberg airport. I could've driven to Paris, but it would've made for a very long day, and I didn't want to spend all that time on the road. Since my trip was short, the budget airline flight with its bag restrictions and minimal space wasn't so bad, and I'd take a train back, which would still be better than driving.

I spent a day touring Reims, mostly thinking about how much more fun the tour would've been with Jen, and then feeling annoyed with myself for doing anything other than enjoying the moment. It'd been the one non-refundable part of our plan, and I'd decided my love of champagne and the fleeting time left in Europe meant I needed to take it. I wished Jen were here. I wished Eric were here.

Dangerous thought. I'd been having them a lot. I'd been picturing spending days and nights together, sharing more and more experiences, ourselves...

The metro car zoomed to a halt, the doors scrolled open, and I hustled out, glad my little travel bag had a backpack function so I didn't have to drag it behind me up the stairs. Each step that took me closer to Eric felt like a step closer to... something.

Ever since he'd asked me to come and clarified that yes, he really wanted me here, I'd had this strange tunneling sensation. Like so much of the last few years had led to this moment. Like the choice to say no to the engagement with Aaron. And the choice to start working at DODEA schools, then move to Germany, then stay with teaching kindergarten when I could have switched to first. Like the choice to break my rules and date a dad, a soldier... like all of it had led here. I'd worked hard to push away that feeling, but whether despite or because of it, I'd said yes.

And now, here I was, ascending the stairs and out onto the Parisian street, inhaling the fresh air and feeling the jump in my chest at the familiar sights of a city I truly loved. I'd visited no fewer than five times in the years I'd lived in Europe. The trip with Jen had been designed to be my last hurrah. I pushed away the disappointment of the foreshortened trip and determined, like I'd told myself I would so many times in the last few weeks, this would be great.

Before I knew it, I'd been buzzed into a building I could only describe as picturesque situated on a quiet street on the Left Bank. I'd stayed all over the city, but not in this neighborhood. Eric had apologized for the location like it was some kind of inconvenience due to its relative distance to the main sights. He'd found a place to stay with a bit more space at an affordable price... I could hardly fault him.

Little voices jabbered behind the door as I approached, and my heart sprinted in my chest from the climb. Definitely the climb, and not anticipation, or nerves, or the sudden thought that it was totally strange I'd come to stay with them—or that I'd been missing them so fiercely since Eric had stopped by my place days ago.

"She's here! She's here! Ari, get the door!"

Ariel's smiling face greeted me, along with a bouncing Robby and Delia. They ushered me in, then hugged me like it'd been months, not days, since we'd seen each other. There was something about reuniting in a new place that necessitated such a greeting.

This was a great sign—I hadn't expected contact so soon from Delia, but Eric had mentioned on one of our phone calls how amazing she'd been doing, and how the therapist had remarked she felt Delia had turned a corner in the last few months. My nervous energy calmed a bit. I knew these people, and loved them. I was glad I'd come.

"Eric's just run out to grab a few things for tomorrow morning. Let's get you settled, and then we can go explore when he gets back." Ariel waved me into the apartment, a truly stunning place with natural light and a white, gray, and light blue color scheme.

I admired the décor as we passed through the living

room and kitchen, then down a hallway where Robby and Delia showed off their room featuring two single beds with fluffy white duvets and adorable art on the walls.

"The books are in French, but the pictures are good." Robby gestured to a basket of books sitting on a table situated between the two beds like a shared nightstand.

This was something I loved about travel. I loved staying in hotels, but apartments were so interesting. Seeing how the owners outfitted a place, enjoying the small thoughtful touches they might include, made each trip all the more memorable. Granted, sometimes it also made them disastrous, but in the dozens of trips I'd taken, I'd only had two spectacularly bad locations.

I left the kids and made my way to the bedroom next door. Two more twin beds sat in an identical set up.

"Wow, they're angling hard for large families on this one, aren't they?" I set my bag down on the small bench at the foot of the unclaimed bed.

"They seem to be. The master suite is really something. Eric tried to make me take it but I refused." She plumped a pillow and sat with her back against it and the wall.

"Would he even fit in one of these beds?" I pulled my toiletry bag out and set a pair of shoes on the floor.

"I would, but I appreciate not having to find out what the consequences for my back would be."

His smooth, low voice came from the doorway, and the sound of it set off a tumbling in my stomach.

"Hi," I said, all brilliance and refined grace as I fumbled with the toiletry bag and it clunked onto the duvet.

"Hey. Glad you made it."

The smile and the stubble on his face were a brutal combination to my coordination and my chest, already so fraught with the flurry of witless little butterflies that I might've been near panting.

"I'm going to go grab some water and make sure the kids use the bathroom and all that. I'll meet you two by the door in a few." Ariel slipped out past Eric, but he made no move to enter the room more fully.

"How were the first few days here?"

He leaned against the doorframe. "Good. I think the kids will be ready for Disney when the time comes, but they've handled the walking really well and seem to be enjoying the city. We tend toward outdoor options when we do longer trips. This is the longest we'll be in a city, actually."

"That's great," I said a bit absently, like I'd heard what he'd said and hadn't been mostly just appreciating the view.

I hadn't gotten to see him much the last few weeks, and it'd been strained before that. His quick stop by my apartment days ago hadn't been enough. Now he stood four feet away looking dark and handsome and rugged, but also ridiculously sophisticated somehow. He wore dark jeans and a button-down white shirt. It wasn't anything fancy but man, he made the wardrobe choice look good.

My eyes returned to his face and found a half-smile on his gorgeous lips, and more than a little humor in his eyes. I'd been caught staring.

"Um, so, yeah. My trip was good too. I mean, a little lonely, but now I'm here with you guys which is great."

His smile widened, and he moved to me, grabbing my hand. "Are you nervous, Livie?"

I swallowed, then exhaled. "I'm trying not to be."

"Don't be. Really. Everyone's glad you're here, and if you get sick of us, it's only two nights." His thumb stroked over the back of my hand.

A nice thought. But the problem wasn't worrying I'd get sick of them. Quite the opposite, in fact.

"I'm just going to take a quick sec to freshen up, and then I'll be ready to go." I dropped his hand and clutched the toiletry bag to me.

His blue eyes pinned me, though. I didn't move, and he didn't... not for what felt like a full minute as he studied my face, eyes dipping to my lips every so often. Just before I lost my wits and pulled his face to mine, he dropped his head and kissed my temple, releasing the butterflies and sending a mildly dizzy sensation through my brain.

"Okay then. See you in a minute."

The afternoon and evening flew by. Seeing Paris through the kids' eyes proved to be an amazing way to encounter my beloved city in a new light. Robby's curiosity and energy paired with Delia's careful, artistic, thoughtful approach brought new appreciation to so many things. Eric mentioned how relieved he'd been that Delia, so far, had handled the travel well. They'd had practice with how best to handle new places, and he'd once explained how he traveled prepared for as many versions of her anxiety to manifest as possible. He had disposable gloves, sanitizing options, even extra changes of clothes when needed.

I remembered him mentioning how the worst trip they'd taken had come a few months after they'd arrived in Germany, just after his ex-wife had canceled the kids' visit to her place. Delia's anxiety had skyrocketed, and she couldn't handle touching anything without immediately sanitizing her hands and in some cases changing shirts, to the point that his mom had ended up staying in their hotel room with her by the last day.

I marveled at her now, wandering around, pointing and laughing with Robby, or at times elbowing him out of her way. One advantage to sightseeing the way we were doing it —by walking—was that it didn't necessitate much contact with things. But even when we stopped for lunch, or took a seat by a fountain in the gardens, she seemed relaxed. Fortunately, Paris was a perfect city to just walk and see, and we'd lucked out with gorgeous spring weather.

Perhaps my favorite part was standing with them in L'Orangerie surrounded by Monet's water lilies in canvases stretched across curved walls. At one point, only the five of us were in the room and like so many of my favorite moments traveling, it felt like we had the beauty all to ourselves.

Robby had lapped around the room several times, looking close, then backing up until the brush strokes became the larger picture again. Delia had lingered, not wanting to leave, asking to buy a souvenir from the little shop and stopping to sit on a bench and jot down secret thoughts in the little journal she carried. I noticed Ariel take a chest-expanding breath and closing her eyes before opening them and staring at a particular section.

Eric reached for my hand and held it tight, sending warmth flooding through me. The smile on his face was appreciative. Maybe because this stop had been my suggestion, or maybe because he was glad to share the experience. Either way, I squeezed back.

By the end of the day, we'd stuffed ourselves with an amazing meal, then dessert, and the kids had passed out in bed while Eric, Ariel, and I stayed up sipping wine and chatting, drawing out the day as long as we could.

"What's Nate doing for his leave?" I'd wondered if he would be here too, but Eric had said no, like *of course not*, as though Nate wasn't at their house and by his or Ariel's side nine days out of ten.

"He's off on some ridiculous trek in Thailand or something." He shook his head like it was an unbelievable thing for Nate to do.

It kind of was.

"Thailand? Wow."

"Yeah, he's a big traveler like that. He toured Europe a lot during college, lived in Italy for a few semesters or something, so when he gets longer breaks he'll go farther afield." Eric removed his arm from where it rested behind me, but quickly grabbed my free hand in his.

We'd always guarded our physical interactions in front of the kids, but today he'd made no secret of holding my hand. Maybe after Robby had reported to Eric's mother that we'd held hands and kissed, he'd decided there was no point. Whatever the case, I enjoyed the closeness, even though it created a kind of hectic, pent-up feeling I couldn't see the end of.

"He's fancy," Ariel said, draining the last of her wine in a gulp.

"I'm surprised he didn't ask you guys to go with him." He seemed to genuinely love the family, and he and Ariel were such close friends. Seemed like more than that, but I believed Eric when he said Ariel didn't have room for something like that right now. Not yet anyway.

"He knows I wouldn't go that far. And Ariel turned him down. Told him I needed help with the kids."

My eyes widened, and I watched for Ariel's reaction. *Nothing.*

"He didn't really mean it. Of course I couldn't go

anyway." She scooted her glass around on the side table where it rested, making little circles with the base. Then her blazing blue eyes hit mine and she smiled. "You guys need to go out on a date tomorrow night."

"Uh, oh. That's nice—"

Eric sat up. "Yeah, that'd be great. We can do a late dinner after we all get in, that way you don't have to wrangle the kids out and about. Thanks Ari."

He patted my knee lightly, then stood and extended a hand to me. I took it, bewildered but pleased at the exchange, which felt a little like they'd planned on that all along but didn't want to make it too obvious.

"Is that okay with you, Livie?" His blue eyes, like his sister's but a thousand times more intense, bore into mine.

"As long as you feed me cheese, then yes."

CHAPTER TWENTY-SIX

Eric

The next day floated by like something in a dream.

We ate pastries for breakfast and wandered the *Jardin de Tuileries* for about a half hour before Robby begged for his next feeding in the form of a crêpe. The kids rode the Ferris wheel at the carnival set up. We snapped cheesy pictures at the Louvre's glass pyramids and took a quick tour of the opera house before stopping for a long lunch. The kids discovered the glories of *mille-feuille*, a pastry consisting of layers of crisp butter puff and cream.

And all the while, Livie pointed out parts of the city she loved, sometimes sharing a memory she treasured. It was always small things, special moments, or embarrassments that had us all laughing.

She'd been working on teaching the kids a few basic French phrases, which Ariel and I had done a bit of but not as well. Then she told the story of asking a woman in the metro ticket office for help.

"I walked up and I said, 'Can you help me find the right line to get closest to the Louvre?' or wherever it was I was heading, and she looked at me, total lack of amusement and said, '*Bonjour*.' Then she waited. Finally, I got the message and greeted her properly. After that, she was perfectly pleasant. From that day on, I have never failed to greet someone before asking for help." She laughed at herself, and Ariel shared a similar story from our first day here.

Every one of Livie's stories served as another hook in my heart, another tether binding me to her.

By the end of the day, which we'd packed full of everything imaginable that we hadn't already done before she'd arrived, everyone was exhausted. Ariel declared they would order in pizza and relax, which would give me and Livie the chance to get out a bit earlier and spend more time together before we left for Disney and she made her way back to Germany.

I loved my sister all the time, but lately, she'd been the best wingman I could ever ask for. Maybe too good, based on the pleased little twinkle in her eye when I stepped out of my room in jeans, a gray button-down shirt, and a black blazer. I didn't plan on anything too fancy, but I hated to look too casual.

"Very nice."

Her approval made me even more nervous, which grated. I didn't want nervous to mix with the anticipation and joy at having this time. I wanted to simply savor it.

Livie wandered out in a soft pink dress that hugged her torso and flared at the hips... just as I took a slug of water, which turned out to be terrible timing because I must've tried to breathe through my mouth at the same time, and came up sputtering. She rushed to me, patting me on the back as I recovered, fully aware any amount of cool or smoothness I might've owned prior to that moment had evaporated.

"You going to make it?" She clapped me on the back again, her lovely brown eyes accentuated with more makeup than I'd seen her wear other than maybe New Year's Eve.

She looked astounding. She wore gloss of some kind on her lips a few shades darker than the dress, and her hair was down, with one side pulled back behind her ear. She looked so beautiful, so so beautiful.

I cleared my throat.

"I think so." I coughed a few more times.

"You guys have fun. I'm going to check on the kids. Don't stay out too late." Ariel winked and wiggled her brows, then wandered over to the couch where the children sat glued to the iPad watching a movie—a rare treat in honor of our busy day.

"I guess that's our cue." I held out a hand, and relief, excitement, desire all coursed through me when she took it.

"Lead the way."

The St. Germain neighborhood vibrated with life and art. Livie had recommended it as a good place to find dinner, and we certainly had our pick. We'd lucked out with a gloriously warm spring day, and though the evening had cooled, it hadn't scared away the artists and street performers of the area.

We finally found a spot, less concerned about the menu since almost everywhere we went had delicious offerings and it didn't seem we could go wrong. If we sat and didn't like the food options, we'd have a drink and then move on.

The waiter flicked his hand at a minuscule table facing the street with two wicker chairs smashed together side by side.

"*C'est parfait, merci.*" Livie's French, like her German, sounded perfect to me.

"You have a bottom to that bag of tricks of yours?" I asked when we sat.

"If I do, I'm not about to tell you." She gave me a dazzling smile and settled into her seat, perusing the menu.

The first of our food came—champagne and a charcuterie selection that barely fit on our table, particularly after a small basket of bread was dropped to the side of the board.

"I love Paris. I love it so much." Her tone was wistful and a bit dreamy.

"I had a few people warn me away from it. They said it wasn't worth it, whatever that means." I sipped the champagne, the crisp, cold drink heightening the moment.

She made an annoyed sound. "I think those people come expecting Paris to bow down to them for showing up. They don't have manners, they don't observe basic customs, and then they get all bothered that Parisians haven't thrown a party when they bothered to wait in line at the Louvre and hike to the Sacré Coeur."

I couldn't hold in the laugh. "But Livie, how do you really feel?"

She elbowed me, which was easy since she was practically underneath me in her seat, close as we were. I dropped my arm nearest her and gripped her thigh over the soft fabric of her dress, then caught her arm with the opposite hand and twisted as much as I could in the chair just as she did, bringing our faces close.

"I feel very, very glad to be here with you, Eric."

My stomach clenched at her words, her breath on my lips, the feel of her so close, and a gratitude so enormous I thought I'd choke on it as it welled up in me. That she'd make the trip, that she'd agree to spend her time with kids and not on some adult adventure, that she'd even consider spending time with an aging single dad who needed glasses to read menus and butchered German and French with abandon...

Despite the closeness, I took her hand in mine. "Thank you for being here. Thank you for coming."

The evening flew by. We ate five courses and watched a few street performers wander through. We laughed and talked and ate ourselves silly—soups, salads, entrees, desserts, cheese. By the time we began our walk home, which we quickly abandoned and ordered a car because the evening had chilled and Livie was freezing, even with my jacket around her, I felt like I might explode.

From the food. From happiness. From the unabated *wanting* I felt, even after being so close to her all night. If anything, that had heightened the desire, a bow being pulled and pulled across a string until one or the other burst.

When the car dropped us at the building where my family likely lay sleeping, it was after eleven. I wished, more than just a little, that the apartment would be empty. That somehow, I could have this night with her, alone.

But the reality of my situation—a father of two, brother to a sister who still needed me... these things were mine to claim. It hadn't scared her away yet... or at least not entirely.

"Thank you. It was so fun to be out in the city with you." She spoke quietly as we took the stairs slowly.

We stopped at the door, and I hesitated, then pulled our clasped hands and clutched them to my chest. She gazed up into my eyes, and my heart thudded heavy behind my ribs. "I don't want the night to be over."

"Me either."

We breathed in sync for a breath, two, and then my ability to resist her collapsed. I wrapped my free hand around her and brought her even closer while she urged my head down with hers at the back of my neck. Our lips met, softly just once, then ravenous, like she'd been needing the contact as much as I had.

We savored each other there in the hallway, silently claiming kisses and stolen touches before a door slammed above us and we jolted apart. Reluctantly, I unlocked the door and we tiptoed inside. All the lights were off except one in the kitchen.

So Ariel hadn't been waiting just inside the door, sitting on the couch reading or just watching for us. I'd wondered. Had I known she wasn't, I would've staged my move inside the door. But now that we'd made it inside, Livie seemed like maybe she was ready to turn in, and I didn't relish the thought of having one of the kids wander out for a glass of water and find us making out on the couch.

"Thank you, again."

I released the hand I still held and ran a finger along her cheek. "Thank you for going with me."

"Good night, Eric." She leaned up and placed a light, too-swift kiss on my lips.

I watched her go, every part of me yelling, demanding I go take her hand and lead her to my room, continue the promise the evening, and the months of seeing each other, had set up. But I forced myself to turn and walk to the oppo-site hall, the main bedroom with a bed large enough for two, that would sleep only one.

I moved through the routine—brushing teeth, slipping out of my shoes, pulling on shorts to sleep in, ditching my shirt, undershirt—

A knock on the door interrupted me, so I quickly moved to open it, wondering if Robby had had a bad dream.

I opened it to find Livie, arms crossed tightly over her chest.

"Sorry. Uh—" She turned to go, then rotated back toward me halfway. "Ariel locked the door and I can't get her to answer. I forgot she sleeps with earplugs. I don't know why she'd lock the door but—"

"Stay here. Stay with me."

God bless my sister.

CHAPTER TWENTY-SEVEN

Livie

So many things happened in that moment.

I never would've guessed Ariel would lock me out. We'd be having words about that, for sure. At the same time, based on her ready participation in getting us out on the town together, I knew she'd done it to give us space... lots of space.

But that made it so I had to come to him. Which I wanted to do, and yet the way my heart practically shook my body, the way it had to be pounding louder than it ever had before, made me breathless before I ever knocked on his door.

Then he opened up, evidently mid-clothing change. The man was shirtless, and if I hadn't been breathing normally before, well...

"Livie? Come in."

His soft words, his hand gentle on my wrist where it wrapped around me, shook me from the daze the moment, the late hour, and his very attractive torso had lulled me into.

"Sorry. Sure. Thanks. I already brushed my teeth while I was trying to figure out if I could pick the lock on the door, but no luck. I can sleep in my dress—it's really comfortable, so that's good. I just need a blanket or something and I'll crash on the couch, no problem."

He shut the door behind me, but didn't step away. The heat from his body, only inches from mine, beckoned.

"I'll text her. She can't be that deeply asleep." He reached for his phone, which he regrettably had to move to the other side of the bedroom to get. He tapped the message while still eying me.

I chuckled weakly, a forced, nervous little sound. "I'm pretty sure she's not going to answer, whether she's asleep or not."

"What makes you say that?"

He set his phone on a table and returned to me, sending little thrills of awareness sparking through my chest.

"I think she's trying to push us together."

A single brow rose in response as he stood close, not touching me yet overwhelming my senses.

"She seems to want us to have time together... alone."

Just that word sent another trill of nerves through me... the anticipation of his touching me, kissing me like he had just outside the door, threatened to steal my breath entirely.

His lips twitched, like he didn't want to smile openly, but couldn't help the impulse. "Is that a bad thing? I thought we were both wishing for more time not twenty minutes ago."

"It's not bad, no. Definitely not bad." I slid a hand up his arm, needing to touch him and to reassure him that though my voice sounded annoyingly weak, I had no doubts about being here. His skin was warm, and smooth, and I wanted to press my lips to his neck, his chest.

His face broke into a blazing smile, and my heart flipped.

"Good. Because I'm having a hard time finding anything bad about this." His voice sounded lower than usual, a little gritty from the late hour and like every good thing combined.

With a hand at my waist, he tugged me close, and we came together, the build-up of the last few months, days, and especially hours sending us from lukewarm to incendiary in seconds. His hot mouth met mine while my hands roamed his chest and arms, ending in the short hair at his nape. We pressed closer, all heat and desire, before he backed me toward the bed. The backs of my legs touched the fluffy white comforter, and I gripped his shoulders.

The response was immediate. He broke away, pulling me up so I wouldn't topple over onto the bed.

"Sorry. I'm sorry." He let go and stepped back, placing a few inches of distance between us.

I smiled seeing his disheveled hair and swollen lips. "Don't apologize. I just... want to make sure this is a good idea."

"It's a great idea."

We both laughed at his quick response, and I set a hand on his chest... his really nice chest. "I mean, I don't want this to confuse either one of us."

His eyes searched mine, and the smile faded from his face. "I can tell you this, Livie. I'm not confused about what a great night we've had. I'm not confused about how much I want it to continue. But I hadn't planned on this—didn't think we'd get the chance here, for sure. I haven't been with anyone since Renee, and I think it might end up being... problematic."

I swallowed, nodding. "Me too."

What I didn't say was that I wasn't confused about anything—not the desires *or* the emotion behind them. Yes, Eric Wolfe was a babe in and out of uniform. But he was so much more than a good-looking guy. He was thoughtful and funny and kind of intense about certain things. He loved his sister, and he adored his kids, and he wasn't afraid to be vulnerable. He was essentially everything I could imagine wanting, except for his career, and even that had made him who he was so I couldn't begrudge it.

But it did mean this building emotion... the one I didn't want to name but felt very clearly—one I'd never felt so clearly before—had shattered the illusion that my heart could remain intact when this was all over.

Taking the next step physically wouldn't help that. And even though hearing him say it would be *problematic* made my heart hurt and my body want to cry, he spoke truth.

My hand curled against his chest. "Okay, then I'll just borrow a blanket and hit the couch."

He grabbed my hand and pressed it into his warm skin. "No, honey, don't do that. Stay here with me. Sleep in the bed, hold my hand while we fall asleep. It doesn't have to be all or nothing."

His soft words and the sweetness behind them made my throat ache and I swallowed. "Okay. I'd like that."

"Wear these, and I'll be back in a few minutes," he said, handing me a clean T-shirt and a pair of boxers, then excusing himself to the bathroom.

I could hear the water running, then the sound of him brushing his teeth. I slipped out of my dress and into Eric's things, my heart tripping at the smell of his detergent and the feel of his clothes on my skin, yet thankful for the moment to get my bearings, though wearing something of his to bed didn't exactly chill me out. When he emerged, he still hadn't put on a shirt, and my blood heated at the sight.

"Can't look at me like that, okay?" he said, a little gruffly, one brow arching to lighten the moment even though his sound and expression were otherwise serious.

I chuckled and ducked. "Then I guess I better not look at you."

He laughed too, then took my hand and led me to the bed. I swear, I tried to act normal, but couldn't ignore the sure, possessive touch of his hand guiding me to the bed. I couldn't stop the excitement at his nearness, or the way he slid in behind me and curled around me, fully nested.

I nearly changed my mind about all of it—everything—when he nuzzled into my hair by my ear and said, "Good-night, Livie. I'm glad you're here."

I whispered, "'Night," and bit my tongue to keep so many other things from spilling out.

I woke sprawled across the bed... not a single bed. And with a large, warm body beside me, which was obviously Eric. My stomach dropped, remembering the night before.

The way he'd wrapped me in his arms, and we'd fallen asleep nestled together. How he'd given us both a few minutes to get a grip before we jumped into bed and pretended we could just ignore the raging chemistry between us, and the desire, and all the feelings, after running full-out toward a finish line.

It was the right choice, and the fact that we'd mutually agreed, that we'd stopped in the moment, only showed how amazing he was. He hadn't pushed, and in fact, it'd been his choice, ultimately.

What kind of man was like that? One who'd been deeply hurt by his divorce, certainly, but also one who cared. I wondered if he cared as deeply as I did.

I shook that thought from my head and tossed on my dress—thankful he'd given me a pair of shorts and a T-shirt to wear to bed since his rotten sister had locked me out. I slipped out the bedroom and out the apartment door before anyone could find me, eager to enact my plan.

Thirty minutes later, I unlocked the door and found Delia and Robby sitting on the living room couch each flipping through books.

"Livie! Where were you? We thought you were sleeping like Ari and Dad."

Robby sprang off the couch and ran toward me without stopping, eventually plowing into my legs. Fortunately, I'd braced myself for impact.

I held up the bags of goodies. "I ran out to get us breakfast."

His eyes grew hearts. "Oh, what did you get?"

Delia joined us at the table where I set a plate after washing my hands, then pulled out the delights I'd picked up down at the *boulangerie* down the street. Croissants, almond pastries, pain au chocolat, among others... every delight times two, at least.

"This looks amazing." Delia's awed statement echoed my own sentiments exactly.

"Do we have to wait for Dad and Ari?" Robby sat, knees jumping, hands clasped together.

"Let's make sure we save them something, but I'd say no. Let's eat!"

And so we shared the French feast, reveling in the perfection of the croissants especially.

"You know, German croissants just aren't this good." Delia pulled apart another pastry, flaky swirling layers revealed.

"You're right about that. It took me a good six months before I believed that they just weren't worth it to me. I kept trying different bakeries, but nope. They're a different animal." I popped the last bite of one of the aforementioned delights into my mouth and savored the buttery flakiness. Bliss in a bite.

We talked about our favorite things about France, and then about Germany. By the time Eric emerged from his room, causing my heart to summersault in my chest at the sight of him, we'd covered a lot of ground, and were completely full.

"You're all up early," he said in a sleep-roughened voice, approaching the table.

I fleetingly wished I'd stayed in that bed and enjoyed the pleasure of watching him wake. I hoped someday I'd get the chance. But my thoughts had been shouting at me, and I'd needed food and fresh air to get my head on straight. Plus early morning pastries were one of the true pleasures of a stay in France.

He leaned down and hugged each of his kids, both of them pressing a kiss into his scruffy cheek. There was nothing rote about the movements for any of them—though clearly routine, the actions were full of genuine affection.

My heart thudded at the sight. Thudded, then broke

open, love for this man and his children spilling out and filling up my chest. Then he came for me from behind my chair, set a hand on one shoulder, thumb stroking the side of my neck and leaning down to place a kiss on my cheek, then just below my ear. I shivered, the sensations paired with the expanding emotion in my body too much to hold inside.

"Of course we are, Dad! We head to Disney today! Disney! Disney!" Robby began chanting and he skipped down the hallway to the bathroom, presumably.

Delia shook her head, but her eyes practically twinkled with excitement. "I just heard Ari get out of the shower. What time are we leaving?"

"About an hour. Better get a move on." He patted her head before she trotted off to join her brother.

Ariel had generously agreed to help the kids pack everything but their clothes and toiletries last night, so all that remained was rounding up the towels and emptying the trash per the owner's expectations, and zipping the last few things into everyone's bags. He must've anticipated a late night, but I also knew he wasn't the kind of man to leave anything to the last minute.

He sat next to me in Robby's recently vacated spot, the table in front of him covered in croissant flakes. "Looks like the kids enjoyed their breakfast, thank you."

I resisted the urge to close my eyes and let his voice wash over me. What was wrong with me today?

"They're so great. We talked about... everything."

He chuckled and grabbed my hand, linking our fingers and then placing a kiss on the back of my hand. The place where his lips had touched seemed to pulse from the contact.

"They were probably elated to have pastries and not

just cereal for breakfast. Thank you for going out to get all of this."

Though we'd done some damage, I'd bought enough to feed a party of eight or more. "Well, go ahead and eat. I'll make us some coffee."

I stood and released his hand, but he didn't let go of mine. Instead, he guided me to stand between his legs where he sat, placed his hands on my hips, and looked up at me.

Wow. Those eyes this close after the last few days... absolutely killer. I held his face in my hands, my palms pressing against the stubble on his jaw, and leaned down to kiss his lips.

"I'm so glad you came."

His quiet, low voice rumbled through me since I stood so close.

"Me too. Thank you for inviting me. Much better than moping around my apartment the whole week."

"You should come with us to Disney. You don't have to leave today." He turned his head and kissed the palm of my hand.

"I do though. It's a memory you should make together."

Without me. I didn't say it, but it hung in the air around us. I hated the thought of them looking back at pictures and thinking *remember that lady who came with us, what was her name?* No. It should be them, just family.

"You being there will only add to the enjoyment. For all of us."

I stepped back, unable to take his sincerity and that look in his eyes at close range. I escaped to the kitchen to start the single-serve coffee maker, a sad drawback to the rental apartment game but better than no coffee. "I think Delia has the whole park memorized from the map you printed for her. They're going to run you ragged."

And if I longed to be there, to join them and witness firsthand the explosion of joy those kids had at the sights and sounds of Disney Paris? I could funnel that into a dream for my own family one day.

One day, I'd have kids of my own and we'd travel to Disney World, a straight shot from Virginia to Florida, really, and I'd get to have it for myself.

CHAPTER TWENTY-EIGHT

Eric

We snuck one last goodbye kiss on the street, and then she was gone, backpack with her clothes and two canvas bags full of French breads and cheese over one shoulder.

She left the same time we did when we checked out of the apartment this morning. She hopped onto the metro in one direction to the train station where she'd catch her train and we went the other way, toward Disney and the madness therein. The air pressure pushed out of the underground, making her hair swirl around her when she waved before slipping down the stairs and disappearing, and a pit opened up in my chest.

Truly, I had to clench my teeth to keep from calling out to her, running after her, begging her to stay. It was ludicrous—made no sense. I'd see her in a few days, and we'd text and maybe even call each other in the evenings. I had no reason to feel the sense of loss I did when she left.

And yet, each day we spent apart, the more I felt the inevitability of our end. Each ride we rode or magical parade we watched or pair of ears the kids donned, I missed her.

I felt the hole in me widen another inch at the thought that kept invading. At some point in the not too distant future, she would leave, and she wouldn't be back. She'd move on with her life, and I'd be left here, scrambling to cobble together a life for myself and my kids, to somehow help my sister climb out of her own damned crater, and I would be hollowed out because Livie would have taken my guts with her when she left.

After two full days at Disney Paris, we surrendered to exhaustion and decided to make the trip back in one go instead of dividing it with a stop-over at Ramstein Air Base where we could get cheap military lodging and an easy fill-up at the gas station using our rations like we had on the way there.

Robby fell apart about six hours in. I regretted the long drive, but it'd give us an extra day to recover before we returned to work and school Monday. This was pushing it for one day of travel, especially for the youngest in our pack.

"I know, bud. We're on the last leg. Why don't you watch a show?" Ariel did her best to console him where she sat, twisted in the front seat and reaching back behind her to pat his leg, I guessed, though I couldn't see and drive safely.

"I don't want to go home. I just want to *be* home."

His tearful voice pulled at a primal part of me that demanded I stop the car and right whatever wrong existed in his little world, and yet stopping would do nothing.

"Only about another hour, Robby. You're doing great." Ariel gave me a helpless frown as she said it.

"Give him a minute. He'll get on top of it."

He'd done a great job, but with super long days and then being crammed in the car, it was bound to happen at some point. Delia would likely cry quietly too. She struggled with the anticlimax of things, or the knowledge that a wonderful experience could never be replicated. A more complex feeling, and one she had to confront each time we went somewhere special and memorable. We'd been working on the flipside—when we feel sad something is over, we can then remember we're only sad because it was so great. Then we can think of that great experience and be happy and thankful we got to have it.

It was still a work in progress for them. Frankly, for me too.

I hadn't stopped thinking about Livie, and sharing a perfect Parisian day, then date, then night together. Well, not exactly *perfect*, but as perfect as we could get without causing irreparable harm.

Had I regretted not diving in and enjoying her more completely that night? Why, yes. Yes, I had. Because I was a human man and hadn't been close to a woman, much less one so purely lovely as Livie, in years. But I also knew myself. I'd been teetering on the edge of falling for her before Paris, even with the shaky ground we'd tread on. The days in the city had made the risk of falling even greater, and our evening spent eating and laughing and talking had pushed me over.

Taking that final step with her would've made it irrevocable. She would've stolen my heart and taken it with her, wherever she'd go. So I'd protected myself. And her, maybe.

Yet the problem hadn't, in fact, been evaded.

"It's crazy they have you guys starting another rotation this week."

Ariel's voice shook me from my morose musings.

"Such is life here. The only way we get these longer breaks is because every other time we're not gone, we're working."

We sat quietly for a few minutes. Robby and Delia had started a movie and had headphones on, so only the sounds of the car filled the space. The autobahn was blessedly well-kempt and we'd avoided any *staus*—traffic jams. We'd made good time.

"You know I love you, but you're wrong."

This, apropos of nothing. "Am I? What about?"

"Your life."

If I didn't love her so much, and know she wasn't trying to be a know-it-all, I would've snapped at her. The drive had worn me down too. "Well, you better tell me about that then."

"You think you can't have a relationship and be in the Army."

I gripped the steering wheel tighter. "I know I can't—at least not long-term."

"And I'm saying you're wrong about that. I know enough to know that it wasn't just *you* who ruined everything between you and Renee, and certainly not you who ruined her life. I know she has you convinced that any marriage where one person is in the military requires too much sacrifice for the other person. But I call BS on that. You should too. Just look at the couples you're friends with. Are all their wives miserable?"

I loosed a dramatic sigh. "No. Of course not. I've seen plenty of happy military marriages. But I know myself. *I* can't be relied upon to place a spouse first, before my career. I proved that with Renee, and I don't want to hurt anyone else."

"Are we going to pretend we're talking about *anyone* or should we be real and say *Livie*?"

My pulse surged at her name, and I gripped the wheel tighter. "We can be real."

"She's a strong woman. About as opposite from Renee as you could get, in fact."

Ariel's voice was gentle and kind in that way she had. She could say things to me my mother certainly couldn't. She'd always been able to, and especially in the last few years as I'd realized how oblivious I'd been to what was really going on with her. But right now, I didn't want to hear her. The heights of our time in Paris were too near— thinking about all the ways we couldn't move forward felt like quick, relentless jabs to the gut.

"I hear you. It's not just me though."

"Fair enough. Just don't give up on yourself."

Ariel's words swirled in my head the rest of the drive, through unpacking and pouring the kids into bed and a restless sleep that night. They invaded the long, slow jog I took Sunday morning, and I had to push away the gloom that threatened to overtake me. I'd talk with Livie later today, and I both longed for and dreaded it. I wanted to hear her voice—needed to at this point. We'd only texted since our farewell in Paris and I missed her.

But I dreaded it because what was left? Where could we go now if we didn't plan to stay together? And how long could I torture myself with being near her and knowing goodbye was looming?

Just don't give up on yourself.

I ground my teeth together and pulled wet clothes from

the washer, then tossed them into the dryer. Ariel meant well. I knew she did. And I could understand her perspective. But she didn't understand that it wasn't just me who'd said we couldn't go anywhere. It was me, my past, my circumstances, *and* Livie's reasons.

But maybe we needed to revisit the discussion. Maybe...

Hope bloomed in my chest at the thought that maybe, somehow, we could figure it out. We could find a way forward...

I didn't know how it'd work, but I didn't want to be someone who refused to try. I'd played that role with Renee in the end, though it wasn't that simple. I didn't want to look this beautiful person in the face and say *I'm sorry, it's just too hard.* What kind of idiot did that make me?

So I'd talk with her tonight, and we'd figure out the next time we could get together. I'd bring it up. Maybe she'd been having the same thoughts. Maybe we were already on the same page.

CHAPTER TWENTY-NINE

Livie

Before I left France, I'd loaded up on enough bread, cheese, pastries, macarons, and wine to last me through the rest of my spring break.

By Sunday night, I'd polished off all the baguettes, croissants, a small round of camembert, two fruit tarts, and two bottles of wine, though to be fair, that'd been spread over four days and maybe it was a bit much but I couldn't deny drowning my sorrows.

And sorrows they were. Ultimately, leaving Eric and the kids had felt like a punishment, not a choice that left them with special family time. But that was the reason, and before the break, it'd seemed like the right choice. For them, and me.

I shut my eyes against the ache in my chest. It hadn't quit since I'd left him, and we'd planned a phone date tonight that was unlikely to relieve it. I wanted to see him but worried what would happen if I did. Maybe he'd felt the same because neither of us suggested seeing each other in person.

When the phone rang, I curled into a ball under my softest blanket and answered, heart fluttering.

"How was the rest of your trip?" Best to talk about specific things and not all this murky mess of feelings floating around.

"Good. Exhausting, but good. Disney Paris is only two parks, which makes me think I wouldn't survive a trip to Disney World."

I'd pictured them all wandering around the parks, though I'd never been. But since I hadn't, I'd looked on the website so I could envision them more effectively, which made me a hopeless nerd and provided even more evidence that my feelings for Eric went way beyond casual. But I didn't regret the half hour I'd spent clicking through images of the place.

"You made their little dreams come true though. You're a very good dad, Eric."

"Thanks. How was your weekend?"

I smile-frowned, glad he couldn't see me.

"It was good. Very low-key. Very chill." Very boring and lonely and pretty sad, frankly, but I didn't want to explore those thoughts with anyone, not even myself at this point. I'd called my mom and dad and basically snapped at them when they'd tried to ask anything about me and Eric.

"Good. Hopefully, you feel rested up to power through to the end of the year."

My head dropped back to the couch cushion, and I shut my eyes. I didn't want to think about the end of the year. "Yeah. Should be great."

We were both quiet on the line until he spoke again.

"Listen, I think we should get together as soon as we can. I know your week is going to be crazy, and mine is too, but I don't want to wait until the rotation's over. Could I see you tomorrow or Tuesday after work?"

"Yes, of course. You choose—either day is fine with me."

He chose tomorrow, which made me bubble over with glee even while my doubts pulled at me.

"I don't want to wait any longer than I have to. I should've come over tonight just to say hey, but I'll look forward to tomorrow."

"Me too."

"Okay then. Tomorrow. I'll swing by after I get home—probably around seven."

"Great."

He hesitated, just a few seconds, then, "And... I just want to say, I really missed you."

"I missed you, too."

I bit my lip to keep from saying any more—something dreadful and too much like *I love you* or *I don't ever want us to be apart.*

Corralling five- and six-year-olds just returned from spring break travel was always a bit like herding kittens. Less so than the beginning of the year, but their attention spans weren't quite up to full operation the first few days.

This meant the day moved slowly. Lots of "one two three, eyes on me!" exercises. And then Principal Crenshaw, caught up with me in the hallway as we walked the students from music back to the classroom.

"Livie, do you have a minute?"

I pressed my lips into a smile. "Of course."

My assistant teacher nodded, acknowledging she'd heard and would deal with the kids solo for a few minutes, bless her. I followed Principal Crenshaw into her office and took a seat when she gestured to the one in front of her desk.

"So."

I had to smile. She never beat around the bush, that was for sure. "So."

"When can I expect your signed contract?"

I swallowed, my dry throat refusing to relax. "I'm... well, you know that I'm—"

I stopped, unable to bring myself to say that I was moving this summer. Despite the promises I'd made to myself about returning to the US this year. Despite my plan for *family phase* to begin soon. In months, not years. I had no good explanation for it other than that I knew how rare the contracts were here, and I didn't want to give it up until I had things settled where I was heading next.

"I know you've been considering a move back stateside. Have you decided what you're going to do yet?" She smiled and her voice held that calm, reassuring tone she used so effectively with hysterical kids, parents, and teachers alike.

I heaved a sigh. "I've got a few things to settle before I can make the call. Can you give me another month or so?"

A regretful frown pulled at her mouth. "I'm sorry you're having trouble figuring out what's best. I can give you until the end of the month, but no longer. I won't have time to hire and contract someone new otherwise."

I nodded once, my stomach filled with lead. That gave me about two and a half weeks. "I understand."

∾

Hours later, I sat at my dinner table, the leave form filled out, my doubts hammering inside my head so loudly, I thought my brain might crack. Or maybe that was the headache that had settled at the base of my skull when I'd walked out of Principal Crenshaw's office earlier this afternoon.

She was a great principal. It was one more factor to consider in deciding to leave. My happiest years of teaching had been at Kugelfels Elementary. Plus the location, the travel, my friendships with Jen, Nina, and so many other great teachers...

A knock sounded at my door, and I glanced at my watch. Seven p.m. on the dot, and there was another reason for my waffling about the move in the flesh.

I opened the door to a stunning man, his dark features serious. Without speaking, he stepped through the door, took me in his arms, and buried his face in my neck. We both exhaled, our bodies relaxing together and closer into the hug.

"I missed you—"

"I missed you so much."

We pulled back, both smiling now at the shared sentiment.

"Thanks for coming over. I wouldn't have made it through this rotation."

The truth of those words resounded through me. I would've had to track him down. I would've had to find him and hold him.

"I couldn't have stayed away any longer. I should've come yesterday."

His blue eyes surveyed my face, a look so soft and warm there, my heart thudded and glowed at the sight of it.

The words were right there, hovering under my skin,

just waiting, but I could feel they wouldn't wait much longer. Not if he kept those blue eyes on mine and his warm hands smoothing over my back.

He saved me from myself, dipping his head to press his lips to mine as he pulled me against him again, the contact pushing heat into my blood. I clutched his shirt, keeping him close, until I felt so much love and joy and sadness building in me, I had to release him.

I broke away from his embrace. "Come in. Sit. Can I get you a drink?"

"No, thank you. Come sit with me."

I'd wanted to see him all day. I'd been counting the hours while I coaxed kids into listening and monitored recess and tried to find clarity about my plans. I'd come to a tentative and terrible conclusion and I had a plan, but I didn't know how I'd go through with it when he looked at me like that.

He took a seat and exhaled roughly. "Listen, I wanted to see you, but I need to talk with you."

That heart pumping in my chest kicked into overtime, the thumping coming loud in my ears and heavy inside my ribcage. I sat by him, and he immediately took my hand.

"I never expected you."

I huffed out a breath, pleasure at his words but a bit of confusion at his tone chasing each other. "Why, thank you."

He smiled and shook his head. "You know what I mean. I wasn't looking for anyone. I certainly wasn't expecting to find someone in Robby's kindergarten teacher."

"Well, I certainly wasn't on the prowl for a hot single dad."

His smile grew. "But we found each other."

I nodded.

He squeezed my hand where he held it. "And we've

always planned on this... running its course. Being great, but being temporary, knowing how our lives couldn't really line up."

A sick, shaky feeling wormed its way into my belly, and I pulled my hand away from his to clasp it with the other and tucked them between my knees to keep them steady. "Yeah."

He eyed where I'd stuffed my hands, then returned his serious gaze to my face. "I've been going around and around about this, and I just have to tell you what I think, and then you can tell me to go take a flying leap, or whatever you need to, okay?"

"Okay."

He paused, seeming to gather himself. Then he took my hands in his again and hit me with those eyes. "I love you, Livie. I'm in love with you."

CHAPTER THIRTY

Eric

Tears sprang to her lovely brown eyes, and my heart clenched.

"No, no don't cry. I didn't mean to make you cry." I pulled her close and kissed her forehead, mind frantic for a way to make this better, to put the words back in my mouth.

"It's a good thing, Eric. It's the best. And honestly... I love you too."

She spoke into my chest, the sound a little muffled.

The last words had come out on a sob, both injecting me with adrenaline and skewering my already weary heart.

I brought my hands to either side of her face and pulled her in for a kiss once, twice, but her tears turned heavy and she dropped her head low so I couldn't see her face.

"Don't—ah, hell, Livie. Why are you crying like this is terrible? Is it really?"

I could hear the mild panic in my words and could

freely admit I wasn't handling this very well at all, but I'd never seen her cry. It hadn't occurred to me until now, but I hadn't. I'd only seen her tear up a time or two, but not really cry, and she was going for it. Full bore. She'd need tissues and a cool washcloth for her face. She'd need recovery time after a cry like this.

She came up for air and wiped her face on the shirt she wore. Even that action made a burst of love spread through me. She had no pretenses and was so comfortable being *her*.

"I didn't expect to cry like that, sorry." She sniffled and wiped under her eyes.

"Let's talk about it. Help me understand."

For some reason, that made her eyes leak again, and she cleared her throat and scrubbed at her face. "I love you, Eric, but I don't think that changes things."

I swallowed what felt like rocks and summoned a response. "What do you mean by that?"

"I mean all the same things that kept us from thinking long-term before are still an issue. You're not any more available long-term than you were before, and I'm not—" Her shaky voice halted, and she pressed a hand over her mouth.

"You're not...?"

"I'm not going to be here."

Hope drained from my mind. Because I'd started to believe maybe I was available. I could be. For her. If she wanted me to be. If it wasn't me putting it on her—the pressure of the military life and all that it entailed. If she chose it, eyes open, then I could live with the ups and downs knowing I hadn't forced it on her. And I had the history and enough experience with the life to tell her honestly about how the pressures would be.

And I thought maybe I'd learned enough about how *not* to do things... I hadn't come out of a nearly fifteen-year marriage without learning some things I'd done wrong. I'd learned how to prioritize my kids and make time for them even when I was stressed out of my mind. I messed that up constantly, but I was trying. It was miles ahead of what I used to do, and whether it was Ariel's insistence or my own mind convincing me, I believed I could include Livie in that. I'd done so already while we were only dating.

But if she wasn't going to be here... wasn't considering staying... I certainly wouldn't ask that of her, if it hadn't occurred to her already.

"So you're moving back home?"

Why did calling it *home* feel so patently wrong?

"I'm not sure. Honestly, I don't know what I'm doing, but Principal Crenshaw needs an answer so they have time to fill the job if I leave. I'm actually going to make a quick trip back home and see if it... clarifies things for me."

She avoided my gaze, her eyes downcast on her hands in her lap.

"That sounds like a good idea." I forced out the thought despite the collapsing in my mind, like every door I'd shouldered open slammed shut with the news.

She nodded but said nothing for a moment. I felt the walls coming up, rising on the sides of my metaphorical heart, ready to lock down the feelings and move forward, to get out of this scenario which felt like an ambush even though I knew it wasn't.

"I'm sorry. I feel like we've been avoiding talking about this, and since I haven't known what I was going to do, I haven't said much about it. It's not because I don't care about you, or even that I don't want your opinion. I do. You can tell me what you think. I want to know." A hand on my knee squeezed. "Please tell me what you think I should do."

Oh, no no no. "I'm sorry, but I can't tell you that. You've had these plans for a long time—you told me months ago you were moving this summer. If something has changed for you, then you should explore that. But I can't be the one to tell you to stay."

Her throat worked, and her chest seemed to rise and fall more dramatically. She pressed her lips together and nodded. "Okay. Yeah. I know."

We sat quietly next to each other, legs pressed together but nothing else. Any illusions I'd had on the way here had crumbled to dust in the last few minutes, and I wanted to both crush her to me for fear this was truly it for us, and run away because I hated to feel this hollow, crashing feeling sitting here next to her.

"Will you... let me know how your trip goes, at least?" I stood, suddenly unable to tolerate her nearness.

"*At least*? What does that mean?"

"I'm not sure what to do here, Livie. We've taken a huge step forward here, and about twenty steps back." My arms hung pointlessly at my sides since I didn't want to cross them and seem angry or prop them on my hips to seem impatient.

"I don't either." Her gaze tracked around the room and returned to me. "I don't know what to say."

I took her hand in mine and kissed it, that caving-in sensation filling my mind, my heart. "Let me know how the trip goes. Let me know what you decide."

She nodded, her lips pressed together, but I could see them trembling. She moved toward the door so I dropped her hand, taking the cue.

"I'll... talk to you soon."

And with that, I left, disappointment and sadness—grief, really—filling me to the brim. Her door shut behind me, and I pulled in deep breaths of the cool spring evening air, wishing that had gone another way. Any other way.

~

The rotation had been brutal. Spring rains meant the box was a muddy mess. Soldiers spent days on end wet and cold, and more than one truck got stuck. Even a tank nearly crushed a vehicle when a mudbank slid out... just cluster after cluster. It felt as though everything that could go wrong had gone wrong, and no one was happy. The NATO forces who'd come for the rotation were unhappy, as was the commander—my boss.

All in all, the rotation perfectly mirrored my real life. I'd stumbled home on Monday night, feeling utterly heartbroken —maybe more than I had with the divorce, except for when I'd thought of my kids at that time. But my feelings for Renee had never been love. In the beginning, it'd been infatuation, maybe lust, and then a kind of companionable co-existence. I'd loved her for giving me children, but I'd never been *in love* with her—I knew that with even more clarity now.

This was a reality I'd only come to grips with as the bright glow of feeling for Livie threw into shadow every other version of love I'd felt for a woman. But Monday's conversation had left us... where?

Apart. We hadn't exactly said we were breaking up, but that's what it was. We'd confessed our love, and then she'd said it didn't change anything about what we'd always planned to do. But it did. Because continuing to be together for the next few months would be a torture I couldn't endure if I knew any moment it would be stripped away.

Plus there was already distance between us. And maybe

her tears had shown me that she really didn't feel good about the situation, but I'd given her ample opportunity to say she wanted to stay. When she'd asked me to tell her what to do... what had she expected? I couldn't be the one to make her stay. I couldn't and so I hadn't.

I sat sipping a beer on the couch, only a single lamp on. The rotation had officially ended, eleven days after my talk with Livie, and though I had to work tomorrow, I needed a minute. Just a minute to unwind before I'd shower and sleep like the dead and then get up to deal with the aftermath of the disastrous training exercise that had taken over my life—and the entire community's.

"She heads to the US tomorrow."

Ariel's voice floated ahead of her as she walked in from the kitchen. I'd never heard her come downstairs.

"Good for her." It sounded as resentful as it felt to say out loud.

She sat in the corner of the couch and sipped her glass of water, not taking her eyes from me. I didn't look at her, but I could feel her focus, the way she studied me where I sat slumped and irritable and drinking my beer from a bottle like it held answers.

"She hasn't been the same. It's like all her bright, Livie energy is dimmed."

Pain pulsed in my gut. What a terrible thought.

When I didn't say anything, Ariel continued. "She won't talk to me about anything, but I've tried. Nina and Jen said the same. I made her promise to text me and let me know how her travels go."

She didn't need to tell me all this, but I suspected she knew my bad mood, the one that had radiated off me the minute I'd stepped in the door after speaking with Livie eleven days ago, hadn't persisted simply due to the bad rotation.

She stood again, evidently abandoning her efforts. "Obviously, you're not going to talk to me, but I just want you to know I'm here for you. And I'm sorry. And if there's anything *you* can do about this, you should do it."

I didn't respond, didn't even acknowledge her comments. I knew I was being a jerk, but I didn't have it in me to respond. What could I do, if she didn't want me enough to stay?

CHAPTER THIRTY-ONE

Livie

I'd been in Virginia for three days. I'd seen every one of my old friends, though the number these days was small, and I found myself missing Jen and Nina and Ariel and feeling a bit like I had very little in common with the handful of women I'd met with.

I spent lovely time with my parents, enjoyed all my favorite restaurants and reveled in free, endless ice water at each of them. I ate guacamole every day of my visit.

But I missed Germany. I missed my students, though I'd only had to take one day of leave thanks to the long Easter weekend. I missed Eric most of all.

Miss was such a feeble word to describe this aching, empty, crumbling feeling that had slowly built ever since I'd left Paris without him. Of course I'd maintained some sense of hope until the night he came over—two weeks ago tomorrow—and we'd laid everything out.

Our love. The impossibility of moving forward.

Until I'd asked him what he thought, I hadn't dared hope he might... *what?*

I let out a long sigh and tossed my e-reader on the worn couch. I'd been getting up super early and going to bed soon after we ate dinner so I wouldn't be too jet-lagged when I returned. I'd have to dive right into the workweek and be ready to finish out the school year. We'd be out end of May, so not much time left. When I left here, the rest of the year would fly, and I'd be ready to pack up.

Maybe not ready, though. I had a little over twenty-four hours left here, and I felt absolutely no confidence in my choice to move back.

As it always did, my mind circled around to Eric. Honestly, I'd hoped he'd tell me he thought I should stay. I'd hoped he'd try to convince me that Germany and life at Kugelfels and being with him was right. I hadn't expected him to totally step out of the conversation.

Granted, staying there didn't mean staying with him indefinitely. He would leave at some point, and that would be in less than two years, if I remembered his timeline right. But we couldn't move forward if I didn't stay, so what did it mean that he wouldn't say he wanted me to?

I'd turned it over in my mind, wondering if it meant he was done with me. That didn't sit right and certainly didn't fit Eric's way of doing things. If he'd tired of me, he wouldn't have told me he loved me. He wouldn't have been so upset, and he wouldn't have started the conversation by hinting that he saw a different way forward for us.

Ultimately, it'd been me who'd shut things down because of the move. I'd made a plan to be back here in Virginia by thirty-five and my time was up. Time to begin *family phase...* right? To honor my parents and show them what they meant to me by living life near them.

But being here had done nothing to cement the decision like I thought it would. If anything, it'd made it all feel so horribly *foreign* and I'd been walking around with a little ball of upset knotted in my belly since I'd departed Munich airport.

No, since two weeks ago.

"What's with the sighs, sweetie?"

My mom came and snuggled herself onto the couch next to me, then handed me a mug of steaming coffee. She held her own to her chest like she'd done all my life—she made it look so cozy and wonderful to drink coffee. I'd been sorely disappointed by the taste at twelve, particularly since she drank it black.

I held my mug, savoring its warmth before confessing. "I'm feeling... lost."

She tilted her head to the side, and I saw myself in the action. Her short blond hair didn't move much, close-cropped as it was. We did look remarkably alike except where her eyes were green, I'd gotten Dad's brown.

"About the move?"

Just the word sent a fresh spiral of anxiety winding its way through my belly, up my throat, and into my mind. "Yeah."

She didn't respond right away, so I chanced a sip of coffee and relaxed a little when the temperature was just right. I stared into the lightened liquid, warm and familiar, a hum of gratitude pressing back against the anxiety at the feeling of being home. My mom had, as always, remembered I took a little milk in my coffee. When I'd arrived, she'd had all my favorite foods and had already set up a meeting with a realtor to see a few apartments. It should've made me feel welcomed and loved, and it did... but it also made me feel wretched and guilty for not feeling certain about moving back.

She leaned an elbow on the back of the couch between us before speaking. "You know, when you said you were coming to visit and prep for the move home, I couldn't believe it."

My turn for a head tilt. "Really? I've been telling you guys I'd make it back here before thirty-five."

We shared a small smile, hers all kindness and mine a mask for the mess in my chest.

She smiled warmly, offering the motherly reassurance I craved like she had all my life. "I know. And I wouldn't have doubted you. But since you've talked about Eric, I thought..."

The sound of his name in the air, in the house... oh, it felt like a slap. I hadn't said it, and neither had she or my dad. They hadn't asked about him, though they knew pretty much everything—how much I'd liked him and how I'd babysat for him, then dated him, then fallen for him. Maybe I hadn't shared that last part in so many words, but as an only child, I had a close relationship with my parents and didn't keep anything from them.

And they knew me well enough, they hadn't asked. Plus it wouldn't have been hard for them to figure out—I'd never talked about a man like I did Eric. He stood out to them because he stood out to me.

"We have no future. We talked about it... he told me he loves me." My voice faded into a small whisp, the words painful and utterly heartbreaking.

Mom reached out and placed a hand on the cushion between us, which I took and held like a lifeline.

"You know, your father and I love you very much."

I laughed at the out-of-nowhere statement. They'd always been vociferously affectionate. Their love was a major reason I felt bound and determined to make this choice. "Yeah."

"But maybe you should consider not moving home."

My head snapped to her and I studied her face, still gentle and loving, no signs of... anything but that. "Why would you say that?"

She let out a small sigh and squeezed my hand. "You've always planned to come home and live nearby and find your happily ever after here. I've admittedly always loved the idea of that. But these last few years you've been in Europe have been so wonderful for you. You've come alive there, and your reluctance to come home could be a sign that living in a small town with your parents around the corner... well, it might not make sense anymore."

I sat up straighter, ready to fight her the same way I'd been mentally battling myself on the very point she made. "I have to grow up someday. I have to get to a place where I can see a future, and living there just isn't going to make that happen. I've always planned on having my adventures, but making the move to a more family-focused phase in my life. I pushed it back a few years already. If I keep going... I need to bite the bullet and be here, finally."

She nodded once, one small concession to my point, but I knew a counterpoint would follow. "What if it's not the place anymore? What if Eric and you could be together? Would it matter so much that it wasn't here in town?"

Something funny happened in my chest—an odd wobble of my heart, expanding with hope at the thought, and then hiding for fear of it. "You always said how exhausting moving around was. And as a kid, it was super difficult. I never wanted that for my life. I love the stability of this place and I miss you guys. Plus, if I have kids, I want them to know their grandparents. I'm your only child."

She squeezed and released my hand, then cupped her mug close again. "We miss you too, Livie. But I suspect that moving with the military and all that entails is both easier and harder than what we did. I also suspect that you have the temperament for it in a way I didn't. You're adventure-some and love a new challenge. I'm a homebody introvert who deeply dislikes meeting new people. You're all your dad when it comes to that, and I think you'll find though the work was difficult, he didn't mind the changes so much."

I pulled in a watery breath, and took a drink of my coffee to avoid speaking.

She rubbed my shoulder gently until I looked at her, then continued. "You've been gone for more than a decade now—not so far away as Europe the whole time, but you haven't been home, not really, since before college. You ran out of here like a shot after Aaron proposed. I know you've always said it was because you weren't ready for the family part, and I'm sure that's a bit of it. But think about whether, just maybe, it might be because settling down here for good isn't actually what you want."

I studied my coffee like it could make sense of this mess, took a sip, set it down. My mind had scattered like a handful of marbles dropped on the hardwood floor. I thought it might shatter with the *crack* that sounded when her words landed, but instead, every thread of coherency shot to a different corner of my thoughts.

"We would love to have you here. You'd be an asset to this place, and I believe you could build a life here and find a way to be happy. We would absolutely love to live near you and whatever future grandchildren might come about. But it's possible that your time abroad has taught you new possibilities, and that with the right person, you could have a wonderful life with adventure and experiences and fulfillment, and still come visit me and your dad."

She brushed the hair out of my face and kissed my forehead, bringing me comfort as I attempted to process her words.

"I hope whatever you decide, you'll know you owe us nothing but your continued love and communication. We expect nothing of you except that you go live a wonderful life and occasionally let us enjoy it with you."

Determination hit halfway across the Atlantic.

I'd mulled over my mom's words the rest of the day, nearly missing the opportunity to take a walk with her and my dad in the afternoon, but fortunately, I'd snapped out of the haze of emotion and self-focus for a while. She must've told my dad about my breakdown because he mentioned more than once how they'd come visit me, wherever I lived, and would be proud of me no matter what.

You'd think that by my mid-thirties, I'd be secure enough not to need that, but it helped. So much. In a way I hadn't ever realized I needed, they'd set me free. The first half of the flight and many hours before that, I'd battled a familiar guilt that had plagued me on and off for a few years and had grown increasingly sharp and loud the last few months. I'd felt so darn guilty about not wanting to move back when I knew how much my parents would love it, and had been waiting patiently for it.

I felt foolish for not having talked openly about all of that sooner, but until this crisis point of forcing myself to move home, I didn't ever recognize how deeply the need to avoid disappointing them had taken root. I'd been stubborn and willfully ignorant—refusing to acknowledge the total lack of desire to move back to their town and confusing my loyalty and love for them with a duty to live next door to them.

Their pledge to continue loving and supporting and being proud of me no matter what, and not just as a pat on the head placating gesture but in a genuine and real way? It smoothed salve over the raw places that'd so feared making the choice between upsetting them or upsetting myself.

I had new clarity, and even if Eric's feelings had changed, which I prayed to God they hadn't, I wouldn't move home. I wanted to continue to see what the world had to offer—whether it be in Germany or Georgia or somewhere in between. I didn't want to pack up and quit the adventures... but I was ready for a new version of them.

And when I left my parents, and the place closest to what I'd call my childhood home and hometown despite only spending the last few years of my teens there, I realized the missing I felt for them was vastly different than what I felt when I left Eric—*every* time I left Eric. I didn't want to keep having to leave him. Terrifying though it seemed, I wanted to be with him. I wanted the place I called home to be where he was... wherever that might be. I wanted to begin this next phase of life with him.

Mom had it right—it wasn't the place. It wasn't being in Virginia, which I could begin to admit wasn't what I wanted, especially since I felt only dread at moving back. The next phase, this *family phase* I'd had set on my calendar for so long... it was the person. The people, really.

It should strike me as insane that I felt this strongly for someone after so short a time. But Eric and I had connected so completely right from the beginning—gotten along and enjoyed each other even before I ever tried to express inter-est. Even though the first few days had been awkward, the experience of taking care of Robby and Delia while Ariel was gone had created a kind of intimacy I wouldn't have had for months with someone I was just casually dating. Maybe that was the reason I loved him so soon... or maybe it was just because we fit and we'd found each other.

Delia and Robby. I'd thought it before, but a laugh bubbled out. Was I ready to become a parent? Was I prepared to dive *all* the way in? The resounding *yes!* echoed through me. I had no idea what that would look like, but we'd figure it out. I believed we could.

My knee bounced in the middle seat, and I pressed my elbows into my ribs to remind myself to stay small. I was a fairly petite person, and even then I felt smashed into the passengers to my left and right. But the short notice of my trip meant I got what I could take and couldn't complain, especially since I'd miraculously managed to find tickets that didn't eat up my entire travel fund.

But now, still two hours out from Munich, I felt a rest-lessness that threatened to drive me insane. I wanted to get home, to get to my car and drive back to my little Bavarian town and run to Eric's house and demand he talk with me.

Which wouldn't work, of course. He'd be at work—it was Monday, and though I didn't think it was a rotation, I'd make it back by no later than noon.

So I'd go to him. Because I couldn't live like this anymore. And I hoped—prayed—he'd feel the same.

CHAPTER THIRTY-TWO

Eric

The briefing dragged, and though I didn't have to stay, I chose to. The men leaving for a short advising trip to Afghanistan had to sit through it, so I stayed too. After, we convened in my office to review details and so I could thank them. As they'd offered to do, they were saving several men who'd been on constant rotation and TDY scheduling for months from being gone yet again. So had these guys, but they seemed not to mind—they'd take two trips two weeks apart, which no one wanted except, apparently, them.

I could see how being here without family of any kind would make it tough—unless you had a good friend or were dating someone, you'd be traveling solo or not traveling at all. That was the *OCONUS Bonus*—living in Europe and traveling, seeing this part of the world on four-days instead of the more seemingly mundane long weekend plans we made while living in the US. But doing it alone?

"Gentlemen, have a seat." I gestured to the chairs across from me, and Sergeant Miller and Captain Waverly sat.

"You'll be gone for sixteen days round trip both this time and next. You've got a thin platoon with you for training and a few tactical exercises toward the end of your time—your leaders are you two, Lieutenant Jacobs, and Sergeant Cross. As you know, Sergeant Masters was injured in the last rotation so he won't be joining you—it's a loss, but I believe you can handle it. You'll be in Kandahar for the majority of the time, maybe a trip off once or twice for training each go-round. Any concerns or questions?"

"No, sir," they both confirmed.

"Good. Then go ahead and get your gear organized and all that. See if you can finish up your work before Thursday and take a long weekend pass before you head out. See you on the other side."

The men bid me farewell, then shuffled out of the office and I sat back and rubbed my tired eyes. How could I be this tired at one in the afternoon?

Nate poked his head in, and I waved him in.

"You look rough."

I glared back at him.

"Seriously. What's going on with you?" He folded himself into a chair and crossed his arms like he had a right to the information.

"How was Thailand? We haven't really talked." I'd kept myself working as much as possible, and beyond that, immersed in the kids, so I wouldn't drown in thoughts of Livie.

"Nope. Not my turn. It's *your* turn. Ariel told me you

haven't been sleeping and you're a moody butthead, I think were her words."

I chuckled. "First, why are you trying to get dirt on me from my little sister? And second, did she actually say the word *butthead* as a woman in her thirties?"

"First, don't worry about it and second, yes, I believe she did." His glaring smile spoke to his delight. He had a knack for finding things hilarious or amusing when I found them annoying or inconvenient.

"Fine. I'm sad, okay? I don't like not being with her." My voice softened. "But I'm trying to figure it out."

"I'm sorry, man. I really am."

"Thanks."

He sat back, slouched in the chair like he owned the place. "I do wonder, though... if she were here, would you want to see her?"

Something in his voice caught my ear. "Why would you ask me that? Of course."

His brows arched high. "Oh! Well, then I guess you *do* want me to send her in?"

I shot to my feet. "Livie's here? Are you kidding me right now?"

He shook his head with a face full of glee that might've made me want to murder him if I didn't feel like fist-pumping and falling to my knees at the same time.

"Get out of here and go get her, you idiot!" I whisper-yelled, because I was a mature adult male who would not actually yell at his best friend.

"I guess I could do that," he said over his shoulder as he wandered out.

I paced the small space behind my desk, thoughts shooting from one possibility to another. Why was she here? When had she come back from the US? Was she here to tell me when she'd move? To officially break up, or...

A lightning strike of hope shot through me head to toe.

Just then, she appeared in the doorway, and my thoughts scattered, my pulse taking off and racing wildly in my veins. She wore jeans and sneakers and a zip-up sweater jacket-type thing, and her hair hung loose to frame her face. *Good grief*, she was lovely.

She held herself close, like she was nervous. "Hey. Do you have a minute?"

I moved toward her. "Always for you. How was your trip?"

I sat on the edge of my desk, wanting to be eye to eye with her. She stood a few feet inside the doorway, and thanks to a fairly small office, that meant we were only a few feet apart.

"It was okay." She frowned, her brow wrinkling with whatever thought occurred. "Actually, it was both terrible and great."

A smile broke through at that. "That sounds... interesting. What made it terrible?"

She huffed a small breath and clasped her hands together. "I realized that moving back this summer isn't what I want."

The words seemed to echo in the small space, which made no sense, but they settled into me layer on layer, like the best news I'd ever heard. Or, like *possibly* the best news I'd ever heard. I stayed glued to the corner of my desk instead of jumping up to swing her around prematurely. That really could mean anything. It could mean she planned to move back tomorrow. It could mean she planned to move to Korea or Hawaii or Alaska or...

"And the great part?"

She straightened her spine and stood tall, her chin raised just a touch so she looked me right in the eye. "I realized that moving back this summer isn't what I want."

Then a smile she tried to tame eventually broke free and shone out from her, bathing me in the beauty that was her joy.

If hope had been a man at the bottom rung of a ladder when she walked in, he now stood at the top, balancing precariously on one foot, touching the moon. I smiled back, unable to resist joining her.

"I'm glad you have some clarity." And so much else. There was so much else to say, but it felt like too much. All she'd said was she didn't want to move back this summer. "So do you know what you *do* want?"

My voice showed the fraying restraint, the tone low and a little rough as I worked to quell the need to crash into her, obliterating the space between us.

She must've sensed that in me, or shared the need, because she stepped between my legs and wrapped her arms around my neck and brought her face inches from mine.

"I do know. I'm hoping there's a way you'll want the same thing I do."

My heart absolutely thundered in my chest. I slid my hands around her waist and then answered, uninterested in any more suspense. "I probably do. But you'll have to tell me, Livie. I can't be the one to force anything on anyone, but if you only tell me what you want, I'll move Heaven and Earth to make it happen if I can."

Her hands tracked up to the sides of my face. "I want to be with you. I don't want to leave. I want to stay here with you."

Our lips touched tenderly once as we both gazed into

each other's eyes, then collided in a tumble of pent-up longing and elation, lips, teeth, tongues, hands, until a sharp knock on the door forced us to disengage.

"As happy as I am for you, *sir*, maybe save the action for after-work hours?"

Nate's snark was softened only by the genuine smile on his face and Livie's laugh, which didn't sound regretful or embarrassed. He disappeared again, and she spoke.

"He's right. I came straight from the airport because I had to see you, but I shouldn't have interrupted your workday—"

I shook my head emphatically. "No, you absolutely should've. You can interrupt my workday any time."

She responded with a pleased grin. "Well. How about I come over when you get home? I can see the kids and Ariel and we can... catch up a bit more."

I tugged at her hand, and she stepped close enough for me to gather her into a hug. "I would love that. Yes. I'll text you when I'm heading home."

CHAPTER THIRTY-THREE

Livie

I couldn't keep the smile from my face or the hope from my heart the rest of the day. I tried to lay down and rest, but that was entirely futile, so instead I unpacked, did laundry, cleaned my apartment, made a trip to the grocery, and sat twiddling my thumbs until Eric called.

Okay, fine, not really. I texted Jen, Nina, and Ariel with an update, which all returned with little explosion emojis and hearts and lots of warm wishes. I reveled in their congratulations, though a sliver of me—okay, a solid little slice—felt it might be a bit too soon.

He'd reacted just like I would've wanted. The whole *I'll move Heaven and Earth* thing? Wow.

But we didn't get to talk about what that really meant, or what we'd do moving forward, or anything.

That kiss though? *Worth it.*

I shut my eyes and fell into the memory of the kiss—the

pure passion and relief that had billowed out around us. The urgency and longing and liquid heat... all standing right there in his office. *Whoops*.

I'd likely face some jokes and ribbing from Nate next time I saw him, but he'd been so happy for us, I didn't need to be too concerned there.

Finally, the message came through—Eric had made it home and asked me if I still wanted to come over. I could understand his question—though we'd planned my visit like it was a sure thing, I'd been all over the place lately. And I couldn't blame him for wondering whether I would really come, or not. Plus we hadn't finished our conversation, and so he didn't know how completely I loved him, nor did I know what he truly felt.

I grabbed my purse and a jacket and burst out the door. The spring night was chilly against my skin as I trotted down the street, not fully jogging, but certainly not patient enough to walk. I'd need the jacket on the way back but for now, I just wanted to get there.

Five minutes later, I knocked on his door. Ariel answered.

"Well hello there, friend." She pulled me inside and into a big hug, which felt like congratulations and celebration and welcome all at once. "So good to see you."

"I saw you last week," I said on a chuckle.

"True. But I have a feeling the version of Livie I've been dealing with for a few weeks before your trip wasn't the same one who I'm seeing now. Am I right?"

She knew she was, and my answering smile confirmed it.

"Livie! Livie! Livieeee!" Robby came at me full tilt, sliding on his socks before he hit me with a full-body hug. "We missed you today but I'm so glad you're back and I think you're going to really like the drawing I started in art but my dad says he needs to talk to you so I have to just say hi and then go get ready for bed so hi."

I burst out laughing, pure joy filling me at his greeting, his breathless explanation and bounding energy, and at the delight he carried with him wherever he went.

"I missed you too. I can't wait to see your picture."

"You're going to love it."

"Okay, bud. Let's get you upstairs." Ariel herded Robby to the stairs and looked back. "He's on his way down—just wanted to change clothes. Delia's actually already asleep or I'm sure she'd be down here to hug you too."

I set my purse and jacket by the door and stayed put. I'd been in the house countless times by now, but somehow, I felt I needed Eric to be the one to tell me to come further in. Like me stepping inside this time meant something more than it ever had, and if he invited me in, it had weight.

That was probably a lot of over-analysis, but I couldn't stop the feeling that I shouldn't just wander in and have a seat at the dinner table, especially now that Robby had scampered back upstairs with Ariel on his heels.

Before my thoughts wound too far out of control, I heard the quick pat-pat of Eric's shoes on the stairs and saw his legs, then body materialize through the space between each stair. My blood thrummed as he approached—he didn't stop walking and didn't speak anything, just took me by the hand and led me up-up-up the stairs to his room.

I swallowed, my throat thick with nerves and my breath short from the quick trip up the three flights of stairs. His room held only a bed with a fluffy dark blue comforter and a dresser. One side of the room's walls sloped sharply over the bed as was custom in a German house like this. It made the room feel intimate and almost small, though there was plenty of space. It felt significant to be here, in this most-private space of his, for this conversation.

"As you know, the walls are thick. I wanted us to have privacy and figured this might be the only way we'd really get it while Robby's up, plus Ariel's got something going in the kitchen so..." He looked around, seeming unsure.

"It's fine. That's a good idea."

"Good. So, uh, I just realized there aren't seats. Do you mind the end of the bed?"

He sat to one side of the middle and I sat next to him, surprised at how nervous and formal he seemed.

"So..." I folded my hands in my lap, nervous energy building little tornadoes in my chest.

"So... I'm glad you're back. And I'm very glad you want to stay."

We shared a smile, but his faded quickly. "I'm... concerned."

Fear zipped up my spine. "About..."

"I won't always be here. And if I'm understanding your meaning from earlier, then you want to be with me... maybe indefinitely." His cheeks colored at that, like saying it was a big leap for him, and somehow embarrassing or risky.

I took his hand and threaded our fingers together. "Yes. I love you. I've never felt this way about anyone, and I've honestly never wanted to change my plans for a man—"

"That's my concern. I have been down this road before. I mean, not this one precisely, but I've been through enough to know that one person giving up their plans for another can be pretty problematic."

His wrinkled brow and the tense energy in his shoulders made me want to shake him, but I knew he came to this with a lot of experience that told him I would eventually resent him and leave him.

I'd been mulling over his past relationship and what I could say to help him understand my thoughts better for days, if not weeks. Of course I hadn't known I'd decide not to move, but I'd been thinking about him, and about how he should try with someone, even though the thought of the *someone* not being me had made me queasy and sad.

"I'm not going to resent you, Eric. If we're talking long-term, and I hope we are, that means marriage. I understand that also means moving, probably several more times, before you retire, and while I don't have any idea what your time-line or career plans are, I'm guessing that's a ways off. The *place* is ultimately immaterial to me. While I visited Virginia, I realized that I missed *you* in a way I couldn't stand. Since I was younger, I had this idea that I'd move back home and live happily ever after, but even in the last few years, I couldn't make myself do it." I waited for questions or thoughts, but none came. *Good.* I had more to say.

"On this trip, I finally figured out I don't want to do that —I don't want to live one place and *settle down there.* I want you. You, and if I'm being really bold, Delia and Robby. You'll be my adventure. The Army life might provide some interesting places down the line, but even if we settle down in one place and stay there forever, I'd still be happy... with you. Because it will be with you."

His intense blue gaze studied my face. "I want to believe you. I really do."

"I'm not trying to make it sound simple, but it is. I know in reality the life you live is *not* easy and the little I've learned about it by working here and interacting with military families is just that—a little. But I also see the way you love your kids, and your sister—even your mother, whom I haven't met yet—and I can imagine that being a part of that family would be worth it."

He exhaled sharply, a gust of air out, and ran a hand over his dark gray and black hair. "Good grief, I love you."

We crashed together, an immediate continuation of the kiss from earlier, though this had less desperation and more relief. Overwhelming gratitude filtered through me as I pulled away to look at his gorgeous face.

"Does that mean we're still dating?"

He laughed, cupped my face, and kissed my forehead, cheek, then lips. "We're definitely still dating. We're never going to stop dating, if I have a say in it."

"Uh..."

He laughed loudly then. "Not like, we're *only* ever going to date. But we'll keep dating long after we're married. And I hope you're willing to marry me because it's not great to just be partnered in the military. They're getting better about it, but I want—"

"I do." I bit my lip, then chuckled. "I do want to marry you. Yes. I mean, I know you're not proposing now, but I do want to be married, and I am pretty sure I know the answer I'd give you if you were to ask me. Whenever such an event should occur."

His smile then was boyish and all charm. "That's good to know."

CHAPTER THIRTY-FOUR

Eric

Livie had left minutes ago, though I wished she could've stayed. She had things to do before she returned to work tomorrow, and I needed to talk with Ariel. I needed someone outside of my own mind to tell me I wasn't insane.

I'd just caught my sister up because she'd materialized with an expectant smile the second Livie left. And then I'd dropped the bomb.

"I'm going to propose. Soon."

She stared at me, a serious look on her face. Serious enough my surety faltered and I wondered if I'd made a mistake in thinking about that kind of commitment so soon.

Just when I started to truly doubt, she burst out in a laugh.

"You were totally panicking."

I just looked at her.

Another minute of laughing, because apparently, seeming disapproving of my girlfriend slash hopefully sooner than later future wife was hilarious. But then she stopped and threw her arms around me, and squeezed tight.

"I'm thrilled for you. You couldn't find someone better because Livie is the best. I can't wait for her to be my sister, so yes. Propose tomorrow, marry her Saturday, and I'll watch the kids for the honeymoon."

I shook my head.

"Probably not *that* fast, but sooner than later." I took a deep inhale. "I feel like things have clicked into place. I'm sure I'll still be angry with Renee at times, especially when she bails on the kids or tells me I ruined her life, but I feel grateful at this point. I wouldn't have found Livie otherwise. I know my baggage has slowed me down, but maybe that was good. I think she needed the time to come to her own conclusions."

She hummed in agreement as we walked to the kitchen.

"I think you're right—though I'm not sure we can really say this was *slow*." She grinned at me and patted my shoulder. "But it sounds like you've both come to the same conclusion."

"We have."

She stopped and turned to me, eyes wide. "When are you going to tell the kids?"

I spoke with Delia first, the next morning. I considered waiting until we got engaged, but I didn't want her to feel left out. I wanted her to have time to process things and be a part of it all. So, I told her we were dating, and that we'd probably get engaged soon, and probably get married.

She shrugged. "Makes sense. I figured."

I blinked back at her, startled.

She craned her neck from where she lay on her bed reading. "Did you think we didn't notice?"

"Uh, I don't know. I guess I didn't realize you were paying attention."

"Well, I'm always paying attention, and even if Robby isn't, he's not dumb. He's wanted you to marry Livie since the day he met her, so you're going to make his dreams come true." She rolled her eyes, channeling the preteen she was fast becoming.

I chuckled lightly, relief and hope swelling in me. "Okay. Well... are you okay?"

She sighed, but smiled. "I'm good. I like her, and you seem really happy with her. I don't really know what it's going to be like to have a step-mom, but it sounds like that's not happening tomorrow, so I have time to get used to it."

I patted her leg. "Yes. You do. And she'll be around more often so we'll get to have some fun all together and I think that'll help."

"Sounds good." Then she sat up from where she lay on her bed reading. "Actually, one more thing. Can I be the one to tell Robby?"

I'd planned to do it myself, but she rarely had strong opinions like this. "Sure."

Without another word, she ran into the room. Seconds later, before I'd even made it to Robby's room, I heard, "YEESSSSSSS!!!!"

Delia appeared in the hallway, beaming. "Yeah Dad, we'll be fine."

〜

I paced the office, rehearsing what I'd say. I'd planned to wait a few months, but just four weeks after our conversation, I had a ring and a plan.

I'd propose soon. I didn't want to be apart from her, and I'd spent the last six months getting to know her. We'd talked a lot, had quite a few shared experiences, and I'd gone through what life without her would be like.

I'd hated it, and I wanted to make sure I'd never have to do that again. As a forty-year-old father-of-two divorcé, I knew what I wanted, and Livie was it. Once that lightbulb had flashed in my mind, there was no going back, especially since she wanted me too.

Army life could compress things like this too, sometimes. Truthfully, it'd been part of the pressure that had made me and Renee jump, and so I'd taken the last few weeks to really dig into my motivations. I came out knowing that even if I left Germany tomorrow, I'd want to be with Livie. I came out knowing if I stayed in Germany another five years, not that such a thing was possible, I'd want the same. Being officially together sooner than later would allow us to plan our lives, would give the kids security, and would let us both begin the next chapter together.

And so, I was going to track her down on her lunch break—the school year only had another week or so left and this afternoon, they had a movie scheduled. Ariel had helped me choose a day. The setting wasn't particularly spectacular, but I had a little surprise to make it special.

"I'm taking off. Wish me luck." I breezed past Nate's desk.

"Luck!"

I smiled as I left, looking forward to celebrating with him. The drive to the elementary school was short, but by the time I pulled up to the guest parking spaces, I was a ball of nerves. It wasn't that I didn't think she'd say yes. I was pretty sure she would, even though this was coming sooner than even I had originally planned. It was just... one of those moments. One I'd never do again, if I had any say in the matter, and one I'd always remember. We both would.

We all will.

I trotted up the front steps and saw she already sat on the bench under a flowering tree. My heart sped up, but I slowed my breath as I approached.

"Hey there, soldier." She stood and smiled, then sat back down.

Apparently, someone had told her it's against regulation to kiss and hug in uniform. Technically true but a rule I'd happily break here in a few minutes.

"What's your favorite sandwich?" I asked, like I didn't have another far more important question burning a hole through me. I'd told her I'd bring her lunch—I hadn't. But I needed just a minute here before I could ask.

"California club with bacon and avocado. *Yum.*" She smiled dreamily, then sobered and frowned a bit. "Wait, did you forget to grab lunch?"

I considered waiting another few minutes, but my thundering heart, dry mouth, and the way my stomach felt like it might turn itself inside out told me I wouldn't make it. Fortunately, I saw Ariel waiting inside the classroom with windows facing the front walk where we sat. She gave me a bright smile and thumbs up, and I nodded to her.

I dropped to a knee in front of Livie and took her hand. She looked up with a pleasant smile, then seemed to register I was kneeling and looking at her expectantly.

"Oh, uh..."

"Livie Anderson, you are a blazing star in a dark night. You are full of life and joy and fun, and I love everything about you. I want to be with you every day, every night, for the rest of my life. I want you to help raise my kids and know my family—to be my family. I have a question to ask you."

Her lashes fluttered, and she nodded. "Okay. Ask it."

"Well, I needed a little help."

I turned and looked toward the front of the school where Ariel led Robby, Nina led Delia, and Jen also followed. They held up the signs saying *Will you marry me?*

Livie burst out laughing and hugged me close. "Of course I will. Of course. Yes."

Robby ran to us, joining the hug, then Delia arrived and stood patiently until I looped her in with us, though Robby's firework of energy made it hard to stay close.

Jen, Nina, and Ariel applauded and hooted and hollered from where they stood on the school's steps. We all pulled back, and the flurry of chatter from Robby, and even Delia, filled me with more joy than I could've imagined— and that was saying something considering the over- whelming glee I'd experienced at Livie's *Of course.*

"Alright guys, come on back." Ariel corralled them, and they both waved before disappearing into the school.

"I can't believe this," Livie said, face flushed and smile blazing.

"Really? I told you I wouldn't be able to wait."

She giggled—a pleased, elated sound. "You did. I guess I'm just... I didn't imagine I could be so happy."

I hugged her close and tilted her face to mine. "Me neither."

When we pulled back, she sat down. "Can we still have lunch?"

"Yes, of course. We're also going out Friday for dinner to celebrate... if you're free."

"Of course I'm free."

I nodded in approval, then grabbed her hand and her purse from the bench. "And now, we're heading into town to eat lunch. Ariel helped arrange a sub and she's staying too, so you're covered. I even cleared it with Principal Crenshaw."

Her mouth fell open, and I laughed, so much joy running through me that I had to let it out somehow.

"You're sneaky. This is all very well planned out." She gave me a sly grin like she approved, particularly of how well-planned it was.

"I'm glad you approve."

We dined on crispy duck and pasta Bolognese, fried savory spring rolls with sweet dipping sauce, and jaegerschnitzel. We toasted with champagne, then drank radlers and got tipsy and laughed, and I couldn't believe how good it felt to be in this moment.

My phone, which I'd ignored until the end of the meal as we stepped out of the restaurant into bright spring sun, buzzed again—for the second or third time, I didn't know. Didn't care, really, because nothing anyone had to say at the end of that line could be that important since we weren't in rotation at the moment. But Livie must've felt it.

"Whoever's calling you is pretty persistent. Do you need to take that?"

"Whatever it is, it can wait five more minutes. For now, please kiss me."

Then we sealed the engagement again, the promise, with a kiss so sweet and achingly tender, I felt more breathless than before I'd popped the question.

The phone buzzed again. Just a text this time. "I'm sure it's just Nate. Probably pestering me for details or joking about how you rejected me."

"He couldn't possibly think I'd reject you, could he?" She hadn't stopped smiling since I'd asked her, and neither had I.

"No. But he'll be very happy to pretend he did." I reached for her, settling my hand at her waist.

"I don't know how he could think that after seeing us in your office a few weeks ago." Her cheeks brightened with the memory.

"He'll figure it out. For now, kiss me again, and then tell me how long I have to wait to marry you now that you've said yes."

EPILOGUE

Nate Reynolds

A familiar muted quality had snapped into place when the soldier on the other end of the line had reported the worst news I'd heard in a long time. Ever.

The words replayed in my mind.

"Sergeant Miller and Captain Waverly were taken in an ambush during a routine—"

I shot to my feet. No time to freeze up. Time to act, and feel later.

I dialed Eric's number. I'd seen him just a couple hours ago, wished him luck on his ridiculously cheesy proposal mission. I hoped it was done.

No answer. I could reasonably wait another five minutes before reporting up the chain. Most likely the leadership in Afghanistan had already contacted Colonel Shoales. *Damn*, this was a mess.

We'd need to send out notification parties to the families, but not just yet. I could get that ready though, have it all good to go when Eric landed back here. We'd need to move fast, and we'd likely be in briefings about what we knew, what anyone knew, and who the special operations folks in theater were who could get them back, or if they'd fly someone in.

Hopefully, Miller and Waverly were still alive to get back.

I dropped into the chair at my desk, signed into the system, and sifted through information until I found the designated points of contact. Katharine Miller, spouse of Staff Sergeant Noah Miller, and Janice and James Waverly, parents of Captain Rob Waverly.

I dialed Eric again. And again.

Damn.

Sent a message. *Call me. ASAP.*

No answer. He still hadn't seen.

He was probably in the throes of bliss, celebrating his engagement to Livie. Good for him—for both of them. The best man I knew and a great woman—they'd be happy.

But I needed him to tune in. I'd have to drive over there and track him down.

A low, sick feeling settled in my gut as panic pulled at the edges of my mind. I pushed out of my chair. *No.* No time for that nonsense. What next? Think of a list, a plan, something.

I texted Eric again. Called him.

I stood, exhaling slowly, and prayed. *God, please let us get them back alive.*

Sergeant Major Allen burst in. "How did this happen? How long ago? What's—"

I held up a hand as my phone buzzed. "Eric. Get over here."

"Whoa, calm down, my friend. I just got engaged, for goodness' sake! Let me have a minute to—"

"Eric." I brushed a hand over my head as I paced.

"What's wrong?"

My tone must've clued him in.

"Miller and Waverly were taken. Their patrol was ambushed. Get back here."

The end... for now.

∽

Did you enjoy this book? Would you consider leaving a review wherever you purchased it? Reviews make a huge difference to indie authors! If you can't wait for more, read on for a sneak peek of SGT Miller's book.

ALSO BY CLAIRE CAIN

The OCONUS Bonus Series continues:

Finding Happiness in a Hoax (Book 2) - Feb 2, 2021

Learning to Fight after Flight (Book 3) - May 2021

The Bright Side of Brooding (Book 4) - Fall 2021

The Rambler Battalion Series

Sweet Military Romance

Where You Go: The Rambler Battalion, Book 1

As You Are: The Rambler Battalion, Book 2

Don't Stop Now: The Rambler Battalion, Book 3

Home With You: The Rambler Battalion, Book 4

All of You: The Rambler Battalion, Book 5

The Silver Ridge Resort Series

Sweet Small Town Romance

Unexpected Love at Silver Ridge, Book 1

Second Chance at Silver Ridge, Book 2

Patrolling for Love at Silver Ridge, Book 3

Fire and Ice at Silver Ridge, Books 4

ACKNOWLEDGMENTS

I'm so excited to begin this new series! Thanks to so many of you for supporting this fun new adventure.

Thank you to my beta readers Emma, Caroline, Ashley, and Daphne. Your feedback and thoughtful comments helped shape and refine this book, and I'm so thankful for it!

Thank you, Jamie, for phone calls and commiseration and swapping and listening to me whine. You are the actual best.

Thanks to Zee Monodee, my fabulous editor, for not shying away from insisting I do better. I am thankful for your hard work and support!

Thank you to Rainbeau Decker for doing a truly astounding job finding the models and taking the cover photo! You've brought Livie and Eric to life! Thank you for your commitment to excellence and your friendship.

Thank you to Emma, because I'm not sure how I function without you. Like, for serious. Thank you for your design, for your insights, for beta reading, for supporting, for talking webtoons and being a nerd with me. I am so thankful for you and your willingness to share your gifts with me and my readers!

Thank you Julie, for being my nightly chat and letting me verbally process both my plans and accomplishments—you've given my little "3" heart a place to breathe in this odd few months. I love you.

Thank you, finally, to A, W, and M, the best kids on the planet, for being so astoundingly awesome. Thank you, Matthew, for doing what you do so faithfully and well, even when it isn't easy or pretty or fun. I admire and love you so.

Thanks to Claire's Sweet Readers, my facebook group, for helping name the places and characters in this book, and for sharing my excitement for the series! This group is one of my favorite places online—thank you for sharing the journey with me!

And to all the readers, thank you for giving this new series a try! I hope you'll let me know what you thought, and consider leaving a review on Amazon. Now back to writing I go!

ABOUT THE AUTHOR

Claire Cain lives to eat and drink her way around the globe with her traveling soldier and three kids, but is perhaps even happier hunkered down at home in a pair of sweatpants and slippers using any free moment she has to read and cook. Or talk—she really likes to talk. She has become an expert at packing too many dishes in too few cabinets and making houses into homes from Utah to Germany and many places in between. She's a proud Army wife and is frankly just really happy to be here.

You can also join Claire's facebook reader group for exclusive content and fun: https://www.facebook.com/groups/clairecain/

Website: http://www.clairecainwriter.com

E-mail: Claire@ClaireCainWriter.com

Newsletter sign-up for new releases, exclusives, and freebies: http://eepurl.com/dGuIBv

SNEAK PEEK - FINDING HAPPINESS IN A HOAX

Katie

The flight attendant dimmed the lights and I shut my eyes, knowing I needed sleep. I had no idea what would happen upon my arrival in Germany, or what any of this meant.

The moment everything changed came tunneling back in my memory.

"Ma'am, your husband has been extracted. We're flying you to Germany to meet him at the hospital."

They'd knocked on my door eight days ago with the news that Noah had been abducted during what they believed to be a planned attack against American soldiers in a southern province of Afghanistan. The Taliban took the two men—one of them Noah— after separating them from the larger group. As of about twelve hours ago, Noah's boss, the man I spoke to most often, notified me a team had successfully rescued him.

After waking hours before to the news I'd been praying for, I could hardly remember the rest of the day. Now, I sat crunched between passengers on a flight halfway across the

Atlantic, en route to see my husband after not having seen the man in almost two years.

I didn't know how to act or even what to *think*. They wouldn't tell me specifics about injuries or any details, only that they'd speak to me when I got there, and that I could see him when I landed at Ramstein Air Base in Germany.

My mind wandered right to Noah while my heart ached. It might've been all in my head, or it might have really been hurting, but I missed him. It was stupid, of course, but I'd missed him. And now, knowing he'd been in peril for more than a week—whether he was alive or dead, uncertain—I missed him in the bone-deep way I rarely let myself feel.

I never let myself experience the love and admiration I would so easily fall into if I didn't watch it. What a stupid thing that would be, right? Loving my husband.

Except the one thing no one knew—no one but Noah's mom, me, and Noah himself—was an undeniable truth. And that truth held the reason it made no sense for me to love him, to want him, to miss him, or to wish to be with him. It had motivated me to banish all those feelings five years ago—and whenever they popped up along the way—and do whatever I could to keep them gone.

Noah had married me to save me from harm. He'd married me because he was too kind and good, and when his mother had given him the idea, he'd done it without a second thought. And now, almost five years in, we still didn't know each other—not really. We'd spent a handful of days together, max. Mostly, we'd lived our lives separately, which had always been the plan.

And yet, I'd been listed as his primary contact on his military documents, not his mother. I'd asked if they'd contacted his mom, and his commander, Lieutenant

Colonel Wolfe, had said he'd authorized it only because of the unique nature of the situation, but that the Army would only fly me to be with him.

I swallowed down the rising panic and exhaled, willing the pressure in my chest to ease. But it kept coming back, right along with the inability to breathe normally or think straight anytime I thought of how terrified he must have been or wondered what it was like. Had they beaten him? Starved him? Shot him?

Please, God, no.

And then the other thoughts came. Would he recognize me when I showed up? We hadn't seen each other in a long time, only e-mailed or texted. It wasn't like we traded photos or stalked each other online.

The last time we'd met in person had only been for a few hours, just to go to the legal department to sign updated wills and get me a powers of attorney before he deployed again. I didn't need many since his assets would go to his mother, but I had to have access to our shared accounts and a few other things that got tricky if I needed something while he was gone.

He'd gotten home from that same deployment while final exams monopolized my brain and time, so I hadn't seen him. I'd felt guilty about that. I'd wanted to see him, but he'd refused to push in on my study schedule. He'd promised me it was no big deal so not to worry, to study hard, and to ace my tests. Then he'd assured me he couldn't wait to get to Germany, his next duty station.

The last time he'd seen me, I'd been twenty-one. It'd been two years since, and I didn't keep a social media presence like he did—nothing my family could use to find me, even still. They would be looking for Katie Simonsen, not Katie Miller, but I didn't need to make it easier for them either. Also, now my hair was shorter and darker. I'd looked almost fully blond the last time he'd seen me. I'd lost weight in places and gained it in others. Would he like that?

Doesn't matter, stupid.

The jerk in my head had been spewing hateful things ever since I'd been notified days ago. I'd worked hard over the years to get past the drowning sensation that came whenever anything went wrong.

I'd talked to my therapist, Maria, once a day since they'd called, bless her. And still, here it was, rearing its head.

I knew, logically, I bore no blame for Noah's capture. Nothing I did—no amount of worrying or crying or begging God—could change that it'd happened. I believed prayer might help him be recovered, but those other things? No. They wouldn't. The voice berating me, telling me it was all my doing and that if I'd just been a better wife none of this would have happened? Nonsense.

I knew it, and yet, I couldn't block it out.

It's all your fault. It's all your fault. It's all your fault.

Sometimes, it sounded like my stepfather's voice. Other times, my stepbrother's. And the worst was when it was my own voice, which proved to be the hardest to ignore. I tried to think about what my therapist had reminded me earlier today. I breathed it in while blocking out the person next to me shifting in his seat and jostling the whole row while children and babies cried from different corners of the packed *Stars and Stripes Express* flight for military personnel and their families.

Maria had asked, "Would you talk to a friend this way?"

"Of course not!"

She only had to give me that look of hers that told me I should draw my own conclusion, and I knew. I wouldn't speak to a friend this way. I wouldn't tell a friend that the

Taliban had captured her husband—something I didn't even know happened anymore—because of her. Never.

So why are you talking to yourself this way?

I exhaled again, letting my lungs empty completely, and then pulled in a breath slowly and steadily until air—not stress or fear—filled my chest.

The real Mrs. Miller, Noah's mom, had called me twice. I'd been too much of a basket case to answer the first time and at work with my phone tucked away the second. I'd texted her back, sharing her hope that we'd hear good news soon. It struck me that I hadn't told her about the flight plans, or anything about my trip here—it'd all been so whirlwind. I'd had hours to prepare. I'd messaged her to say they'd rescued him, but after that...

I'd always assumed he'd list his mom as his primary contact, not me. In fact, I was pretty sure during that first deployment or so, he'd listed his mom as such. It didn't make sense for it to be me—I had nothing to offer him and owed him everything.

I forced away those thoughts, the fear and genuine worry that I had no idea how to act in this situation, and started the count. From one thousand back to one, and I'd repeat it if I had to until I got some sleep. I wouldn't think about him not recognizing me, or how bad this could be if anyone noticed how nervous and unprepared I was. I wouldn't think how quickly everything could crash and burn.

Can't wait for Noah and Katie's story? Grab the pre-order now—Finding Happiness in a Hoax releases February 2, 2021.

Made in the USA
Monee, IL
13 January 2021